They crossed
the boundaries
of the heart
to unlock a
sweeping passion....

Critical Acclaim for All the Exciting Novels of
Jill Barnett

WONDERFUL

"A sizzling romance filled with passion and a love that brings tears to the eyes. *Wonderful* has a sexy hero, a spirited heroine, sensuality, and a fast-moving plot."

—*Rendezvous*

"A *Wonderful* reading experience. . . . A humorous, fun-to-read medieval romance due to its varied, eccentric, and exciting characters."

—Harriet Klausner, Amazon.com

"*Wonderful* will find a way to curl up in your heart and stay there, keeping you warm and wonderful. Jill Barnett brings a unique joy to writing that is infectious and makes her books shine like a priceless gem."

—Kathe Robin, *Romantic Times*

"I enjoyed this book so much! *Wonderful* is enchanting and uplifting. . . . I laughed and cried."

—Laurie Shallah, *Under the Covers Book Reviews*

"*Wonderful* is fast paced, a lighthearted romp that will tickle your funny bone and touch your heart in perfect Barnett style. It is, simply, *Wonderful.*"

—Jamie Ann Denton, CompuServe Romance Reviews

CARRIED AWAY

"The marvelous cast of . . . characters . . . along with an ideal balance of poignancy and humor bring together the best of Jill Barnett's talents. Read this just for the pleasure."

—Kathe Robin, *Romantic Times*

"A sweet story."

—*Atlanta Journal*

"This one has humor, unusual pairings, settings and surprises. It's like a beautiful fairy tale."

—*Rendezvous*

IMAGINE

"Jill Barnett has written a wildly romantic story! Just 'imagine' if it could really come true!"

—Gloria Miller, *The Literary Times*

DREAMING

"Barnett has a rare knack for humor. Her characters are joyously fresh and her style is a delight to read—a ray of summer sun."

—*Publishers Weekly*

"There is so much happiness, magic, and pleasure in the pages of *Dreaming* that you'll believe in the magic of love!"

—Kathe Robin, *Romantic Times*

"Positively stellar! This book is not only funny, it's caring and compassionate . . . and magical!"

—Julie Mesinger, *Heartland Critiques*

Books by Jill Barnett

Wild
Wonderful
Carried Away
Imagine
Bewitching
Dreaming
The Heart's Haven
Just a Kiss Away
Surrender a Dream

Published by POCKET BOOKS

JILL BARNETT

WILD

POCKET STAR BOOKS

New York London Toronto Sydney Tokyo Singapore

An *Original* Publication of POCKET BOOKS

A Pocket Star Book published by
POCKET BOOKS, a division of Simon & Schuster Inc.
1230 Avenue of the Americas, New York, NY 10020

Copyright © 1998 by Jill Barnett Stadler

ISBN: 0-671-00413-1

First Pocket Books printing November 1998

10 9 8 7 6 5 4 3 2 1

POCKET STAR BOOKS and colophon are registered
trademarks of Simon & Schuster Inc.

Front cover illustration by Lisa Falkenstern
Tip-in illustration by Steven Assel

Printed in the U.S.A.

For Chris

What chance is this? How is it I see you here?
Ye are in my power at last; are in my power.
Yet fear me not; I call mine own self wild.
—*Idylls of the King*, Alfred, Lord Tennyson

Chapter

1

~

The Welsh Marchlands, 1280

Legends were born here.

With good reason. High in the hills, the mountains took on odd shapes like that of King Arthur's crown, the Devil's giant hand, or even God's profile. Ancient stone rings with mysterious pasts marked the countryside. It was here where the Druids once roamed, and the fairies had been known to bury their treasures under old oak trees—the ones with branches that looked like they were trying to climb clear up to heaven.

Sometimes, when the wild wind blew down from the hills, the trees in the woods sounded as if they were singing, the stars fell right down from the sky, and people's lives could change over the space of one night without them ever knowing it.

If you looked down from the tall mountain called *Craig y Ddinas,* the sleepy hamlet of Bleddig appeared to be nothing more than a cluster of neatly thatched roofs threaded with winding paths, the colorful splash of a garden here or there, and large, square patches of farm fields.

1

But this was Wales.

The village that sat there so innocently was surrounded by rolling hills and thick, dark woods. Above it stood a plateau, where a ring of giant blue stones had towered over the whole valley for as long as anyone could remember.

If the superstitious villagers happened to look up and see a young woman walking toward that huge and eerie stone ring, they would cross themselves and mutter the names of all the saints, for that was the place, they whispered, where Teleri of the Woods conjured up her evil magic.

Did you know she could call down healing powers the same way witches called down the moon? Aye, she could. She had claimed it was the stones, but they, the villagers, knew better. Wicked, that's what she was.

Some of the villagers had threatened to stone her, because they sought to kill anything that was different.

Others didn't threaten; they did throw stones.

Whenever the wild young woman named Teleri looked at her reflection in the water of the brook or in a glassy forest pond, she saw a small, star-shaped scar just below her right eye where a sharp rock had struck her. It was a scar that went so much deeper than just the white mark on her skin.

She talked to the forest animals, because animals didn't hurt a person just to make themselves feel better. Unlike people, animals only attacked to protect their young or if they were cornered and feared for their lives.

She stayed away from the village of Bleddig. Instead she lived deep in the darkest part of the Brecon Wood, a place where the fireflies danced wildly on dark summer nights, where the trees would moan from the wind, and insects sang so loudly they scared the world away.

Over time, Teleri of the Woods became part of the local folklore. The villagers claimed she stalked them on moonless nights to steal their souls. If the wheat grew slow, they would say 'twas because she walked past the field. She had cloven feet, you know, like the Devil Himself.

It was easier for them to make up tales and spread lies than to understand a young woman who was so pure of soul that she could simply look at them and see the malevolence hidden deep inside their hearts.

Some of the village children scared young babes with fearful tales they would tell in their beds on dark winter nights:

If she looks at you during a full moon, you will change into a statue of stone. If her tall shadow crosses your path, you will become a wild bird, destined to forever chase after the sun. Her kiss is so wicked just the touch of her lips can turn you into a toad.

Sometimes the children made up cruel rhymes which they sang at the edge of the woods, where they chanted and threw sticks and stones. "Be leery of Teleri!" they called out. "Run! Run! Or you will be done!"

She was the Devil's spawn!

The daughter of Satan!

But Teleri of the Woods was not the daughter of the Devil, for if she were, she would have known who her father was.

Her mother had been Annest, daughter of the Druid woman Gladdys and a wild beauty that no mere man could conquer, though many had tried. One day Annest had just disappeared.

'Twas said that a mysterious knight in a golden helm rode down from the hidden caves in the Welsh hills on a wild white horse with a mane and tail blacker than the River Styx. The knight had reined in the horse the moment he saw the fair Annest. His horse had reared and pawed the air as if in protest. But the knight only leaned down and held out his hand to her.

She calmly placed her hand in his and rode off with him toward those high dark hills, only to come home months later alone and heavy with child.

On the very day Teleri came into the world, her mother Annest left it, taking with her the one secret Teleri longed for. Her father's identity.

Brecon Beacons, Wales

Sir Roger FitzAlan rode across the Welsh Marches by order of the King, an honor that today he did not welcome. For Roger had a weakness. He loved women, the wrong women. And last night he'd spent too long in bed with one.

Today he had a duty to perform: to eye the land King Edward himself had chosen for the building of his newest castle on the border in southern Wales. Roger also had been given the select honor of overseeing construction. Once done, the castle would be his.

Yet at that moment he didn't feel like building anything but a pile of pillows for his throbbing head.

Behind him a few paces rode his men-at-arms, one of them carrying his pennant, which snapped loudly in the gusty wind, then snapped again, and again, sounding as loud and as final as the crack of a mace handle when it breaks in battle.

The snapping sound made his eyes throb. His head already ached from lack of sleep and the incessant, tinny jingle of a brace of golden bells on his mount's trappings, an annoying royal ornament that actually did serve a purpose. Those ringing bells told anyone with half an ear that he rode at King Edward's command.

Ring! Ring! Ring!

Hallo world! I am Sir Roger FitzAlan. I am on the King's business!

Ring! Ring! Ring!

King Edward wants another border castle built!

Damn! Damn! Damn!

Sir Roger wanted a new head.

He reined in and let his mount rest, leaning down to

give the beast a stroke. He almost slipped from his saddle and had to quickly hook his leg around the pommel.

He looked down and groaned.

I must look like one of the queen's ladies.

He put his boot back in his stirrup and stood. He was studying his saddle when Sir Tobin de Clare, the newly knighted son of the Earl of Gloucester, rode up to him.

Roger gave him a quick glance.

De Clare stiffened in his saddle the way he always did before he said something that made Roger want to clout him. De Clare's face held that quick, easy-to-anger look that mellowed with a man's age and experience. "Are you trying to drive every last one of your men into the bloody ground, sir, or just me?"

"You?" Roger laughed; it was a brittle sound even though he hadn't meant it to be. He sat back in his slippery saddle and rested the reins on his leg. "Why would I want to do anything to you?"

"Elizabeth is my sister."

"An unfortunate accident of birth for which I've never blamed her."

"God's eyes, but you can be an ass!"

"Aye," Roger said in an indifferent tone. "My father trained me well in the art." He fingered his reins absently, then rested an arm on his pommel and leaned closer to the dark-haired young knight. "My father also taught me how to take care of lads who have more tongue than sense. And speaking of asses, de Clare," he added pointedly and almost laughed when de Clare scowled at him, "it's my ass that concerns me. I'm trying to keep from falling on it."

De Clare looked confused. Still annoyed, but confused, too. 'Twas easy to play with the young man's mind. An enjoyable game Roger would have continued if he did not have to worry about keeping in the saddle. He adjusted his seat again, then mumbled to himself. "This blasted saddle feels as if it's been slathered in goose grease."

De Clare made a strangled choking sound and looked suddenly away.

Roger eyed him for a moment. "You find that amusing?"

De Clare was looking off toward the hills. He did not answer him.

"Look you. Because Earl Merrick is my friend, and because you are here with me at his request, we are stuck with each other for the next two years. Until then, I am your liege."

The young knight turned back around. He had more arrogance than wit. The fool was grinning. "Aye, sir."

"Surely you would not be so foolish as to laugh at me."

"No, sir."

"Then what is so bloody amusing?"

"As I recall, Thwack polished your saddle this morning."

"Ah," Roger said, nodding. He had his answer. Thwack was a good-hearted lad, a ward of the Lady Clio, Merrick's wife. Thwack also created disasters with the same frequency that rabbits created offspring.

"I'll wager he did use goose grease." De Clare was still wearing that stupid grin. "Do you want me to ride back to Camrose and fetch him?"

"No." Roger dismounted. "Lady Clio and Lord Merrick both would have my head on a pike if I chastised the lad. No doubt as usual he was trying too hard and only meant well." Roger inspected the ground, then grabbed a handful of grass, which he began to smear on his saddle.

"Aye, sir. He usually does."

"Just before one of his good intentions comes crashing down on one or all of us." Roger finished smearing grass and dirt on his best palfrey saddle. "And now, unless this mud works, I'm stuck with the distinct possibility of finding myself lying in the road like a tavern drunkard." He dusted off his gloves. "'Twould not be the most dignified position for a knight of the realm, particularly one who is on the King's own business." He mounted his horse.

De Clare was quiet for a moment, as Roger remounted, then said, "Sir?"

"Aye?"

"About Elizabeth—"

Roger raised a hand to cut him off. "Not now." He took the reins as his horse shifted back a pace. "Not ever. I do not want to talk of Elizabeth with you or anyone else. Wait for the men." He tapped his spurs to his mount and took off down the grassy hills, leaving Sir Tobin de Clare and the others behind.

He rode hard over the low hills. The King's blasted bells still rang clear through to his teeth. Cursing, he grabbed the bell strap and tore it from his trappings, then tossed it away into the high grass the way one flings away an apple core. A fortune lying in the grass for some lucky soul to find.

But Roger did not care about fortunes. He had made one of his own, and his teeth had stopped ringing. Thank the Almighty. The sudden silence was almost better than a good night's sleep. Almost.

He leaned low as his gray horse sped over the ground, leaving the king's golden bells far, far behind. He would be the luckiest of men if he could only leave behind what was truly eating at him. De Clare had known what bothered Roger, had seen through his gruffness, even if he refused to admit it to de Clare's face.

Elizabeth had broken off their affair.

She was the first woman other than his mother and sisters that Roger had ever loved. And he had loved her since he was fifteen, had wanted the fair Elizabeth de Clare since he had first laid eyes upon her at a Twelfth Night feast, where the two of them had been made King and Queen of the Bean.

Had it been luck he had chosen the cake slice with the bean? To him it had been fate.

But his father had laughed at that idea and called him foolish, then refused to agree to a betrothal. For two years Roger tried everything, anything. Baron FitzAlan would not betroth his only son to Earl Gilbert's daughter.

The day Elizabeth de Clare was betrothed to someone else, Roger stopped speaking to his father. The day of her wedding, Roger left England for the tourneys in France, then on crusade with his friend Merrick de Beaucourt.

It had been years since Baron FitzAlan and Roger had crossed paths. He only returned home to visit his mother and sisters when he was certain his father was not there.

So today he rode hard, trying to outride his own devils. Up the green hills they flew, man and horse, with his small troop of a dozen men following at the same thunderous pace. The earth trembled beneath his mount's churning black hooves the same way that war drums made the air tremble just before a battle.

Now this was a sound Roger felt akin to. It was not the foolish tingling of bells, like some court jester tumbling for the King, but instead a deep pounding sound. One that held power and freedom.

He shifted. Again he almost slipped, so he tightened his thighs, pressed his heels down and concentrated on staying in his bloody saddle.

He wore heavy mail that day; it further weighted him and seemed to drag his legs lower when he was forced to halfway stand in his stirrups. It was like being stretched on a dungeon rack. Mail was a strain when he was tired. But far worse was full armor, which felt as if he had a prized ox hanging onto his back and neck.

Over his mail he wore a surcoat of the FitzAlan colors: gold chevron device over a blue field quartered with the emblem of the first FitzAlan to achieve knighthood: a black hawk which stood for bravery slashed with a bar sinister, the mark of a bastard.

An illegitimate son of Alan, Comte de Caux, the first FitzAlan won his title and lands by cunning and sword, then had the good fortune to marry the sister of the English king and set about producing legitimate male heirs and generation after generation of kin who had close ties to the Crown.

Roger proudly wore the FitzAlan colors and emblem, except he had altered his device from his father's. The chevron was upside-down, a brash act of public defiance that proclaimed he was not like the Baron Sander FitzAlan.

Roger's mount sped up. He realized suddenly that his whole body was tight with anger at the thought of his father. The poor horse was only thinking he was urging it onward.

A split second later he laughed bitterly at himself, at the ironic fact that the mere thought of his father could still make him feel anything. He didn't want to feel contempt. He wanted to feel nothing. Yet his laughter hung around him in the air, mocking, until wind and distance swallowed all but the bitterness of the sound.

Roger turned his face into the cool air as if to prove he did not weaken to such mundane and human things as exhaustion and reason.

Riding helmless into the autumn sunlight kept him awake.

Riding helmless let the cold wind whip all thoughts of caution away.

Riding helmless across the wild Welsh borders was dangerous; it was something his father never would have done. So Roger did.

A figure atop a horse stood still as stone against the western horizon. Neither horse nor rider moved, but the sun broke through a white cloud and glinted off the rider's dark hair and the same black color of the horse's mane.

The rider raised one hand to block out the glare of the sun, then watched Sir Roger FitzAlan and his horse ride over the Welsh hills. Roger's red hair gleamed like a copper penny as he went down into the valley of Brecon, south of the high Black Mountains and north of the vast forest of Brecon Wood.

You took freely what was not yours to take, Roger FitzAlan. And I vow I will see you dead because of it. I will see you dead.

But the rider did not go after him, only sat atop the horse on that hill where one could see everything from the mountains to the distant sea, and as Roger became little more than a small, dark silhouette in the distance, the rider raised one fist to the sky and laughed.

Chapter

2

~

Just for sport, a group of village boys stoned a pheasant. Teleri was out picking herbs not all that far from the fields when she heard the boys' laughter and saw a stone fall. She'd hidden in the bushes, afraid that the stones were meant for her.

She then saw what they were aiming at. She rubbed old leaves and moss mixed with mud into her hair and smeared it all over her face. Humming sharply, as if someone had cut out her tongue, she leapt out of the bushes waving her arms and trying to look wild like her grandmother, Old Gladdys, who sang magic hymns, spat curses, and still practiced the ancient ways of the Cymri.

The mean little boys ran off and left the bird lying on its side in the dirt. She'd put the poor thing in her willow basket and brought it home, where she spent the last day and night tending its wounds.

Now, the pheasant was lying on a bed of straw and soft moss in a wooden manger that stood in a warm corner of her cottage. Draped over the edge of the manger were the bird's tail feathers, which were exquisitely beautiful, tinted all the shimmering colors of the forest.

The God-given colors which were supposed to protect the bird had not done so. The pheasant's tail feathers looked so perfect; its poor battered body did not.

She placed two fingertips on the pale down of the bird's breast next to a jagged spot of dried blood. Its heart pumped weakly, and so slowly that she could feel life just dying away with each heartbeat.

Out of habit she reached for the pouch of stones that hung from a chain belt at her hip, but it was not there.

She turned and scanned the room, looking past the silly old squirrels that sat every morning at her rough old table as if they were guests just arrived for a fine feast, past the hairy pig with the goshawk perched on its head while it stood in the corner munching on a wad of marsh marigolds, and past the plain brown sparrows and wild doves perched in the open windows and singing so brightly.

She grabbed a nub of wax that used to be her finest beeswax candle, a gift from her grandmother. As she moved past a stack of willow cages, a bald ermine reached out from the top cage and playfully grabbed at her skirt.

"Stop that." She turned around and plucked her skirt from its sharp claws. "I've no time now to play."

She hurried across the room with the pig suddenly snorting at her heels while the flightless hawk squawked and hopped up and down the pig's back, wobbling to and fro and just carrying on something fierce. "Get back to your meal, Pig. I've nothing for you. And hush, Hawk. Your brother the pheasant needs me now."

She lit a blackened candlewick that barely stuck up from the wax and cupped it with her hand to keep the flame lit, then she stepped into a small room with low oak beams that slanted from the ceiling to a hard-packed dirt floor.

It was here that she slept on a roughly-hewn bed made of fallen oak branches and covered in a plump tick stuffed with heather grass and wild thyme.

Her red leather pouch was sitting on the mattress. She tied the pouch to one of the chain links in her girdle as she rushed back toward the manger, then lifted the limp bird gently into her arms.

Outside her cottage, she turned and ran across a small stone bridge that arched over a brook. After the heavy winter rains, the same brook would flow so close to her home she could reach out her window with a bucket and draw up water that was clear and clean, so much so that when she washed her hair with that water it would shine for over a week.

But it was nearly autumn and the brook was narrower. She stepped off the bridge onto a small, rock-strewn path, where she stopped, hugging the bird to her, and gave a shrill whistle.

A moment later her horse came prancing through the trees, tossing his head so his long black mane whipped majestically through the air. When he was in front of her he stopped, standing still as fallen snow. She snapped her fingers once and he knelt down.

"Good, Horse," she told him and mounted astride, her arms still filled with the body of the dying bird. She pulled up the frayed hem of her rough woolen tunic, wrapped the bird, and tucked it safely between her legs.

She gripped the animal's long sleek mane in her fists, leaned forward, and put her heels to his girth.

They rode off toward the hills, out of the safety of the deep woods and toward a circle of healing stones that stood like giant blue guards over the valley.

Late that afternoon, Roger rode up a steep hill toward the ridge above Brecon Valley. Ahead and above him was the plateau marked on the map, the exact position Edward had chosen.

Roger planted his hand on the rump of his horse and

turned, making the leather of his saddle creak. Just from his vantage point here near the base of a ridge, he could see that the plateau must have a commanding view of the valley below, the golden fields of early fall and the dense woods that ran for miles along its eastern edges.

Even from here, beneath the plateau, he could understand the possibilities of such a castle site. He could see clear to the borderlands.

No one could ever dispute the fact that Edward knew well how to plot his defenses. He was a king respected for his shrewd mind.

As a young prince he'd learned strategy under the tutelage of one of England's master warriors, Simon de Montfort. And Edward had learned well. Years later he would use those same strategies and a few of his own invention to defeat the barons in their rebellion against his father, Henry III.

It was a tribute to Edward's sharp mind that the defeated barons had been led by his own mentor, Simon de Montfort.

Roger leaned back in his saddle and stared up at the ridge. He could hear de Clare riding toward him. Naturally the young knight had picked up the King's bells. *Ring! Ring! Ring!* Part of him hoped the damn things had rung the arrogant young man's ears off.

De Clare reined in next to him, then looked up at the site and whistled softly.

Roger nodded. "Edward knows his business well."

"Looks impregnable, even from here." He shifted, then handed Roger the bells. "Here. You lost these."

They both knew he hadn't lost anything.

"Wipe that stupid grin off your pretty face." Roger glared at the bells with a look that should have melted them. "Keep the bloody things. That constant ringing drives me mad."

His mouth still in a half-smirk, de Clare took a length of woolen cloth from his satchel and wrapped up the bells, muffling them so they could hardly be heard. He stuffed them in the sack and retied it to his trappings.

Roger raised his hand high, a signal to his troops to close formation for the steep climb to the top of the ridge. He tapped his spurs and a moment later his horse was picking its way through rocks and boulders.

As the hillside grew steeper, his horse slipped backwards occasionally, sending shale and dirt from the face of the cliff tumbling in dusty clouds back down the hillside. For balance he leaned low over his horse's neck. Ahead of him he could see the jagged lip of the ridge.

Not far. Just an arm's length or so.

A short moment later his horse stepped onto a large plateau and Roger exhaled a breath he hadn't even known he'd been holding.

He reined in and studied the sight before him.

A second later he swore under his breath. Two foul words.

It was the perfect site for a castle, except there was a ring of massive blue stones in the way.

Behind him, de Clare's mount scrabbled over the edge, and he heard the same telling silence.

"Jesu . . ." de Clare mumbled. "How in the name of Saint Jude are we supposed to build a castle on that?"

"We take them down . . ." Roger said, then caught something out of the corner of his eye. A flash of color.

He whipped his head around as his right hand went for his sword.

"What is it?"

"Quiet." Roger signaled de Clare back, then pulled his sword and leaned forward, listening.

There was a soft cooing sound coming from inside the stone ring, a sound he'd remembered well from his childhood, one he'd heard whenever he was near his mother's dovecote.

He kneed his horse forward so he had a clear view inside the stone ring.

A girl—no, she was a woman, with long brown hair, wild, curly hair, that hung down her back—was kneeling in the dirt at the center of the stone ring.

Clad in the rough woolen gown of a crofter, she had her face turned upward. Her hands, palms up, were held out from her sides; it was as if she were waiting for something priceless to fall into them—manna from heaven or a feather from an archangel.

He'd seen statues in Rome that looked like this woman: Mary Magdalene at the foot of the Cross and Ruth praying for the gift of a son. Their faces wore the same look, an expression filled with desperation, a pleading need that was carved so precisely into the stone countenance that he had felt as if he could almost see those statues weeping.

So while she looked to Heaven, he looked at her. He did not move; he was frozen in place as if he were carved from the same stone. Even had he wished to, he could not have turned away.

A strange power held him where he was: curiosity? Reverence? What? He studied her the way one studied a piece of bone or a corner of Christ's shroud—a relic in a reliquary—as if he couldn't believe what he was seeing right before his eyes.

He noticed for the first time the bird lying near her knees; it looked dead. A pheasant cockerel. He could see the bright colors on the tail spread out in the reddish dirt.

Was she praying over it?

Had he found a dead pheasant, he would roast it, not pray for its soul. If animals even had souls.

The cooing sound came again. It was not from her, but from the bird, which suddenly rolled to its feet and stood for an instant, then began to peck at its wing, ruffling its feathers as if it had not just come back from the dead, but was picking at nits.

The girl lowered her arms, scooped up some rocks that were scattered on the ground, and tucked them inside a red pouch tied to her waist. She dusted off her hands and stood, then bent down again and touched the pheasant on its back.

The bird cocked its head, plainly unafraid, and looked at her, then it scurried off into the brush.

A sharp whistle pierced the air; a horse trotted into the ring, tossing its regal head. It stopped in front of the girl.

Roger's mouth dropped open. By God's blood! He hadn't seen that horse in nearly five years.

He had to look twice, then thrice before he believed his tired and bleary eyes. It was Merrick's prized Arab—a gift from a grateful sultan during the last crusade, the same horse for which Roger had almost been willing to sell his soul.

Five years ago, when the horse was stolen, he had chased it and its devil of a rider all over Glamorgan. About broke his neck trying to catch them. And now it was standing a few lengths away from him.

He slid his sword back into its sheath just as the sound of his men approaching came from over the lip of the ridge. Their harnesses were jangling and their voices cut through the silence.

He heard the woman gasp as she looked at him, stunned.

There was the flash of a silence, the kind of eerie, taut instant which happens just before an event that changes one's life. Then she moved before he could blink an eye, grabbing the sleek Arab's black mane in her fists and swinging up onto its back.

"Stay here," Roger ordered his men.

An instant later she took off and disappeared over the opposite side of the hill.

"What is it? Where are you going?" de Clare called out.

"I gave you an order! Stay there!" Roger shouted, already going after the girl. He didn't need de Clare's help, the green fool. He did not have to answer to anyone here but himself.

The girl and the horse were cutting a jagged path

down the Welsh hillside. He rode to the edge of the hill, then urged his mount down after them. This time, he vowed, as his own horse slid down the hillside, he would catch the rider—a woman.

God's eyes! The horse-thieving rider was a bloody woman!

Chapter

3

~~

She saw the *English*. The blue knight who wore his chevron the wrong way. What odd turn of the moon had caused him to find her again? Here, where she lived?

How could this be when she had since been so careful? Now she always walked all the way to see Old Gladdys. Once though, a few years before, she'd been foolish enough to ride into Glamorgan.

This *English* was the one who had chased her then. And he was after her again.

Teleri sat atop Horse as stiff and straight as a forest pine. The trail was so steep here that Horse half-slid his way down. She twisted his black mane more tightly 'round her hands and pressed her knees against his sides.

At the bottom, where the hills rolled out before her, she tapped her heels, that was all, and off he went.

"Run, Horse!" she urged him. "Chase the winds!" She leaned low and let Horse take over. He loved to be ridden, to fly over the hills and valleys as if he were free.

She leaned low and looked back over her shoulder.

The knight was giving chase, more swiftly than she'd expected. His horse was a strong one, too.

If he caught her, he could choose to kill her. The English law was his. Horse was not rightly hers—not that right mattered. Any knight could make his own laws; it happened often enough along the Marchlands.

She turned away from the direction of Bleddig, away from the west side of the woods. Still she rode hard, darting past trees and bounding ahead. Horse was strong and well, because she'd made him so. She fed him rich forest grasses and fine oats mixed with the clearest water in all of Wales. She rode him to keep his fine muscles lean. And she loved him; he was her friend. So for those reasons, and the right of nature and survival, he should be hers.

She had been the one who found him down and wounded. She had been the one who pried two deadly arrows from his neck and who washed his wounds, the one who took care of him in the woods of Glamorgan, had nursed him with her grandmother's chants and her potions until he was well enough to slowly walk all the way to Brecon.

And when one of the wounds had opened and festered, she had been the one to take him up to the ring and lay her stones on him.

She had earned the right to call him her own.

With her he was wild and free and simply happy; he was safe. They were alike in that way—free, happy to be hiding away from the world that had hurt them, the world that had left them both scarred.

He was hers and he was going stay hers. Horse could outrun any Englishman's puny-spirited mount. Even a knight. And surely this knight, she vowed.

Again she turned and headed north, taking the long way 'round Brecon Wood. In the distance, the trees cut a sawlike pattern across the horizon. She rode until the sun had slipped lower, until it was hidden in the red and gold clouds to the west of the rising moon.

To hide her tracks she rode along the tape grass and water weed that edged the River Usk, then splattered right through the river at a place she knew to be most shallow. When Horse stepped onto the opposite bank she looked back.

It had been in water where she'd lost this knight the last time; he had fallen in.

She grinned. Even now she could still remember him sitting in the mud and water and cursing down all the saints of heaven while he shook his fist at her.

But this time he didn't fall. He reined in his horse and looked at her from across the river. A shaft of light from the setting sun cut through the clouds and shone on him, making the red in his hair look even brighter. An instant later he maneuvered his mount into the river.

She rode off toward the woods, the wind catching her hair and making it fly back, then whip across her mouth.

"Go, Horse! Go!" She laughed into that same wind, knowing it would carry her voice back to the river. "Show the *English* who can ride!"

She could hear her laughter echoing behind her. She leaned low again. Only a few more lengths to go. She looked back again, then smiled.

He was at the far edge of the river, but struggling to get his mount to go up the muddy bank. From the angle of his head she could see that he was looking right at her.

She laughed again.

Ahead was the Devil's Woods, the part of Brecon where the trees grew so thick it looked as if they had grown together, where the thicket were full of thorns and bramble and as tall as a man, where the underbrush did not make passage easy.

It was a place where one could not ride a horse, but had to walk through—if one could find a way. There were at least a dozen paths from this side of the woods alone. Some led into the woods, some led to dead ends.

But Teleri knew which path led home. This was the surest place for her to lose him.

She slowed Horse with a soft command, and he stopped at the forest edge, where the brambles were twisted like tangled hair. She slid off his back and stroked his muzzle.

Then, just as the knight rode up from the river bank, as the wind grew still and a sliver of a moon crawled up the eastern sky, Teleri and Horse disappeared.

Camrose Castle, Glamorgan

A fat, one-eyed orange cat called Cyclops lumbered across the inner bailey, heading for the castle brewery where Clio de Beaucourt, wife of the lord of Camrose and Earl of Glamorgan, was busy testing her latest batch of ale.

Now Lady Clio had a goal, one she'd had for years. She was determined to discover the secret of heather ale, a magical and secret brew that died out with the Picts.

At least once a year she still made an attempt to brew the infamous ale, even though after years of mishaps and strange results—usually on her husband or his unsuspecting men—Lord Merrick had forbade her to continue to try to brew the stuff.

His mistake of course was in forbidding his lady wife to do anything, for that was like putting hot coals next to dry straw and expecting nothing to happen.

So on this day when Merrick had been gone for nigh on a fortnight, on business with King Edward, Lady Clio had business of her own. She was busy concocting.

It had been just that morn when Old Gladdys the Druid claimed tonight's moon would be blue. A grand sign. Only two days before the rare red heather they had planted months ago had finally bloomed. Surely 'twas written in the stars that this time, she would discover the recipe.

So Cyclops the cat leapt up into an open window and plopped down where he could rest his head on his front paws, bask in the afternoon sunlight, and watch his mistress get into trouble all at the same time.

In a large black ale vat, the brew was bubbling to a froth. The scent of barley and herbs filled the warm room and steam rose up to the roof of the brewery and drifted outside the open windows.

Cyclops lifted his lazy head and sniffed the fumes. He sighed contentedly, then lay his head back down and fell asleep.

Clio stuck her thumb into the pot and held it high. The ale dripped off slowly in a trail of bubbles and each drop was honey-colored and looked perfect.

"Done!" she said with no little pride.

A blond lad of ten and five dressed in hose and a tabard of the earl's colors was intently sweeping the stoop. He looked up, then leaned the broom against the doorway and came to her side. He stretched his long neck out and peered into the vat. "'Tis ready?"

"Aye. Fetch the barrels, Thud, and we shall start filling them." She paused. "Where is your brother? Does he not wish to help?"

"No. Thwack is polishing tack and working with the earl's horses this week, my lady."

She nodded and soon the two of them were siphoning the brew into two large wooden barrels. Clio corked one barrel just as a trumpet from the parapet blew in five regal blasts.

They both froze, then looked at each other from wide and surprised eyes.

Clio cocked her head and listened to the sound again. "Saint Paul and Peter! He's home!"

"'Tis Earl Merrick," Thud said.

"Aye." Clio wiped her hands on her apron and rushed around the room closing the shutters on the brewery windows. "Get down, Cy."

The cat yowled in protest, but he leapt down from the window and moved to the open door.

"Quick." She untied the cook's apron and tossed it in a corner. "Finish filling the other barrel and I shall distract—I mean, I shall greet my lord husband." She brushed the herb bits from her skirt and swiped back her damp hair from her face. She rushed across the brewery toward the door.

"Where shall I hide it this time, my lady? In the laundry?"

"No! 'Tis where he found it the last time." Clio stopped, chewed her lip thoughtfully.

"The chapel?"

"No. Brother Dismas keeps too close an eye on goings-on there."

"The buttery."

She shook her head, then her face brightened with one of her wonderful ideas. "Roll the barrels over to the stable and put them in the old stalls, the ones we only use when the castle is filled with guests. They will be safe there for now. We have not had great company for over two years."

She stopped and for good measure, grabbed a large earthenware ale jar off a shelf of like jars and hugged it to her chest as she left the brewery. She moved through the bailey, threading her way among carts and geese, 'round children and guards. She walked with determined steps toward the stairs to the main hall, her long, blond braid swinging down her back with each step as she practiced an innocent smile for her lord.

'Twas not that she did not sorely miss him. She loved her husband and missed him terribly, but she was truly peeved with him, for the oaf had sent her no word, not one message, nothing, since the day he left.

At the pounding sound of horses hooves behind her she turned, only halfway up the steps, a strained smile on her face.

Handsome as sin, looking tall and powerful as ever, Earl Merrick rode up to the steps with his men behind him, his black pennant with a white cross and rearing red lion snapping in the air. He reined in and a page came up to claim the reins of his horse.

But Merrick did not dismount. He leaned one arm on the saddle pommel and looked squarely at his wife. His gaze wandered over her, from the top of head to her toes and slowly back up again.

She knew that look. He knew exactly what he was about.

He stopped studying her and stared at the ale jug. "What is this, my sweet? Have I been gone so long you've taken to hugging jars instead of your husband?"

She raised her chin and tried to look indignant. "Has it been long? Seems like you just left."

He dismounted then and walked up to her and made a small bow. He said quietly, "'Tis hard, like your husband."

"Aye. I have found this jar to have great similarities to your head, my lord."

He took the ale jar from her hands and tossed it to one of his men. Then his arm was around her, lifting her into the air and he was kissing her senseless, right there on the steps for all the castle to see.

She heard the whistling and calling of his men, the banging of shields on the castle walls and the cheers of those in the bailey. She grabbed handfuls of his hair, but he deepened the kiss until she slowly let go and slid her hands around his neck and kissed him back.

He pulled back after thoroughly tasting her, then dropped a soft kiss on her brow and whispered in her ear, "I think you missed me, my sweet."

"I think your heart is as black as the hair on your head, my lord."

"You are angry."

"Aye." She gave him a haughty look.

He pulled a cluster of rolled and sealed parchments from inside his cloak and held them up. "About these?"

She stared at them. "You wrote to me?"

"Aye, to you and to our son. Every night."

Her anger was waning swiftly.

He gave her a sheepish look that was so very male, so very Merrick. "I just forgot to send them."

She looked at her husband and laughed. Shaking her head, she sighed, then turned back to the man with the jar. "Bring the ale inside and refresh the men." She took the parchments from Merrick and slid her arm through his as they walked up the rest of the stairs and entered the castle. " 'Twill take me years to teach you how to be chivalrous."

"Aye. 'Twill keep you out of trouble."

"Me? I am not the one who ignored his wife and son."

"How is the lad?"

"Sleeping. He had a hard day running both his nurse and me ragged. He hid under the altar drape in the chapel and scared the wits out of Brother Dismas."

"Brother Dismas has no wits."

"Merrick!"

" 'Tis true. And I do not wish to argue. I am only glad to be home. Come." He opened the door to their chamber. "I have much to tell you."

They chatted over a few things as Merrick settled into a chair and Clio poured him a goblet of ale.

He took it, then stared down at it. "If I drink this will I speak in rhyme or giggle like some goosegirl?"

" 'Tis only ale."

"No heather?"

"No heather," she assured him, though he eyed the goblet a little longer before he took a long drink of it, then sighed and rested his head against the high back of the ornately carved chair.

"You came home early. Did the meeting not go well?"

"The lords all agreed on most of the issues. Edward sent us away early. He wanted to go back to Leeds."

"Roger did not come back with you?"

Merrick shook his head. "He is on his way to Brecon."

Clio turned around and looked at her husband. "Brecon? Why?"

Merrick took another long drink of ale and stared at the goblet in his hand for a long time. Finally he said, "I believe Edward wanted him out of reach."

"I don't understand. Explain."

Merrick looked up at her. "Hugh Bigod is alive."

"Lady Elizabeth's husband?"

"Aye."

"Does he know about Roger and Elizabeth?"

Merrick looked at her as if she were mad.

Shaking her head, she waved a hand. "Fine. That was a foolish statement, I know. I was not thinking. *Every-one* knows of Roger and Elizabeth."

"Aye. Everyone."

"But what can he do? We all thought him dead."

"When a wife sleeps with another man, it matters not to the husband, my love, if he was believed dead or not. Bigod has his pride and he loved Elizabeth well. He is a powerful man, with important lands in the north. Edward is caught between his respect and continued need for Bigod's support and his long-time friendship with Roger. I believe he sent him deep into Wales to keep him out of the way. At least until he can determine Bigod's intention."

"He was gone for five years. If Elizabeth had not refused to marry Roger, she would have two husbands now. What a fix!" She took some cheese and bread off a platter and handed it to Merrick. "Roger could have stayed here. Young Edward adores him, as do I. He is your closest friend. He could stay here for as long as need be."

"I could not think of enough excuses to keep him here for as long as need be. Roger would get restless in a fortnight. He does not know he is being sent somewhere safe. 'Twould not settle well with him, if he did."

27

"No, Roger has his pride, too." She stood behind Merrick and began to rub the tension from his tight shoulders.

He sighed and closed his eyes.

"Is Brecon safe?"

"Until we know what Bigod will do, Brecon seems a safer place for him than here on the Marchlands or in England."

Chapter

4

The next day was one of those strange times of year when the weather didn't seem to know what it wanted to be: summer or fall. Last night, after Teleri had lost the knight in the woods, the air had grown cool enough for Teleri to keep the shutters tightly closed, but this morning the sun rose bright, and the air warmed up so early the dew had turned to steam before she could break fast.

By mid morn she was outside her cottage, her hands stuck inside her saffron-colored tunic, her head down, intent, as she studied the pebbled ground.

She'd lost her red pouch again.

This time it wasn't just sitting on her bed, or on a window sill, or tied to her girdle where it belonged. It wasn't slyly tucked away into the corner of one of the willow cages by her weasel or the fox, or stashed away in the squirrel hollow—a hole inside the thick trunk of the elm standing just outside her east window.

It wasn't inside or near her cottage anywhere. She planted her fists on her hips and tapped her bare foot on the ground.

Think, silly goose girl. Where did you last have it?

She did remember having it when she jumped off Horse, just before she entered Devil's Wood, but all she'd had on her mind then was escaping the *English*.

She crossed over the stone bridge and moved out into a small meadow beyond, where the grass had only just started to turn golden on the tips and where it was still green and soft on the soles of her feet.

A few ducks and wild geese pecked at the ground near her, searching for crawlers that came out to bake themselves in the sunshine. A white dove flew down from a nearby tree and landed on a crusty stump left over from an old hemlock tree, and Horse was slurping up water at the opposite side of the brook.

This time, Teleri feared she had truly lost her bag of stones. So she turned her face up to the sun. She believed what her grandmother taught her: the sun, the moon, the sky knew more than man ever could.

Because while man was sleeping, the moon was awake, while the sun was shining man was too busy to stop and look around him. Man was small, his eyes made so he could only see so far, yet the sky could see far beyond forever.

Teleri closed her eyes, holding her arms out from her sides the way she did when she was at the stone ring. The sun was warm on her face. The rays prickled her skin and made her feel so alive her worry and fear just melted away.

She stood there taking in deep breaths of warm summer air. Then, slowly at first, she began to turn, 'round and 'round in a circle. Her saffron tunic and the skirt of her leaf green gown belled outward as she spun, sending the ducks and geese scurrying away. Then she recited:

> "Oh Sun so high, so warm, so gay
> Help me, please, I cannot delay
> I'm out here spinning 'round and 'round,
> Something is lost and cannot be found."

Teleri slowly stopped spinning and opened her eyes. She was dizzy for a moment, seeing stars, the way she always did when she chanted down the sun, or moon, or sky. She shoved her loose hair back from her face and looked around her.

Sunlight spilled like long golden fingers pointing to a narrow path that led back toward Devil's Wood.

She took that direction, humming to herself as she walked, searching the ground and the small furrows along the path's wooded edges. Thankfully the pouch was red, so she would have no trouble missing it, even here where the woods grew thicker.

There had been no rain for so long the tree branches had started to change. They looked like thirsty hands reaching out to the clouds begging for rain. The leaves of those trees had long ago given up and fallen to the narrow footpath, their edges turning crisp. When she stepped on them, they crackled under her feet as if they were crying out for a drink of water.

She had been walking for a while, and was far into the woods when a breeze whistled through the crowns of the trees, making them sing lightly as a few of their leaves drifted down on the path and over her shoulders and head. She looked up and could see the sun cracking through the high branches as if it were following her.

An old wrinkled oak stood just ahead of her near a fork in the path where another group of paths veered off in different directions. The tree was a favorite spot of hers because the knotted tree trunk looked just like the face of a wizard.

Sometimes, like now when the sun was high, the wizard's face looked as if he was smiling. Sometimes he frowned. Most times he just stared at her, as if he could read her thoughts and dreams and wishes.

"Hallo, Tree," she said in passing fancy. "You look very wise today. I need a wise man." She plucked the seams of her tunic and curtsied as if the tree were truly alive and not just so in her imagination. "Tell me, please, Sir Wizard-Face-in-the-Tree, have you seen my red stone pouch?"

She straightened and looked at the paths in the road. The sun shone down on the two paths that the tree split. Teleri pointed back and forth between the paths as she spoke an ancient Druid chant, Old Gladdys' favorite:

> "Eena, meena, mona, mite,
> Basca, tora, hora, bite,
> Hugga, bucca, bau,
> Eggs, butter, cheese, bread,
> O-U-T . . . Out!"

Her finger was pointing at the left path. That's the one, she thought, and ducked under the low branch of the sprawling oak tree, then moved along, past a thicket of wild white rose where the bees buzzed madly, over a fallen elm tangled with ivy and vines, toward the dark parts of the woods—the place where the twisted brambles grew, where the insects buzzed but she could not see them, and where the air grew heavy.

And it was there she saw her red pouch caught on a thorn as long as her finger. She snatched it away and tied it to her girdle with five tight knots. She would not lose it again.

She turned and moved back down the path, into the light, where she had to wave away the bees. At the fork in the road where the old oak grew, she stopped and curtsied her thanks to the wrinkled wizard face, then turned toward home.

You did not find that which is lost. . . .

A voice?

Teleri froze. She turned back, slowly, expecting to see a man standing behind her.

The *English!*

Her throat grew tight with fear. He could have hidden here all night and been waiting for her.

She looked everywhere. Nothing moved. There was

no sound, not even the bees. There was no one there. She looked at the tree for a moment, searched its branches.

Nothing.

Frowning, she stared at the wrinkled wizard face. Although it looked as if it were staring back at her, truly it was just a tree trunk rippled with age and nothing more. Shaking her head, she turned back and took a step.

You did not find that which is lost. . . .

She spun back around. "Who is there?"

There was no answer, even when she waited. So she bent down slowly, her gaze darting left, then right as she picked up a broken branch for a weapon. She needed some protection. She took slow, small steps until she stood in front of the old tree.

The breeze ruffled through the treetop again.

She looked up.

Was that only the wind?

Perhaps. She remembered how at certain places in the distant hills, the wind could whip through the spindly trees and sound just like someone was crying.

Something cried out then.

She jumped, swinging the branch like a sword.

There was nothing there, nothing but a black rook circling overhead.

She took two steps, moved closer to a path she had not chosen, leaning forward to peer deeper, where it was dark and twisted, the kind of frightening place here in the woods where even a soul could not rise.

Again the wind whistled, but this time it did not sound like a voice.

"Hallo?" she called out. "Hallo!"

Still there was nothing.

She looked down and spotted footprints in the earth. She knelt for a moment. The prints were fresh, no more than a couple of days old. She looked up, still holding the branch, then back down at the imprint in the damp earth.

She reached out and touched the footprint.

He must be tall and strong to leave such deep footprints in the earth.

She did not move, but stayed there almost frozen, touching the outline of the footprints and watching them the way one looks at a man through the eye slit in his helm, foolishly staring as if the metal will merely fade away and suddenly reveal the face behind it.

It could still be the *English,* hiding. She looked up again, then slowly rose to her feet. She looked down the paths before her. If she went home along the path she had come by, he could follow her. If she went down this path, he could grab her and kill her.

Something cracked. Like a footstep?

She just ran, ran as fast as she could, away from the tree, along another path that didn't lead to her cottage, but went around, deeper into the woods and nearer the river.

Her feet crunched on the fallen leaves and twigs. Her heart pounded in her chest. Her breath pounded in her ears. She ran, swiftly as she could. Branches scratched her. Thorns caught on her clothes. But still she ran, fast.

Faster.

Then she took a chance—one quick glance over her shoulder.

She tripped and hit the ground face first. Leaves went everywhere. It took her a moment to realize what happened. She lay there face down, panting.

Under her bare foot was something hard and rough and cold. She pushed herself up, shoved her long hair from her face.

An instant later she screamed.

Chapter

5

~

Someone had hanged him. The *English* lay sprawled face down at the base of a chestnut tree. There was a noose around his neck, a black blindfold knotted at the back of his head. On the ground, a short distance away from his head, was a broken tree branch with the other end of the rope still slung around it. The branch was splintered so the raw wood showed.

Her hand covering her mouth, she sat there, taking in what she was seeing. He was a big man, and that, coupled with the weight of his mail must have been too much for the tree branch. The image of this big man dressed in mail, blindfolded with a black rag and hanging by his neck made the blood drain from her face.

Frozen with horror, she could only stare at his long body. His boot was beneath her foot. She'd tripped over his leg. The sharp prick of his knight's spur was still pressed against her ankle.

She closed her eyes. Tears she didn't know were there dripped down her cheeks, which grew hot, then suddenly cold. She was clammy. Her body broke out in cold sweat and the trees, the bushes, even the light and the air around her began to spin.

She took in deep breaths, trying not to gag, then crawled away and placed her hand against her churning belly. She heaved into the bushes. Over and over.

When her belly was empty, she rolled away and buried her hot face in her arms. She just lay there, crying so hard she couldn't catch a breath.

A sound came from behind her.

Her head shot up. She stared at the dead man.

He lay there still as stone. Still as death.

She realized then that the person who did this could still be here. She slowly looked around her, then reached for the branch and stood with it. She moved toward each bush, slowly and deliberately, then slashed at them with the branch. Each time there was no one there.

She moved closer, her eyes locked on his back, watching for the motion of a breath—and saw none.

She was afraid to turn him over. Afraid to see death on his face. She had heard that people gathered at public hangings the way hungry vultures circled around the dying.

But until that very moment, she herself had never seen someone hanged. People with souls and hearts and minds could do this horrid thing to other people, to their own kind. They could stone them. They could hang them.

Frightened as she had been of this man who was her enemy, who could have killed her, who had chased her, she would not run away and leave him here, like this, with no dignity, no compassion, no last moment to honor the fact that he had once lived in this world.

She needed to put his body to rest. Bury him. Build a pyre. Something.

Take off the noose, she thought, then started to reach out toward him, but pulled her hand back when she saw it was shaking worse than leaves in the wild wind.

She waited, and waited, working up courage, talking

to herself. *Now Teleri . . . He cannot harm you. He is only a man. Someone like you. Silly goose! You have touched dead animals. Ravens, fox, even a wolf. This is no different.*

She took a long deep breath and reached for the knot in the rope.

His body twitched.

She screamed and scrambled back, her hand pressed against her mouth.

He was alive?

She cocked her head, watching.

Perhaps. Perhaps not. When she was very young, yet old enough to still remember, Old Gladdys had butchered a chicken for their meal, had chopped its head clean off. But the headless body had chased Teleri all over the place, like her shadow, until the chicken suddenly just stopped and fell over.

Her grandmother swore to her that the bird was dead the whole time it chased her. Teleri still did not believe that tale and did not eat chicken ever again.

She made herself pick up the noose that was still taut on the back of his neck. He did not move. She slowly loosened the knot so she could slip the rope over his head and lay it flat on the ground where it surrounded his head like a halo of death.

She stared at the back of his head, then placed one hand on his shoulder, the other on his hip. She closed her eyes as tightly as she could, then tried to turn him over.

Moving the huge, ancient blue stones would have been simpler. She took a deep breath and tried to turn him over again. She failed.

Finally, she grabbed his mail in her fists, dug her bare feet into the dirt and pulled with all her might.

She felt him give way and roll over. An instant later his mailed arm hit her chest and almost knocked the wind from her. She lay there, her eyes still tightly closed because she was afraid to open them. She shoved his arm off her and took two deep breaths.

"I cannot look at your face, English." She just lay there. She searched for the courage to open her eyes. She pushed herself up and folded her hands tightly in her lap, then she counted. At one hundred she finally found the courage to open her eyes. She stared straight ahead at the tree trunk.

He groaned; she looked down.

That raspy sound was no trick of the wind. The sound came from his mouth.

She placed her fingers against his throat, where the hanging noose had cut deep and bloody rope burns into his neck.

He was alive. By the sun and moon, he was alive!

His heart beat weakly against her fingertips, as weakly as had the pheasant's, which did not bode well for this man, for the heart of a bird was so much smaller than a man's heart.

She leaned over him. "You're alive, English. Can you hear me? You live!" She patted his cheeks which were covered in a neatly-clipped red beard that hid most of his chin and circled his mouth.

His eyes remained closed. She patted his cheeks again.

"English!"

Nothing. She studied his face. The skin around his cheekbones was bluish, but it was not the gray color of death. Just pale and speckled with dirt and pieces of crushed leaves.

She brushed his cheeks clean. His skin was warm to the touch.

He lived. Barely.

Now what? She could not move him alone, yet she had to do something.

"Horse . . ." she whispered aloud. She would get Horse.

"Stay here," she said as if the knight could understand her, then paused, shaking her head and muttering, "What do you think, Teleri, that he will just rise up and walk away?"

She turned then and ran, ran as fast as her bare feet could run over the leaves and fallen trees, through the bushes and past the bees. She ran for a long time, her paces rhythmic, like drums. Run! Run! Run! Run!

Until she was finally on the path that led to her cottage. Her breath came fast. Her chest was beginning to burn. She couldn't get enough of a breath to whistle for Horse.

Still running, she broke from the dark forest into the sunny meadow. She stopped, bent down and put her hands on her knees as she tried again to catch her fleeting breath. After a few more breaths she straightened and managed enough air to whistle. But it was so weakly done she was surprised when Horse raised his head and looked at her.

"Come, Horse! Come!"

He moved toward her.

She stroked his muzzle once, then hopped on his back and rode him over the bridge to her cottage, where she grabbed a coil of rope from a wooden peg on the wall and jerked her only blanket from her bed.

A moment later she was on horseback again, the blanket and rope tucked in front of her as she rode deep into the forest, heading for Devil's Wood and the knight she prayed was still alive.

Chapter

6

~

The English was worse. Teleri had not thought it possible for him to be worse and still be alive.

But he was.

Never once had he opened his eyes or spoken, even when she'd removed his heavy mail. He did not awaken when she'd fashioned a sling from rope and her blanket, then harnessed it to Horse and slowly drew this half-dead English back home. The only signs he lived were a few raspy groans that came from his swollen throat when she'd moved him. But those noises sounded more like a cornered animal than a man.

It was night, now. He lay quietly atop her mattress which was no longer on her bed, but tucked into a corner of her cottage, beneath an open window. He was clad in only his undertunic and hose, and covered in her one blanket, which she'd had to beat clean after using it to drag him through the woods.

A cambered sliver of a moon rose in the dark sky. Chilly night air was beginning to come through the window, and if the air grew as cool as last night, she would have to close the shutters soon.

Gnats buzzed around the flickering light of her small candle, which she'd set on the window sill so the light would spill over him. Caddisflies circled outside the open window, leaving thin streaks of light in the cool night air. An owl called out to the moon and she could hear Horse slurping a drink from the brook. Outside there was life and the stars and moon. Inside there was this man, who might die.

She dipped a small piece of worn cloth into a wooden mazer filled with cool water from the brook. She bathed his face and neck, which was turning dark red and fevered. A green poultice of moss mixed with herbs was beginning to dry into cracks along the wound where the rope had cut his neck.

She worked for a long time to remove the healing plaster in small amounts, just chipping pieces away so she wouldn't hurt him any more than she had to.

The rope burn beneath the poultice had grown angrier and was starting to turn purple and swell even more. The edges of the wound were festering, so she washed it with cool water, hoping that would soothe him.

It didn't. He was in pain.

She flinched every time she touched the cloth to his neck. Each time he moaned she stopped, until she could not see him because of the tears welling in her eyes. Finally she sat back on her feet and wiped her eyes with the back of her hand, calling herself silly and wishing she had a thicker skin like Old Gladdys.

When she was small, she would cry when a fly died or when she stepped on a spider. Old Gladdys claimed that when she would give Teleri a honeycomb to suck on for a sweet, she was so generous she would put half of it outside for the ants. She wondered what her grandmother would say about this knight. If she would call her foolish for giving succor to a man who if he lived, could harm her.

She closed her eyes because she was torn between her sense and her heart, and she knew she could not change even for someone who was her enemy. Because when she looked at this man, she saw a man, a human—someone like her. And he had been horribly tortured, this man who had been hanged and lived through it.

When she looked at him, it was not fear she experienced but an aching for what he had been through, and it felt as if someone was pulling her heart right from her chest. This kind of inhumanity only served to remind her again how very dark and cruel this world could be.

She stopped and just stared at him as if she were waiting for some miracle to fall from the sky. Again she tried to wash him, thinking that taking rests might make it hurt less.

But he reached up with his big hand and pushed her away, making harsh rasping sounds from his throat. No words came out, nothing that sounded like speech, but she knew the sounds of anger when she heard them. In whatever place his mind was—between heaven or hell—he was furious, fighting with something deep inside of him even if he did not open his eyes. She could feel the emotion emanating from him the way you could feel fear coming from a cornered animal.

He began to toss and turn. She tried to grab his arms, but he was too powerful. To keep him still, she had to lay across him. He ceased moving suddenly.

She pressed her ear to his chest because she feared that he might have died right there beneath her. But she could hear his heart still beating. She slowly crawled off him and knelt there, watching him.

He moaned again.

She leaned closer, confused and worried and feeling a little more than helpless. No animal or man should suffer so. Even this *English* who had the power to destroy her.

To calm him, she reached out to lay her hand over his

heart the way she would do with a fallen bird or a wounded fox.

He twisted suddenly. Violently.

His arm came at her.

Before she could think to duck, his fist slammed into her eye.

She fell flat on her back so hard, her breath left her. Stars flickered before her for a brief moment that seemed to last forever, then she gasped to find air. When she found a breath, she drew her knees up to her chest and curled onto her side, her hand over her eye, for the pain came then, fast and throbbing; it was so sharp she felt as if her head would crack open.

She lay there and knew then she had little choice. When her head stopped ringing and she could move again, she did what she hadn't wanted to do—she bound his hands and feet.

The small contingent of men-at-arms that Sir Roger had left behind was gathered by a smoking peat fire when a rider approached.

Payn Godart, master of the men-at-arms and a dark-haired man the size of a small giant, stood abruptly.

Sir Tobin de Clare rode up and reined in his palfrey.

"You were gone a long time, Sir Tobin." Payn said pointedly. De Clare had ridden out to look for Sir Roger the night before last, after they had waited far longer than any of them thought they should. When de Clare had ridden out, so had three other men, each going in a different direction. Those men had returned the next morn with no clue to where their master had gone. De Clare had not returned readily.

But De Clare said nothing to any of them about how long he had been gone. It was well known who Tobin de Clare was. His father was one of the most powerful earls in the land; the son was too arrogant and hard-headed, even when he had been squire to Merrick de Beaucourt, Earl of Glamorgan.

So in typical de Clare style, he did not explain

himself and the men noticed, but said nothing more. De Clare dismounted and flung his reins over the saddle, then strode toward the fire and squatted down to warm his hands. After a moment spent staring into the red glow, he spoke without emotion. "I followed his tracks, but lost the trail to the south, at the river."

Payn reached down and tossed de Clare a plump leather wineskin shaped just like the crescent moon and a loaf of bread and some cheese. Sir Tobin raised the wineskin high, took a drink, then wiped a hand across his mouth. He looked at the other men whose faces were golden-red from the glow of the fire. "I take it you found nothing." He tore off a hunk of the bread with his teeth and began to chew.

"No," Payn said, shaking his head.

"I wager he's with a woman again, while we're here freezing off our ballocks," John Carteret said in a disgruntled tone.

Payn punched the man in the shoulder and told him to shut up. "You know he would not leave us here, not even for a pretty face and soft thighs. Sir Roger might be wild and reckless in his sporting time, but he is no coward. He knows his duty is to Edward. He's on the King's business, not at an alehouse."

Some of the other men grumbled in agreement.

De Clare looked up after he finished off the last of the cheese. "He was chasing a rider. I saw that much when I looked down into the valley. No one knows why or who?"

The men shook their heads and one said, "John asked at that village in the valley."

"Aye," a man said in a disgusted voice. "And a superstitious lot, they were. Could talk of nothing but Druid witches and the Devil's rocks." The man named John took another drink of wine. "The Welsh are a strange lot, spitting nothing but twaddle. I stopped asking questions when the second villein crossed himself and rushed away as though I had asked for a meeting with the Devil himself. Then I rode through the village," He shook his head. "There was nothing in Bleddig to lure Sir Roger. No tavern. And no wenches."

"What about a horse?"

"The only horse in the village was a twenty-year-old plow mare."

There was silence and someone tossed another peat square on the fire.

"Perhaps," one man said without thinking, "Lady Elizabeth changed her mind and chased after him."

De Clare stiffened and pinned the man with a cold stare. "My sister is with her husband at Atherton. I'll warn you now. Do not speak of her again or you'll regret it."

The man hung his head and muttered an apology. Once again the air grew thick with tension and the silence of men who did not favor de Clare's company.

"We shall leave in the morning," Sir Tobin informed them as he stood, then walked to his mount. "The King will need to be notified."

"I'll wait here," Payn said stubbornly. "Sir Roger will return."

De Clare spun around. "FitzAlan is not coming back."

"You do not know him as I do," Payn argued. "I was with him in France, in Rome, and when he was with the King and Earl Merrick in the East. He will come back." Payn crossed his hammy arms over his chest. "It has only been two nights. I will stay."

"You will ride with us." Sir Tobin closed the distance between them and faced him as if he weren't the size of a battering ram. "That is an order. With FitzAlan gone, I will decide if we go or if we stay."

The two men stared each other down.

"Do not mistake me, Godart," de Clare warned. "We ride tomorrow to tell the King. Edward will decide what to do." He turned then and pulled a pack from the back of his horse, spreading it out on the ground. "And now we will sleep." He sat down on his pallet and looked directly at each man. "That, too, is an order."

Then while Sir Roger's men made their pallets, Sir Tobin de Clare lay down, pulled up his blanket and went to sleep as all knights did—with his hand resting on the hilt of his sword.

Chapter

7

～

The English knight was quieter that next morning, and his skin felt cooler to the touch. After three nights his neatly trimmed beard had grown so much more that the new whiskers on his neck grew stiff and began to curl, which made the cleaning of her poultices difficult, especially when the wound, too, had swollen more.

So Teleri shaved the beard off with a sharp knife, which was tricky, since she only had one good eye. The other eye, the one he'd hit, was swollen like his neck and so very sore to the touch.

She set down a wooden bowl filled with fresh water and had to chase the pesky squirrels away from it and from him. Pig was in the opposite corner eating dandelion roots and ignoring her, his punishment to her for not paying attention to him.

As usual, the flightless goshawk was perched on Pig's back as if he had grown roots there. All her other small animals were in their willow cages or outside. But the wild mockingbirds and curious sparrows stayed atop the window sills, pecking at bits of dried bread she'd left for them.

She began slowly and carefully, dipping the knife into the mazer filled with cool water then drawing the blade slowly over his skin. He did not move while she did it, which was fortunate because the only practice she'd had at this were the few times she had shaved away the hair from a wound on a fox or squirrel.

When she pulled a knife blade over his rough beard and skin it made a rasping sound, just like his voice. She shaved over his chin and up to his cheek, which turned pink after the blade passed over it. Her task was more difficult around his mouth.

Chewing on her lower lip for a brief moment, she stared at his mouth, trying to decide how exactly to do the coarse hair around it. Finally she lightly pinched his lip between two fingers and pulled his mouth taut while she drew the blade slowly and precisely over his skin.

When she finished she sat back on her heels and blew out a breath of relief. Done.

She stared down at him.

To her surprise and dismay, his red beard did not hide a weak chin; it hid an even stronger one. This English was a handsome man, too handsome.

His face was harshly angled, his features as noble as a hawk. His cheeks were hollow where the beard had been and his lips and mouth were stubbornly firm even in his unconscious state. There were small lines at the corners of his eyes, lines that said this man had often laughed.

For just one moment, she wondered what this man laughed at. His children? His wife? He wore no marriage ring, no jewels at all, not even a signet ring.

His brows were darker than his beard, the same deep, dark red as his hair. If he ever opened his eyes, what color would they be?

His skin, which had been cooler to the touch that

morn, must have been so from the cold night air, because by midday he was fevered again. A flush spread from his neck to his forehead and droplets of sweat began to bead on his face.

She made a soup from dandelion tops, garlic mustard, and fresh clover, then spooned it into his mouth to give him strength to fight this recurring fever. She bathed his face, then applied fresh poultice to his neck.

Later that day, when he grew restless again, she cut away his tunic and lay cool, wet cloths on his broad chest, where a mat of curly red hair grew as thick as moss in the forest floor.

By evening, he struggled over and over with the ties that bound him, and she had no choice but to lay on him again to cease his tossing and turning. But it was so strange, for when she placed her cheek to his bare chest he stilled so suddenly, like before, and once again she lifted her head and stared down at him to see if he was still alive.

He rasped a single word. And his expression grew tormented, that universal look of someone who has suffered such pain and heartache that just the look on their face says more than words ever could.

The name of a woman. She believed that to be so from the way he tried to speak. The sound came from his lips so softly, almost tenderly, in the way of a lover.

Then tears dripped from his eyes, over those laugh lines in the corners, streamed over his temples, then spilt into his hairline, where they disappeared as if they had never been there.

His Elizabeth is standing in the arched doorway of the room. A deep blue cloak covers her hair and casts shadows over her face. He has not seen her for a fortnight. He has not slept with her for longer. He lays awake at night, thinking of her. It is her face he sees when he closes his eyes, as if over the years her image has been etched there. She holds his heart, and has for what seems like forever. He has waited so long to see her again. And here she is.

She whispers his name and he walks to her, takes her hands in his. He sees she is crying. He tries to hold her, but she breaks away, turns her back to him so swiftly the hood on her cloak falls away. Light spreads over her hair from the thick candle in the sconce above, and shines so he can almost see his reflection in it.

"I cannot see you again, Roger."

He hears the words but does not believe them, not from Elizabeth. She is his and always has been his.

"No, Elizabeth," he tells her, laughing. "You do not mean those words."

She turns back around, her shoulders straight, her manner strong. Her eyes are dry now because she is angry with him, and they flash with her spirit. "I do mean what I say to you. Yet you will not listen because it is not what you want to hear. That is why I waited so long to come to you."

"I will listen then. Tell me what the reason is that makes you think you will not see me again."

"The best of all reasons." She pauses and gives him a direct look. "Hugh is back."

"Your husband is dead."

She shook her head. "He was held for ransom with Neville. He was ill for a long time, but did not die."

Her words were choking him like hands on his throat. "You do not love Hugh Bigod."

She looks away. "You do not know what is between Hugh and me. You, Roger, do not know what we have or have not."

"You have always loved me."

She draws her finger over the lines in the top of an oaken table. "I do not think that which you and I have together is love, Roger." She looks up at him. "We were too young when we met. We did not like being told by our fathers who we could love or not love. That is what we have together."

He closes the distance between them. He knows what he feels is love. He forces her to turn around and kisses her to show her what they truly have between them—this wild thing that eats at him night and day like something that is alive in the deepest part of him. If that is not love, then he must be mad.

She does not return his kiss. She does nothing but stand there. Dispassionate. Cold.

He pulls back and looks into her eyes, wanting to see her need for him there. There is no need. There is no love. There is nothing he wants to see there.

Because what he does see is worse than anything he could ever imagine. What he sees there in her eyes is pity. He curses and turns away before he does something foolish like shake her. "You do not have to choose between us, between Hugh and me. I will stay in your life, even if Bigod is still part of it."

"Yes. You would. But Hugh will not. And I refuse to willingly cuckold him. He is my husband. In the eyes of the law and of God. He is a good man, Roger, and I will not hurt him."

"Yet you will hurt me."

"Find someone who will love you the way you should be loved."

"I did," he tells her.

She shakes her head. "That person is not me." She walks to the door. "Goodbye, Roger. I wish you well." And Elizabeth closes the door.

He can hear her footsteps on the stone stairs, a soft and eerie kind of tapping that is little more than an empty echo, the way a messenger taps at your door before he tells you that someone has died.

Elizabeth is walking away. The silence she leaves behind is deafening. He stands in the middle of the room staring up at the dark wooden beams in the ceiling, and yet he sees nothing.

He can hardly breathe. His emotion, his soul, this pain in his heart are squeezing the life and breath from him. He hears her horse ride away. She is leaving him now. With nothing.

And Roger cries.

Chapter

8

Teleri moved methodically, trying not to panic as she drove stakes into the hard ground at the center of the stone ring on the plateau high above the valley. She used a flat rock to pound the stakes down, then she bound the knight's hands so he had to lie flat on his back. She raised his knees a little and placed his feet flat, then tied them together and wrapped the ties around a single stake.

The higher and fuller the moon, the stronger the power of the healing stones. A quarter moon had been enough to heal a pheasant, but she had never tried to heal a human.

Sometimes the stones would work and sometimes not. It was as if God chose when to wield the miracle of life, even between these massive granite stones.

She fell to her knees beside him and untied the red pouch of stones, then poured them into her hand. Each one had an odd marking. By trial and error she had learned there was an order, an arrangement she must make.

One by one, she lay each stone with its unique

marking face up in a pattern on his chest, the same pattern as the shape of the moon. Then she straightened, still kneeling but stiffly erect. She lifted her face toward the coolness of the moon and spread her arms out from her sides. She took a few deep breaths.

And she prayed.

He is so cold his skin burns. It hurts to swallow. Every time he does swallow it feels as if his ears are on fire. He is laying on something hard—the ground? Rocks?

What are they doing to him? Is he dead? Do they think he is dead and he is not?

Is this heaven? His skin is too hot now. This must be hell. Do you wake up in hell or stay like this—in the Purgatory Rome always warns of.

He cannot move. He cannot will his arms to move, his feet to move. His body is not working. Why?

It is so hot. Then the heat wanes.

Swiftly, too swiftly, he is so cold.

A woman is near.

Elizabeth?

No. She is chanting a prayer.

A nun?

His arms are stretched outward from his sides, like Christ. Any moment he expects to feel nails going into his palms.

The heat is back, then it wanes again. Yet though he expects it, he is not cold.

A strange feeling comes over him, almost as if some cloud is around him, as if he is being carried by angels. His neck burns still, choking tightly, but the pain is growing cooler. He feels as if all of his skin is shedding away.

Something floods through him, not his blood, but something clear and clean . . . cool, like holy water.

His body is floating now. Light, so light, lighter than the air around him.

A feather.

A star.

A hawk soaring toward the heavens.

His pain disappears. So swiftly that the moment he realizes it has gone, he wonders if it was ever even there.

And then, he sleeps.

Teleri was sitting on a wooden stool, her chin resting atop arms, which were propped on the window sill. Her bare toes were curled around the rough spindles of the stool. That was the most life she had left in her—the ability to curl her toes. She was so tired, so numb that it felt as if she had no bones.

She stared out at the eastern horizon, just above the crowns of the trees, where the sunrise was beginning to turn the sky the color of moor heather. There was an utter stillness in this moment before dawn, a time when everything in the world seemed to be asleep.

Except her.

Finally she straightened, stretched her arms high into the air and twisted, this way, then that. She reached out through the window and pulled the shutters closed, then turned around.

The English lay sleeping. His breaths were even, his sleep easy. For the first time, he truly looked as if he was sleeping instead of dying.

Healing humans was not an easy task. She stood and padded across the dirt floor to stand over him. It did her heart good to see that his color was better. She studied his face for the hundredth time because for some reason she could not will herself to look away. There was something about him that could draw her the way bees were drawn to the wild marigolds.

He took up a great deal of space with his solid body. She wondered what it must be like to watch him walk into a room. He did have fine features. For an English.

His nose was not snubbed, like the fat Brother Dismas at Camrose Castle who was so afeared of her grandmother. His brow was strong, not flat like some of the farmers in the village.

His profile reminded of her of the profiles she had

seen carved on the priory gate at Aberhonddu, strong and lean and sharply cut. The profiles of kings.

She liked the red in his hair, had remembered the way the sun glinted off it when he'd been across the river. He had the longest eyelashes. They were dark, like his brows, and looked like feathers against his skin. She leaned over and brushed her fingertip across one to see if they were truly as long as they looked.

They were.

She shook her head. Her wits had gone walking. Probably from lack of sleep. But before she went to lie down, she leaned over him, pulled her blanket up and lay it gently over his shoulders. She straightened then, and shivered a little.

The air in the cottage was cool, and it chilled her, made the gooseflesh prickle her skin. Hugging herself, she rubbed her hands up and down her arms as she crossed to the opposite corner, where she had made a bed of straw on the hard-packed dirt floor.

Pig was already there, sound asleep, snoring as he always did. Hawk was in his usual spot—asleep on Pig's back. She sat on the straw bed, then lay down on her side, curled into the same shape as the slivered moon, her head resting on Pig's plump and warm belly.

She sighed a little, because she felt as if she truly could go to sleep, then she drew her knees up and pulled her kirtle over her cold, bare feet. Finally, she tucked her hands beneath her cheek.

A moment later she was sound asleep.

Chapter

9

❧

Roger opened his eyes. They felt gravelly and blurred, like he'd slept for a year. It took a moment for his sight to clear. It was dark, yet he was staring up at roof beams and at crude, straw thatching above him.

Where was he?

His gaze darted left and right, taking in the dark, dank room that smelled of farms and dirt and strangely of sweet herbs and fresh flowers. It looked to be a cottage, with a fieldstone base and walls of wattle and daub.

He tried to raise up his head.

A bolt of searing pain encircled his throat, both inside and out.

He moaned. It was a strange, rough sound that was foreign to his ears and a strain on his voice, which felt lost and swollen, as if he had swallowed an egg and it was stuck in the place from where he spoke.

The hanging.

God in heaven . . .

He closed his eyes again, because he had to. All that

had happened came back to him in a rush of horrific memory.

It is barely dusk. I follow the woman and the Arab horse into the tangled woods. It is dark here, black as the King's dungeon and more confusing than the mazes at Leeds, for all around me are paths that lead nowhere. I walk toward one, then another. My sword is raised. The carvings on the hilt press into my palm.

There are dead-ends. Little more than walls of thorns and thickets so twisted I cannot cut through them. I think of hell. This the kind of place where even a soul can get lost.

Someone calls my name. A deep voice that does not sound real, but as if it comes from above me, from heaven.

It calls me again, but the voice changes to a voice that comes from hell.

Something strikes me from behind.

How much time passes? I know not. I awake. Ropes bind me. A blindfold covers my eyes. I see only black. I feel as if my head is lolling back, and then I realize I am atop a horse. A standing horse.

God in Heaven . . . A noose tightens on my neck.

I cannot slide out of the saddle. I would hang myself. I fight at the ties that hold my hands together. Suddenly there is nothing around me but wicked and haunting laughter. The sound echoes in my mind and ears. Am I dreaming? This is not happening. It cannot be happening.

But it is. Fear breaks out on my skin like sweat.

It is no dream. I am going to die.

Someone is standing nearby. I can hear them breathe; the sound is rapid and excited. I feel the evil around me; it permeates the air and touches my skin. It is so real I can almost smell it, the way you can smell rotting meat.

Deep inside, my blood seems to stop flowing in my veins. It freezes. I know this feeling. An instinct that always warns me just before someone goes for my back on the battlefield.

"I am Sir Roger FitzAlan. I ride under the protection of King Edward."

No one speaks to me. There is only that same laughter again.

Then I feel it, hear it—the ominous slap on the rump of my mount.

I am falling, slowly, distant, as if this is the dream I want it to be and not something real. I want to awaken.

I am awake.

The noose chokes me. My own weight and my chain mail pull me down. Down to death and hell.

I can get no air. I struggle. Then I twist. My chest is swelling. The air in there cannot get out. 'Twill burst. My head swells with it, too. I am dying. There is nothing I can do, so I stop moving. I wait for the swelling air to burst from my body, for then, I die.

But he was not dead. He blinked and stared above him at those rafters. His heart pounded in his chest, pounded out the truth: *I live. I live. I live.*

He could feel the sweat pour from his skin, his memory still so close to the truth that he went through the horror all over again.

He had been hanged. Hanged, and the searing pain was still there in his neck and throat. He could not be dead and feel like he did. Only in life could you feel this hellish.

He lay there very still, cautious. Slowly he tried to raise his hand. He could not. He tried to move his feet. He could not.

He was tied to stakes in the ground. He felt the sudden flood of anger go through him, and he pulled at the ropes, bucking and trying to free himself.

He tried to speak, to call out. To shout. Nothing came out of his open mouth but a strange half-growl. His words were blocked by that egg in his throat. His neck hurt inside and out. Swollen huge. He could feel where the rope had been, where it had tightened on his skin.

He had to close his eyes against the pain, the fear, and worse—the humiliation.

The effort to move was so difficult, like he had been running for miles and miles or as if he had no blood left to fuel him. Too weak to do much else, he let his head fall back on something soft—a pallet.

He took quiet, short and even breaths.

Calm yourself. Calm yourself.

How the hell could he be calm when he was bound to the ground, a prisoner in a place that looked like a crofter's hut? Did someone hang him for torture, then cut him down before he was dead? Was this the Purgatory Rome warned of? Where was he? Wincing, he slowly turned his head to the left.

It was dark inside, but his night sight was coming true. Not far away stood a sturdy oak table and chairs with wicked willow twig backs that looked like the claws of a witch's bony hands.

Cages were stacked along the wall, filled with other captives—caged animals. A fox. A weasel and badger. Small hares and others.

Being tied to the ground made him feel like an animal caught in a trap. He tried to raise his head again, despite the pain in his neck, despite the shafts of pain that ran across his head and down to his neck.

He stopped, his head half up, his breath held.

He heard something. A sound from the dark. He could feel the presence of something.

There was someone in the room. Not just one of the animals. A human. His executioner?

He tried to find the strength to turn onto his side. His back, shoulders and arms, and every part of his body was stiff and sore and aching. He winced, sucking in air, and shifted his weight.

A snort like that of a pig came from nearby. His gaze followed the sound. It took a moment for his eyes to adjust.

Sunlight, the fair kind that came with dawn, was just

creeping through the closed shutters. A small ray of
light fell inside.

He stared at the opposite corner.

There was human lump on a nearby pallet of straw. A
lump he recognized by its wild and curly hair.

It was the horse-thief. And she snored like a pig.

Teleri awoke to a thrashing sound. Her eyes shot
open and she froze.

The English was awake.

She sat upright and looked at him.

He was twisting and moving.

Then she heard sounds—harsh noises that came
from his throat. She stood swiftly, tugging down her
gown as she moved over to stand above him.

He jerked hard at the ties that bound him, pulled and
pulled. Then he stopped with a sudden stillness. Had
he been an animal of the forest, his ears would have
perked. But instead he slowly turned his face to look at
her.

She couldn't see his expression, so she reached over
him and shoved open the shutters. Early morning light
spilled inside and over his face.

Those eyes she had wondered about were blue, the
color snow turned when it was deathly cold. But
nothing could have been as cold as the look from them.

She felt the sudden urge to rub her arms.

His face was taut, from anger or fear or both. This
man was twice her size, English, and a knight trained
for war and to kill. And knights did not like to be tied
up and held captive. He looked ready to kill something.

She looked directly into those eyes that frightened
her and tried to mask what she was feeling. "Someone
tried to hang you."

His expression grew icier, something she would have
thought was impossible.

"From a tree."

He made a low noise that sounded as if it came from
a dark cave.

"The branch broke," she added. "I found you."

Though she tried not to show it, she was so very afraid of him, even though he was tied down. She stood a little taller to hide the fact that her knees were turning weak as water.

She wanted to run away and hide instead of look him in the face. "You have been ill. Very ill."

"Ah . . ." The sound escaped his open mouth. He shook his head and pulled at the ropes, bucking and twisting when he could not pull his hands and feet free, when he could not speak. "Ah! Ahhhh!" He was fighting.

She could not believe the same half-dead man had strength left in him to pull and twist like he was. She was thankful, right down to the tips of her bare toes, that she had tied him down again. She watched him struggle. "Hear me!"

He looked at her, his eyes narrowed and savage as the animal noises he made.

"Do not." She shook her head. "If you keep pulling at those ropes, your wrists will turn as raw as your neck."

He grunted something feral, but did not stop trying to get free. His face was so tortured.

"Who could have done this to you?"

The only answer she got was a growl of anger. She thought about how it was for him to awaken like this, especially after what he had already been through. She squatted down next to him and placed her hand softly on his shoulder. "Please. Stop."

It was like he could not hear her, or did not want to hear her. He growled—a sound from deep in his throat like some wild animal.

"Hear me, English. When you are well enough, I will take you to the edge of the forest, then you will be free."

He turned and glared at her from sharp and angry eyes. Then he jerked at the ties and made that sound in his throat. Had she been in his place, the tone would have sounded like a plea. He didn't; it sounded as if he was ordering her to untie him, and the sound was fairly ferocious.

"I will not untie you," she said stubbornly.

His face grew taut. His eyes were so furious they could have burned holes into her skin.

She stood up and turned away from him because the stubborn fool began to struggle again. She moved to a rough-hewn oak table that always wobbled when she placed her elbows on it. She always liked the table because its motion made her feel as if it were a live thing. But she did not smile and talk to the table as she frequently did.

Instead she picked up a shallow wooden bowl and her one spoon, turned and went back to stand over him. She knelt down and held out the bowl so he could see the liquid inside. "This will make you feel better. It will take away the pain and help you heal."

His eyes narrowed dangerously as she tried to spoon some of the medicine into his mouth. Just as she held the spoon to his lips, he jerked his head away.

The motion must have hurt him. His eyes closed in pain.

"This will make you feel better."

He would not look at her, would not cooperate.

"You think I would go to the trouble to save your life just so I could poison you?"

Then he looked back at her.

She held out the wooden spoon. "Here. Take some. Just a small amount." His expression did not change. His look was black, as if he were the one in power. As if he were not tied down.

Again she tried to feed him the liquid, but the stubborn man would not open his mouth. He just pinned her with that cold and fierce look and kept his mouth clamped tightly closed and his jaw so strained she was certain it had to hurt him, for the muscle in his injured neck tightened and in a few places the red burns began to turn deeper and bleed.

"I will not harm you," she told him as calmly as she could. "I swear to you."

It was as if she had not spoken. He did not relax. He did not change his look.

She sighed in a search for patience, found little, then sat back on her heels and leaned over him, watching him closely as she grabbed his chin in two fingers and pinched it. When he opened his mouth to protest, she shoved the spoon inside.

"There," she said and couldn't help feeling as if she had just won a war. She sat back and looked at him. "The herbs will make you feel better."

He spit it out.

She shook her head at him. Men were like children, only worse.

The two of them exchanged glares, a kind of battle of the eyes that within a few moments she knew neither of them was going to win. 'Twas a foolish game she refused to continue.

She shifted places so she was positioned behind him, still kneeling, and placed her hands on his ears. She forced his hard head back against her thighs, almost into her lap.

This way his chin was pointing up higher than his forehead. She held him by one ear, then pinched his chin again, none too gently this time. "It is a good thing for you I shaved your beard, English," she said in an even and calm tone. "It would have hurt more if I grabbed the hair on your chin to pull your stubborn mouth open."

From the expression on his face she was certain he had not yet realized his beard was gone. He did now, though.

She had been wrong before.

He was not furious then.

He was furious now.

"That small amount of red hair will surely grow back," she told him. "Believe me when I tell you, English. It is the least of your problems."

The look he shot at her was one that promised dire retribution.

She just smiled sweetly, released his ear but not his chin, tilted the wooden bowl up, and poured the whole bowl of herb broth into his mouth.

He sputtered and snorted and coughed, like she had almost drowned him.

But at least he swallowed some.

Chapter

10

❧

The little witch had drugged him. Roger's head felt as if he had drunk an entire cask of wine. His tongue was dry as spring fleece. He felt like hell.

His throat was still sore and felt knotted and swollen, but he managed to swallow without feeling as if he were swallowing something almost as large as his head.

When he got his hands on the person who had hanged him he would take every moment of pain out of the man's hide, just before he killed him. He did not know who would do this to him.

Someone who knew him. The coward had called him by name. He heard the voice again calling his name. He heard the laughter and suddenly it was as if he were reliving the hanging.

He began to shake, his fingers, his hands. He clenched them into tight fists and lay there, waiting for this to pass.

He did not know how long he lay there, or if he had slept, but when he opened his eyes his hands were flat against the mattress. He was no longer shaking.

He lifted his head off the tick and looked around the room.

She was gone.

There was no one inside the cottage, nothing but the animals—a badger, a fox, some hares and a couple of weasels—in cages. Even the pig was now tied by a small piece of rope in a far corner. A hawk paced the pig's back the way King Edward paced his war chamber. That one bird was the only animal with any freedom.

The sound of chattering in the window above him made him turn and look up. Some squirrels were perched on the window sill, their tails twitching as they sniffed at some berries that had obviously been placed there.

Lures, he thought.

The squirrels looked down at him, then chattered to each other as if they were ladies of the court busy with the latest, tasty morsel of gossip. He growled at them—the only sound he could seem to make—and the squirrels scampered away.

Thank me, you vermin, for it looks as if I just saved you from being locked inside a cage like that fox and the badger, or worse yet, trussed up like I am.

His head fell back against the soft tick and he lay there for a moment, still and thinking, looking at nothing but the same thing he'd been looking at since he awakened—the dark, heavy wood rafters above him.

Then, out of frustration, he pulled at the rope around his wrists, an action that was a habit by now, for it seemed as if he pulled at the ropes almost as often as he took a breath.

But this time he froze. He made a fist and pulled his left hand again. Either he was still groggy or the rope on his left hand was loose.

He wiggled his hand. The rope *was* loose.

For the next few minutes he wrenched, twisted,

pulled . . . pulled, twisted, wrenched, until his hand came free. It slipped through the rope as if it had been greased. He swiftly reached over and worked as fast as he could to untie his other hand. This was his chance to get away.

He sat up quicker than he should have and the room swam. He held his head in his hands for a moment, then took a deep breath to quiet his churning belly, and he began to loosen the ties around his ankles.

He crawled to his knees, then used the window sill to help him stand up. His legs felt like they had been stewed, and he had to steady himself on the wall lest he fall back down. Using the wall for support, he moved carefully toward the door, then stumbled slightly as he went outside in the afternoon sunshine.

She was nowhere around.

He took a few steps, edging near the corner of the cottage, where he looked around for her.

The Arab was in the meadow beyond a stone bridge that traversed a running brook. Still no sign of the woman.

He looked in all directions and moved as swiftly as he could with such weak and stiff legs and bare feet. His muscles felt light, jellied, and as if he could not tighten them should he wish to. Small sharp stones poked painfully into the soles of his feet. He stumbled forward in lurches, for he could not truly run. Try as he might, his body would not obey the commands of his mind.

He staggered across the ground and over the bridge to the meadow. He slowly approached the horse, which was grazing on the grass. As he came closer to the animal, he tried to speak out of natural habit, to soothe the horse and keep him from moving away.

But when Roger opened his mouth nothing came out. Only that strangled sound.

The horse looked at him, its head down, its eyes turned upward while it chewed on some of the grasses. The Arab raised its proud equine head. Slowly, Roger

reached out and stroked the horse's mane and the white
mark on its muzzle, moved the flat of his hand gently
down the horse's neck and he touched its mane.

Then, before the Arab could see what he was about,
he swung onto its sleek back. He twisted the Arab's
mane around his hands and dug in his heels.

The horse stood still as a stone.

He kicked the Arab again, then again, and finally
managed to cluck his tongue.

The horse cantered across the grass toward the edge
of the meadow.

He did it! Roger laughed to himself, feeling cocky
and free. He was away! *Away,* he thought as he and the
horse headed toward the trees and freedom.

Ride to where? To the stones? He did not know if his
men would be still there. Slowing his mount he looked
between two directions. For barely a hair's-breadth of a
moment.

There was a high and piercing whistle.

The Arab made a sharp turn to the left.

And Roger fell right.

Teleri stopped beating the grass and dirt from the
blanket and took a few steps to the closest window. She
looked inside at the English. He was still unconscious.

She went back and whacked a willow broom on the
blanket a few more times, then she pulled it off of a tree
limb and folded it over her arm as she moved back
inside, where she covered the unconscious knight who
tried to steal Horse. Crossing the room quietly, she sat
down at the trestle table where her friends the squirrels
were nibbling on some walnuts and berries she'd placed
there for them.

Chin in her hand, she drew imaginary circles on the
tabletop while she distractedly watched the squirrels
with their plump, twitching tails. She gave a huge sigh.
"I've gotten myself into a fine mess."

They looked at her and popped more gooseberries
into their plump cheeks. She sighed again and switched

hands for resting her chin, then drummed her fingers atop the trestle table.

As if finger-drumming could ever solve her problem—an English knight who must weigh close to fourteen stone. One truly angry English knight who was not going to be any happier once he woke up.

It was the way he looked at her that made her nervous. He did not need his voice to intimidate her. He could just look at her from those blue eyes of his, eyes that didn't need words to threaten.

From the moment she'd found him, she had been worried only with saving his life. She had not even cast one thought toward what she would do once he awakened. What a fool she was!

And now that he had awakened, now that he had glared at her from hard eyes and fought at the ropes, she saw what a difficult and dangerous situation she was truly in.

So she sat there, wondering what she should and could do. The mazer was before her, sitting on the table, filled with the cold herb broth that would make him sleep. Certainly she could not keep drugging him indefinitely.

Or could she?

Chapter

11

"Do not move, English!"

Roger stared at the young woman who was sitting on a roughly-carved stool and holding him at bay with a pitchfork.

'Twas hard to believe she was the same woman he'd seen at the stone ring, the one with the pheasant, the woman he'd likened to Mary Magdalene and Ruth.

The bloody horse-thief.

She watched him from a pair of sharp eyes the color of the forest. One of those eyes was bruised and swollen.

Her hair was a strange color, nut brown and golden, and was still wild and curly and full, as if the wind were trying to steal it from her very head, and some of that mass of wild hair fell over her breasts and hung past the seat on the stool.

Her age was somewhere near twenty, perhaps eight and ten, he could not tell. She was young and her features pleasing for a witch. She wore rough clothes, but looked surprisingly clean. Her dusty bare toes were curled over the rung of the stool, the only outward sign that she was truly tense.

Then he looked down and realized why.

No ropes. No stakes in the dirt floor. He was no longer tied down.

Her chin up in defiance, her leaf-green eyes were on him, staring boldly, or perhaps intently, for she watched him in the same way a cornered animal watches for the first flinch, the first movement of its attacker.

He opened his mouth and tried to speak. *"Uhhhrrr."* The low moan of a noise that came from his mouth and throat sounded closer to words. *"Uggggh . . ."*

Now he sounded as if someone had cut out his tongue.

She looked as surprised as he was to the change and cocked her head as if that would help her better understand him. "Does your throat hurt?"

He shook his head, winced, then held up a hand in front of the pitchfork and sat up slowly. He'd been hanged. He didn't need to be stuck too.

She jumped off the stool, her face taut and she jabbed the pitchfork near his face. "I am warning you, English. If you try to hurt me or make any swift movements, I will use this."

English. She spoke the word as if it were dirty. He looked at the pitchfork, her weapon. She was not a tall woman, but small. She would not even come to his chin—his bare chin which the ferocious little horse-thieving Welsh witch had shaved.

No mere wooden pitchfork would protect her should he choose to do anything. He was one of Edward's knights, not some animal for her to capture and keep the way ladies keep gyrfalcons and songbirds and kittens.

Yet he did not think he could make any quick and controlled movements. His head felt light, from drugging or the fall or both, and the room was still moving slowly, as if it were dancing 'round a damned Maypole.

Cold sweat beaded on his head and chin, and his belly bounced up near his throat. God . . . if he had to heave out his belly with his throat so sore, it would about kill him. He took a deep and even breath.

"You fell on your head."

He slowly looked at her. For a brief moment she had two heads, a few noses, and a blurred face.

"Off the horse," she added, as if she were trying to help him remember.

Ha! He remembered the horse well. The stolen horse. He scowled at her.

She did not back away or move forward. "Surely it is a good thing you fell on that hard head of yours, English, else you might have been badly hurt."

He scowled at her, an action that sent a jab of pain shooting over his head and temple. He flinched, a small moan escaping his dry lips. He tried to swallow and wanted to shout at the thickness he felt—the whiplike burning in his neck.

He gave her a look that should have cooked her. Men had been known to run from that look. Turks turned and ran from it on the battlefield. His sisters used to scatter like hens, screaming to their mother if he should look at them like he was looking at this Welsh witch with the wild hair and bruised eye.

She only raised her little chin a notch, looked him straight in the eye, and brandished the pitchfork closer to his face.

Had he trusted his sight or his strength, he would have reached up and grabbed the thing, which was making him light-headed, the way she was waving it around. But he did not trust his body to obey the commands of his head.

"You owe me a debt for your life."

He looked at her, not used to being spoken to as boldly and arrogantly as she was by anyone, with the exception of his mother or the Queen. Usually women tried to flatter him.

But she stood in the center of the cottage with its

packed dirt floor, stood there proudly in her peasant's garb and shoeless feet, arrogantly confident, like she wasn't a flea trying to take on a hound.

She was wearing a rough brown gown and saffron tunic, which was belted with a linked belt from which hung a pouch of soft and pliant red leather with braided drawstrings. That pouch caught his eye, for it was an expensive item and clashed with such plain and crude clothing.

Like the Arab horse, he decided the leather purse was most likely stolen. And he did not like to be reminded that he owed her; it only reminded him that he had failed as a man and a knight. No knight wanted to be reminded he was so mortal, yet the scars on his neck were there to remind him *ad infinitum.*

"I will make a bargain with you, English knight," she said, her nose stuck up in the air as if that would make her taller. "You may stay here until you are well, then you are to leave and never come back here."

He said nothing.

"And you will not take Horse with you," she added. "He is mine."

Roger knew he would do what he wished.

"I will share my food with you. I will help you heal, but you will not repay me for saving your life by taking my horse."

He tried to tell her it wasn't her horse.

"Do not try to speak, English. Your words will soon come back to you."

Speak? He looked at the hand she held up. He did not need her to tell him what to do. He tried to speak but that huge lump in his throat did not let the words come. All that burst from his lips were noises. He wanted to scream curses to the heavens when he could not speak the way he wanted.

So instead, he tried to stand up. His height would work to his favor. 'Twould show her she could not order him around.

Standing up was a whole new mistake. He swayed so

suddenly he almost fell on his face. He reached for the wall and shifted his weight.

Pain shot up his foot. His leg gave out, just buckled underneath him. He sat down hard on his hip, then shook his head and stared down at his feet.

One of them was swollen to the size of a cabbage.

He turned to look at her.

"Did I forget to mention your injured foot?"

He tried to move toward her, half crawling, but he stopped. He already sounded like some animal. He didn't need to crawl on all fours like one.

He froze on all fours, breathing hard against the storm he was feeling. He took a few deep breaths to calm down. It hurt to breathe that quickly. Then he folded his leg under him and just sat, his hands clenched, his gaze locked with hers.

"If you want to hobble back to wherever you came from, feel free to do so." She jabbed the pitchfork into the ground and half leaned on it as she casually crossed one bare foot over the other. "Or you may stay here until you are well enough to leave."

Silence filled the room. Tension was a live thing between them. He could almost hear the thrumming of it, like the snap of a pennant on the battlefield, that eerie motion of air that happened before danger hit hard and fast.

"I hear you English knights have a code of honor. You must give me your word that you will not take Horse."

What did she know of honor? She stole horses and purses and lured forest animals into cages. She had tied him to stakes, yet she stood there waiting and demanding for him to forswear.

His options were few. He looked at his swollen foot. The pain was still in his neck and head. He was weak, his limbs sluggish. He did not like her ultimatum, did not relish giving her anything but the trouble she deserved. Yet sense told him that for now, he had little choice.

"Do you agree, English? Do you give me your word?" She cocked her head and gave him a look that dared him to say no.

Time and silence hung there between the two of them, heavy and still.

Roger closed his eyes in frustration. And he nodded.

Chapter

12

❧

Kent, England

A horn blew loudly into the tepid air, warning of riders approaching the Royal Castle at Leeds. Within moments, the sound of horses' hooves clattered over a winding river of stone pavers which led from the edge of rolling English hillsides, around a moated lake fed by the River Len, and on toward the castle gatehouse.

From a corner of the gatehouse tower flew a standard of red with three golden walking lions, and all along the upper walls stood primed archers and spearmen, their helmet visors down so they looked like man-sized playing pieces from a giant chessboard.

The air seemed to tense for a moment, filled with only the sounds of the grinding stones of the castle mill, the soft rush of water and the distant hubbub inside the inner baileys.

The group riders slowed their pace as they moved closer to the gate, then their leader reined in his mount and looked up.

A stern-visaged guard poked his head out from the upper crenels and called out, "Halt ye!"

The leader held up his hand and the troop behind him stopped.

"State your purpose!" The guard's voice was strong and demanding and the men along the wall stayed primed at their targets: the riders.

The knight at the forefront of the troop flew no pennant of his own, but he wore a deep blue cloak beneath which was a tabard of the de Clare signature. He sat atop his sleek gray palfrey with distinctive markings of black, unmistakably bred from the Earl of Gloucester's prized stables, and the mount was equipped in expensive trappings of heavily tooled Spanish leather trimmed in gleaming silver.

"Sir Tobin de Clare," the knight called out. "Son to Gilbert de Clare, Earl of Gloucester; vassal to Merrick de Beaucourt, Earl of Glamorgan and liegeman to Sir Roger FitzAlan!"

His mount shifted backwards as he pulled out straps of leather and gold from his saddle pack. The sudden, tinny sound of the King's bells signaled to all his Plantagenet favor.

"Hear you! I've urgent business with the King!"

Two trumpet blasts sounded and within mere moments the outer portcullis slowly creaked open like the jaws of some giant animal. A heavily armed group of royal guards wearing the *gules trois lions passant guardant un pale d'or* rode out from within the dark bowels of the castle.

They met the knight's troop and escorted them through the gates, the second portcullis, and across a stone bridge that led to the barbican, which was situated on a man-made island impossible to breach.

The men of the troop rode two-by-two, Sir Tobin de Clare and Captain Payn Godart in the lead. When the crowd stopped near the entrance to the main castle, Payn turned to Sir Tobin. "I still contend that one of us should notify Sir Merrick. He should know Sir Roger is missing. He is his closest friend and a powerful man. Earl Merrick would stop at nothing to find Sir Roger."

"No one is to be told before the King." De Clare's tone was cold and curt, one that said he would take no argument. A few moments later he dismounted, obviously frustrated by the wait of the milling crowds. He wove his way through, his height and manner enough to make the crowd part like Moses parted the Red Sea.

Payn ground his teeth in frustration and tried to follow, leaving behind his horse and his men, and the royal escort who had led them as far as the main castle doors.

Sir Tobin de Clare took the steps to those doors two at a time. He pushed his way inside, his blue cloak billowing out behind him and his boots of Spanish leather tapping loudly on the stone floor of the entrance hall.

Payn ran up the front steps and slipped inside the huge doors, then strode swiftly to catch up with de Clare and a sputtering royal servant who was trying to get the willful Sir Tobin to listen to him.

"Not now, man!" Sir Tobin barked and shrugged off the man's pleading as he strode through the castle toward the royal private apartments in the Gloriette. "I have urgent matters with the King!"

"But, sir . . ." The servant found a burst of stamina to run in front of Sir Tobin and try to block his way just as he approached the doors to the royal chambers.

Payn placed his huge hand on Sir Tobin's shoulder. He stopped and turned around, his face angry.

"Perhaps we should listen to the man, de Clare." Payn nodded at the two huge guards armed with small but deadly weapons, a crossbow and drawn sword, and who stood at the doors to the royal compartments. "Pray man, listen!" he said in a sharp whisper. "Before you manage to get our bloody heads lopped off!"

"The King is gone hunting, sir knight," the poor servant said in a half-breath. The man was panting from trying to keep up with the knights and their long strides and quick motions. He took another gasping breath, his pale hand against the royal placard covering his heaving chest. "He left this morning in the company of Earl Rannulf and the royal falconers. They are not to return here for two days."

Sir Tobin grunted something, tightened his fists, and cursed under his breath.

Payn tried again. "I beg you, Sir Tobin. We should leave now for Earl Merrick in Glamorgan."

"No." De Clare shook his head stubbornly, then set a hard look on Payn. "Go tell the men to check with the captain of the King's guard for quarters. We will wait here for Edward's return."

O, what can ail thee, knight-at-arms
　　Alone and palely loitering?

I met a lady in the meads,
　　Full beautiful, a fairy's child,
Her hair was long, her foot was light
　　And her eyes were wild.

　　—"La Belle Dame Sans Merci," John Keats

Chapter

13

❧

Words would not come from his throat.

Roger lay atop the tick trying to find his lost voice. If he spoke swiftly, the sounds were garbled and low, like that of water bubbling over rocks. If he spoke slowly, the words clawed their way out, scraping and scratching and in the end, sounding nothing like words. Even though he could feel the tremor of speech in his chest and back.

He slammed his fist against the hard-packed earth floor and closed his eyes so tightly it hurt. His ears rang with anger he felt; it ran through him so completely it was as if it was part of his blood.

Here in this cottage he lay, a cripple who could not speak, could only hobble, not walk. He had always believed he could handle any enemy, since he had done so in battle and tourney. He always had the arrogance needed to be a knight, for men who lived by war held the strict belief, deep down in their souls, that they were invincible.

He was not invincible. The truth came home to him swiftly and without any ease, a bitter bite for him to swallow, for it tasted like the one single thing any man of pride would abhor; it tasted of cowardice.

So he lay there for a while, his confidence shaken, his mind filled only with self-loathing and pity. That defeated feeling. It started at the crack inside his pride and moved swiftly to consume his mind and heart. It pricked his skin and made him quiver with shame and anger. It made his eyes burn with humiliation and seemed to sap all the strength from him.

A man like him was not supposed to feel things. Proud and strong. Warriors. That's what men were.

She came inside the cottage then, at that very worst of all possible moments.

"Good morning to you, English." She stopped and eyed him with her good eye, her stance cocky, a fist on her hip. "You still lay there, I see."

He did nothing, only looked at her standing there just inside the door, her voice cheery and bright while the dark remnants of what he was feeling only seconds before still hung over him. That pig followed her inside and snorted at her heels. She shooed it away with the end of a staff she held in one hand.

"I have brought you this." She held out the staff.

He noticed then that it was not the pitchfork. It looked to be an elm branch, long and sturdy with a V at the top where branches had once begun.

"A crutch," she explained as if he did not have the puny sense it took to figure that out.

"Do not scowl at me as if you want to boil me in oil, English. You cannot speak, so I do not know if you understand me. If you do not want me to explain my thoughts and actions to you, then nod your head, raise your hand, or some such thing so I know you understand me."

She was a brave and mouthy little witch considering she had no pitchfork to wave under his nose. Some perverse part of him wondered what she would do if he shot up on all fours and snarled at her.

When he made no move to take the crutch, she said, "The day is warm and golden outside. You should come."

He did not respond swiftly, but eventually he shook his head.

She chewed thoughtfully on her lip for a brief instant, her bravery slipping.

He wondered if she even realized it, this woman who suddenly did not look as brave as her words.

"If you want to get around, you will need this. I cannot make you use it, so I will leave it here." She leaned the crutch against one wall, cast him one more odd glance that held something that looked disgustingly like pity, then she turned, the pig sniffing impatiently at her skirts as she walked outside the open door.

He did not know how long he sat there, staring at the crutch, not knowing if he wanted to break it or use it. He looked away then, annoyed at everything in general. He leaned back against the wall and rested his hands on his raised knees, then winced and extended his leg with the injured foot straight out in from of him.

He turned then and studied the crutch. It had no voice, yet in his mind could have sworn he heard it calling to him, saying coward . . . coward . . . coward. . . .

He was a fool. It was only a piece of wood.

He tried something different—cursing every vile swear word he could think of, but to his ears they sounded like weak moans and pleas instead of foul words and curses on the heads of saints.

He looked away, his face tight, his jaw tense, his fists laying over his bent knees but still tightly clenched. Then he found his gaze drawn back again.

A stick leaning against the wall stared back at him.

When he could not stand it any longer, he crawled toward the crutch.

* * *

Cabbages were tucked into straight, neat rows on the west side of the cottage, where they would get the most sun. Teleri squatted down to examine them. A moment later Pig trotted over to her from the brook and trampled through her cabbage bed, snorting and sniffing and being a pest.

"Scat! Off with you!" She shooed him away, then picked off the crushed leaves and patted the earth around the cabbage heads he had stomped over.

Her cabbages had grown, so much so that their leaves were beginning to touch like the hands of young girls dancing around a Maypole.

Now all she needed was to keep Pig from destroying her garden. She turned and looked at him. He was sitting across the yard, his hooves stretched out in front of him and his snout resting on them. His eyes were closed.

Doubtless he was dreaming, not of cabbages and kings, but cabbages and turnips. She shook her head and her gaze traveled past the brook.

In the meadow beyond, Horse was munching on grass while Hawk was perched on his back, wings out as if he would take flight, something he had never done, for Hawk did not fly.

She had found the goshawk with wounded Horse and had brought the bird back with them. Hawk had stayed ever since, melding in easily with her other animals, some that should have been his natural prey. But he spent most his days on the back of Pig or Horse, or hanging from Horse's mane or tail. The batty bird liked to swing back and forth.

Shaking her head, she pulled up one fat cabbage for their meal and set it aside, then tilted a bucket and spilt some water into the soft dark dirt around her cabbages. Since she was already on her knees, she just crawled over to a nearby planting bed and pulled up a few turnips and carrots, shaking off the dirt clods, then she moved back and placed them and the cabbage into a

willow basket that was already filled with plump berries, leafy vegetables, and freshly clipped herbs.

She stood then, bent and brushed off her gown where
marks of the damp dirt had made wet brown circles in
the shape of her knees. Rocking back a bit on her heels,
she pulled up her skirt and examined her bare feet.

There was mud between her toes and all the way up
to her ankles. She dropped the skirt and with the back
of her hand she swiped back a swatch of curly hair that
fell in her face. She had the same mud all over her
hands, too. She used her short apron to wipe them off
and managed to only smear dirt and mud all over it.

She stared down at her dirty palms, then pulled
down a shock of wild hair into her face, sniffed it and
wrinkled her nose. She needed to wash her hair, and to
bathe. The brook was so close and the sun was warm
enough.

She looked at the cottage window and listened,
tentatively, wondering if the English was still lying
there. She heard no sound, so she took a couple of steps
around the fat cabbages and placed her palms against
the wattle and daub wall, then very slowly, she peeked
into the cottage.

He was down on all fours, the crutch lying next to
him.

She held her breath.

He shifted to his knees, then grabbed the crutch and
used it to help him stand erect.

You did it! She ducked her head quickly, afraid that
she had spoken aloud. She huddled down beneath the
window for a moment, her hand covering her mouth.
She had spent most of the morning making that crutch.
She wanted it to work for him.

There was a soft thud. She heard him grunt. She
slowly raised her head again so that just her eyes were
peering over the window sill. He was sitting down, the
crutch fallen at his side, and he was glaring at it with
the same black look she refused to cower under.

He tried again, his face so determined and fierce she

was surprised he did not breathe fire. To his knees first, then standing.

He did it! She let out her breath and grinned.

He did not smile as she would have, did not let out a whoop of success, but instead he stood there, a little straighter than before, with his chest puffed out the way Hawk did when he was pleased.

Arrogant English. But she was smiling proudly when she thought it.

Roger turned and limped angrily toward the door, where he had to duck under the top of the door frame before he hobbled outside. He was still angry, angry because he felt as if he had gained his life, but lost his ability to ever speak again, at least in anything other than a harsh croak.

He stood outside for a moment, not realizing until then that he truly needed fresh air, and even more so, he thought, he needed privacy. He looked about him for the closest direction to the bushes—the thickest bushes where he could relieve himself.

He started to move forward, his crutch sliding into the soft dirt in places. He struggled with it, then managed to move with more ease because the earth was harder packed the closer he got to the bushes.

It took a moment for him to realize that she was there moving with him, taking two small steps to his limping strides.

He glanced down at her, staring at the top of her head as he took two more steps.

She was walking next to him.

He stopped and frowned down at her. Surely she did not think she was going with him?

He took two steps.

She took two steps.

He did not move, but looked down at her. When she returned his look, he shook his head.

For a moment she stared at him as if she were confused. Then her good eye grew wide and too merry for his liking. She could not hide her knowing grin from him, though she was wise enough to try.

Glowering, he turned away and began to limp forward.

"It is not something I haven't seen before, English," she said, walking at his side again.

He planted the crutch into the dirt with as much speed as he could. Annoyed. Though he was not certain which bothered him more, the fact that she was trying to go along with him or that she claimed to have such certain and intimate knowledge of men. Which sense said should not matter to him at all.

"English!"

He stopped, his hand tightening about the crutch, and he turned slowly to look back at her.

She stood a few feet behind him, her hands on her hips and her chin stuck up high. "Who do you think took care of you when you were ill?"

He did not acknowledge her, but turned and limped swiftly away because he did not like it one hair when he felt his face burn red with color.

He was a knight. Not some green lad who blushed when he was with a woman. He did not know why he felt embarrassed, unless hanging robbed him of the man he had been.

Enough women had seen him. He could talk freely of cocks. 'Twas the usual conversation of men.

"Truly, English, yours is no different than any others I have seen," she said as if she had a world of experience with men's privy members.

He kept moving.

"I suppose, though, it is somewhat different," she called out.

Different? He ignored her and headed for the trees.

"It is smaller than most."

He stopped as if suddenly rooted to the ground. Slowly he turned around.

She was not smiling. He could see from her face that she was completely serious.

Smaller? His eyes narrowed and his breath came out in the sound of a hiss.

Her look was thoughtful when she added, "Horse is much bigger."

He stood startled. He was not certain then if it soothed his pride that she was comparing him to a stallion. No man liked to be told he was small.

None of that mattered, however, because she would not be going with him into the woods. He reached out with one hand and pointed toward the meadow.

She stared at him, at his finger, and looked back to his face again. "You want me to go."

He nodded.

"You are certain you do not need me?"

He said nothing, just narrowed his eyes at her, a warning she should be gone quickly.

"Fine." She sighed, then added with a flick of her hand. "Be on your way. The cess pit is behind those trees. Over there. After you get into the bushes just follow your nose into the woods."

He turned then, a few swear words clogging his throat, but they came out scratchy and rough and more like growls.

"I shall stay here in the meadow if you need me," she called out to him in a merry little voice that did nothing for his dour mood.

Need her? He hobbled away as quickly as he could toward a spot in the forest where the trees and bushes were thickest.

He was no horse, but he had never had any complaints. Most women would gasp at first, he thought with pride, limping through the trees and bushes with good speed.

Anyone with experience knew it was not size, but what you did with it. And he was a man who knew how to wield both his swords.

"English!" she called out. "How long do you think you will be?"

Was she daft? He could not shout out to her. He swiftly retied his chausses—before she decided to join him—and he turned and struggled back through the woods until he could stick his head out from the thick bushes.

"Oh." There was a wealth of meaning in that one single word. "You could not answer me, could you?"

He just glared at her.

"Oh," she said again as she looked at him with the first sign he'd seen of embarrassment. "I shall leave you alone then." She finally turned and walked toward the stone bridge.

He grunted under his breath the whole time he moved back to finish his business, annoyed that he could fall into such silliness.

Smaller? He was bigger than his own hand. And for the next few moments he stood there . . . looking down.

Teleri moved across the meadow, laughing because Horse was nudging her with his muzzle. It was a game they played on sunny bright days like today. He followed her like a puppy, step for step, moving whenever she did, and when she stopped, he would butt up against her with his muzzle and push her forward, then shake his head and mane as if he were laughing at her.

Soon he tired of the game and trotted off to munch on some high grass that held more appeal. Animals were not like people. Animals moved through life one need at a time. They did not need everything at once, only what was necessary at that single moment.

Teleri walked through the grass, just feeling its coolness on the soles of her feet. Before long she began to gather autumn wild flowers for the table and soon her arms were full of white and blue campion and cornflowers, pink and yellow chicory and fairy flax.

Then she turned and saw them, a doe and her twin fawns. She knew them all well. The fawns had been newborns that very spring and now they were larger, their legs less gangly. She squatted down in the meadow and stayed very still.

It did not take long. The doe came out from the shelter of the trees and walked toward her, trotting a few feet, then stopping, unsure, in the way of old friends or family when they had not seen each other in too long a time.

Teleri held out a stalk of cornflowers. The fawns took a few small steps from their shelter, their ears perked, their bright eyes following the doe. They watched eagerly when she ate the flowers Teleri held out to her. Then the doe turned and made chittering noises, a call for her babes.

Meanwhile Teleri reached over to a nearby basket and grabbed up some of the sweet berries she had picked. She held out her hands, palms up, filled with plump gooseberries. The fawns followed their mother and soon nibbled the berries right from her fingers.

She laughed, because it tickled and because she loved looking at these animals with their silky fur and delicate features, their big brown eyes and peaceful countenance, things that seemed to stand for all the natural good in the world.

She sat down in the fresh grass and the deer folded their legs and sat there with her, unafraid, as one of the fawns rested its head in her lap with a soft sigh. She stroked him for a few minutes.

She stretched back with her hands flat on the ground behind her and held her face up to the warmth of the sun. She stayed that way for a long time, long enough to have her cheeks grow warm. Then the deer shifted and looked up suddenly with its ears perked.

Teleri followed the doe's intent stare.

The English stood across the meadow at the edge of the forest, his hand resting against an old hemlock tree. He just watched her, his expression unreadable.

She had no idea how long he had been standing there, watching. Part of her wished she could look away and pretend he was not there, pretend that neither of them noticed each other. But she could not.

He did not choose to stay there watching her. He turned and limped back to the cottage, leaving her with that same odd flutter inside of her, the one she had thought was fear, but now realized was something else altogether, something she had never, ever felt before.

Chapter

14

Roger had been wrong.

He would have discovered so even if he had not come upon that scene in the meadow. He had heard of people who had an uncanny ability to tame deer, birds and horses, even great beasts like elephants and lions.

But he had never seen it with his own eyes. A deer with its head resting in her lap?

Stunned and feeling strange, he went back to the cottage where the small world around him was natural. But he went inside with a new perception.

On closer look, he saw that the animals in the cages were no more captive than he was. He stood directly in front of the top cage.

The badger inside it was blind, its eyes milky and unseeing as it looked out at him from behind the wooden bars of its cage. Its flat black nose twitched and its ears perked up.

Roger picked up a small berry near the rim of the cage floor that the animal had been chasing. He balanced the ripe purple berry on his finger in front of the badger's nose. The badger froze for a second, then sniffed some more. Suddenly it plucked away the berry and popped it into his mouth, leaving a small drop of bright purple juice on Roger's fingertip.

He wiped his hand on his chausses, then studied all the caged animals along the wall. Next to the blind badger was a lop-eared rabbit with only three feet. Another hare had a scab which sliced across its haunch in the jagged imprint of an iron trap. It did not take a great thinker to figure out what had happened to both of these animals.

Angry red spots covered the pale pink skin of an ermine weasel in a nearby willow cage. In fact, he could only tell it was an ermine because of the few stray red hairs that poked out from its head. The tips of those hairs were just beginning to turn ermine white in preparation for the coming winter ice and snows. The scrawny-looking, naked weasel had no sign of stubble, so he knew she had not shaved the weasel as she had done to him.

Leaning his weight on a crutch, Roger reached up and rubbed the stubble on his chin and cheeks. It felt strange. As if he were standing naked before the world. He had not been without his red beard since he was just a lad and had grown it solely to spite his father for laughing at him in the great hall and saying to all that he was too young and too green to even have face hair.

The beard would grow back, should Roger choose to look the same. Perhaps he did not wish to, though. Perhaps he would like to face his would-be assassin from a clean-shaven chin and cheek, so his face, every measure of it, would be the last thing the cowardly bastard would ever see. The man who hanged him would take Roger's image with him to Purgatory and to haunt him in whatever hell awaited him when Roger was finished with him.

One of the cages rattled, and he lifted his gaze. The wooden doors looked loose, but not loose enough for the fox inside it to slip out. The fox gripped the door with its black paw and cocked its head at him. Its dark brown eyes were alert, darting left and right, then holding his own gaze for a moment of assessment that made Roger feel as if he were looking into the eyes of a man, not an animal.

Then it tried to turn around and move toward a small pot of water tucked into the cage corner. But the fox could not move well; it dragged its right hip and stumbled, falling flat on the floor of the cage. It lowered its small head to the cage floor and just lay there, defeated.

Foxes were the fastest animals in the woods. They could dart across the fields and moors with speeds that were a pure challenge to man and horse.

But not this fox. Because one of its rear paws was limp, as if that whole back leg had no bones.

And he was a knight who could not avenge the wrong done him any more than that fox could run through the woods. He was lame, maimed liked these animals, left to lean on a crooked crutch made from the branch of an elm tree, his voice little more than a whisper and his throat raw and swollen from being hung.

Hung. They hung thieves and poachers and defilers, not knights of the realm.

It was humiliating and he wanted to scream out his anger and frustration and worse . . . the horrific shame he felt at what had happened to him.

His jaw grew tight and his whole body began to quiver the way an arrow did after it struck a tree. Any huntsman knew the arrow quivered from the power shooting uncontrolled through its shaft, power that did the arrow no good because it could never move on; it must stay where it stuck.

Roger could do little but just stand there, stuck like an arrow. He gripped the crutch so tightly he lost feeling in his hand, and his free fist was tighter than his jaw, and began to shake, too.

It took a long time. How long, he knew not. Because

all he could do was stand there seeing nothing but rage.

When it was finally over, he sat down hard on a wobbly stool, exhausted. He looked around the cottage, his only refuge for the time being.

He had choices. He could limp and hobble his way back to Glamorgan, but he did not intend to. He was too weak now. He needed to give himself more time to think and time to heal. Time to plan.

Someone wanted him dead. Wanted it enough to hang him.

For now, he would let them think he was dead. At least until he had the strength to fight back, then he would leave this place and find the man who did this to him. He reached up and touched his swollen throat, then closed his eyes because it still hurt.

A few minutes later he opened his eyes, seeing nothing but feeling everything, and he took a vow, on his honor, that he would make whoever did this to him suffer.

Not more than a heartbeat later he heard her laughter, distant, clear and clean as the wind. It came from out in the meadow, he supposed. The sound of it came through an open window and washed over him, seemed to permeate his skin and sink inside of him with something light and free, something that was the complete opposite of what he had just been feeling. Light flooding the darkness.

Here he was shaking with anger, mentally plotting revenge, while she was outside in the field laughing and humming and hand-feeding wild animals. He felt as if he were in a strange world—a middle ground between battlefield and some kind of enchanted forest, where nothing was as it appeared, where the real world disappeared with a wish or a hope, where pain was replaced by happiness. Although it had been so long since he'd experienced happiness he had forgotten until this very moment exactly what it felt like.

He had assumed she was nothing but a thief and a

half-mad witch who would grow into an old hag someday, one who got some kind of sick pleasure from keeping animals locked in cages and grown men tied to stakes.

Yet the evidence was all around him. These animals could not live in the wild with such afflictions. She saved them, the same way she had saved him, a fact he had not thought much about, even though she kept reminding him of it.

He owed her; she was right.

But it had taken him a long time to notice the truth. She was responsible for saving him, the same way she had saved these animals. He must have sensed that about her at the stone ring the first time he saw her. It had hit him again when he stood at the forest, leaning on that tree and watching her, unable not to watch her.

He should have trusted his first reaction, for his instinct was usually true. But he had not. His anger at being hanged had taken more than his voice and his pride.

It had blinded him.

Time to brave the beast.

Teleri picked up the basket and looped its rung over her arm. She padded on bare feet through the warm dirt and around the corner, then stood in the open doorway, watching.

He was sitting on her stool, now, the elm crutch gripped tightly in one white-knuckled hand.

He looked as if he wanted to murder the world.

The thought crossed her mind that perhaps she should not have untied him.

For luck she broke off a sprig of rosemary from her bundles of herbs and stood on her toes, reaching up. Rosemary would ward off the Devil if one hung it near the door, so she stuck it into a crack in the doorframe. She figured it couldn't hurt her to be cautious, for she carried no pitchfork or staff, only instinct and blind faith.

He did not seem to notice she was even standing there. His eyes and thoughts looked to be far, far away.

She took a deep breath and walked inside. She let the basket slide down her forearm to her hand. She swung the basket back and forth by its handle, secretly gathering momentum.

She figured she could clout him with it if he went back on his word and attacked her.

But he did not. He looked up and seemed genuinely surprised that she was even there. He did not try to speak, but looked at her from eyes that were strangely curious, not threatening, more as if he were seeing her for the first time.

"The crutch works well?" she said, because the silence was worse than this kind of foolish, one-sided conversation.

He nodded.

"That is good." She moved past him, but not too close, and placed the basket on the table, grabbed the herb sprigs, then crossed over to a carved box and pulled out a small ball of flaxen string.

She wrapped the string around her herb bundles, but was acutely aware of his gaze following her every motion. His eyes were like fire crawling up her back. So she began to hum a ditty, pretending that she did not know he was staring at her or that if she did, it bothered her little.

But inside her emotions were all mixed up, fear and nervousness and something else she could not name all fluttering in her belly like the wings of a hummingbird trying to burst its way out.

She stared down at the ball of string. She did not have her knife to cut it.

But common sense told her she should not bring the knife's hiding place to his attention, so she raised the string to her mouth and bit off a length of the string with her teeth. She finished tying the herb bundle and measured out another arm's length of twine, clamped down on it with her teeth and tugged on it. When it did not break, she chewed and chewed, trying to break it off. Still it did not break in two.

Why was it when she wanted string to break did, it held fast, and when she wanted string to hold, it always broke?

She kept tugging and pulling and chewing on it, watching him from the corner of her eye.

He straightened.

She looked up mid-bite.

He hooked the crutch under one arm.

Her breath stopped in her chest and her gaze followed him as he hobbled across the room, then pulled her knife from its hiding place as if he were the one who hid it there.

She was so surprised she could not move, not even take a single step.

He turned and limped back toward her with the knife in his hand.

Her heart shot up to somewhere near her throat and she forgot to breathe. She was a fool!

He looked up then and stopped moving suddenly, staring intently at her face.

She felt her blood drain down to her feet and wondered if that was the last thing she would ever feel.

He swiftly turned the knife around so the blade was against his palm and the hilt was out, facing her. Clearly offering her the knife, he took a few more ragged steps.

She supposed if he was going to slit her throat, he would have done so. Instead he had read her thoughts or her face or something, none of which truly settled well with her. She preferred to be a stranger to him.

She took the knife as if nothing was out of the ordinary, as if her heart was not beating a little too fast and her knees were not locked, and she cut the string, then set aside the last of the herbs. She cut another few lengths of twine.

For his part, he continued to watch her, his head cocked the way the animals did when they did not know what one was about but wanted to.

"I have finished tying up my herbs," she explained lamely because she could not stand the silence *and* his staring. "This . . ." she added, holding up another length of string, ". . . is to catch the flies and gnats."

Her voice sounded quiet and calm. A shame she was not feeling so inside.

With the knife still clutched in her hand, just for safekeeping, she turned and took down a pottery crock of water and honey that was on a shelf, then dipped the string inside a few times until it was well-coated. She held it up to check the sweet coating, then walked over to the center of the room and with one hand dragged the wobbly stool beneath one of the roof beams.

She started to climb on it.

He made a muffled noise and shook his head.

"What?"

He pointed to the stool, then placed a hand on it, showing her how it rocked.

As if she did not know that it rocked. Did he think her addled? Over time she had learned to balance on the rocking stool very well. 'Twas the only way she could reach higher shelves and the cottage beams. "I must use the stool to tie up this string. There." She pointed to the one of the knobs where she tied her fly strings.

It was little more than a small peg on the roof beam. If he was concerned over her standing on the stool now, he should have been there the day she tried to pound the pegs up. She fell twice and limped for days and days.

She caught his perplexed look. "I shall tie this string

up there," she explained again waving the honeyed string around.

He stared at the peg on the beam, then his look darted back at her and he shook his head.

"I have told you. This string is for the flies," she repeated, trying not to scamper back as he came limping toward her. Then he was standing not more than an arm's length away, glowering down at her as if she should be able to read his mind.

"The flies and gnats will go to the string, stick," she explained simply. "Then I can take them outside and set them free."

He looked at her for a long time, then he smiled, grinned actually.

He could have knocked her down with one of Hawk's feathers. Her surprise must have shown on her face because he began to laugh.

The sound was muffled and thick, as if he were doing so underwater. The odd noises that came from his throat seemed to surprise him as much as her. He quieted and raised his hand to his neck as if he just remembered what had happened.

They both stood there, silent, him touching the red rope burns on his neck, and her staring at it.

All around her, things were the same. Familiar. Her cottage surrounded her, its wattle and daub walls and roof thatched of broom and heather, the only home Teleri had ever really known. And it was still the same as it had always been. The same doves and sparrows chirped in the windows. Flies still buzzed toward the honey string on her hand.

But a soft wind picked up a little and rustled in the trees outside before it slid in through the open windows and ruffled her hair and dried out her mouth. She could taste and smell the scent of fall, that dryness in the air and the odd odor that signaled the changing of the seasons. But there was more than the scent of the air.

Something more than just the seasons was changing. The change was happening now. This very moment. To her.

In most instances, she never realized something had changed until it was too late. She would suddenly look up and see things were different.

But sometimes, like now, when she was just living her life as best she could, eking out some kind of quiet existence in a world where quiet was not easy, something would happen. Nothing she could pinpoint. Nothing she could grasp or control. Yet she could actually see the change coming at her.

She knew she still couldn't do anything about it, for fate did as it pleased and only fools tried to fight the laws of the sun or the moon, of nature and destiny and God. But she knew. She still was aware that her life would never be the same.

And she knew this was one of those moments.

His gaze met hers and held it. An unspoken emotion hung between them. His hand still touched his neck, almost as if he were afraid to let go.

A knight afraid of something? Foolish thoughts, but she could see his fear. It was there in his eyes. It was in the air, suddenly, strung tautly between them, that sharp, distinctive smell of fear—not unlike the odor of blood—that every living thing emitted when it was frightened.

She had seen enough wounded and hurt animals. She knew exactly what fear felt like. She reached up and touched her finger to the scar near her eye. Fear was the reason she lived in the woods, hidden away from a world that was cruel and made no sense.

And after what had happened to this man, who was a man first, not only a knight, she knew he had as much reason to be fearful as she did, as did the hare who had gnawed off its back leg and left it in a poacher's trap at the edge of the woods.

"I am sorry," she said, dropping her hand from her

cheek, wishing the words she had just spoken could be enough to soothe him, and knowing they were not.

He nodded, then with eyes that were not hard, he held out his hand, palm up.

She stared at it, then frowned. "What do you want?"

"The string," he whispered the words clearly. "Give me the string."

Chapter

15

~

Roger watched her mouth fall open and she gaped at him. She shook her head as if she had imaged hearing his words, then frowned at him.

"You can speak."

"I can whisper." He kept his hand outstretched, waiting for her to hand him the string.

Her gaze went from his face to his hand, which she stared at. She started to hand him the string, but pulled back suddenly when his hand came closer to hers.

"I am not going to choke you with it."

Her chin shot up in that defensive manner. "Of course not. I never thought you would." She easily handed him the string.

They both knew that was exactly what she had been thinking. But he understood pride and would not prick hers.

"Does it hurt?"

"What?"

"To talk. Does it hurt your throat?"

"No." He reached up without much trouble and

strung her fly string over the peg in the low beam above his head.

The pig came inside, its snout to the ground, and it sniffed the dirt, then trotted over to her and snorted at her skirts.

"Outside, Pig!" She shook her skirts at the thing. "There is nothing here for you to eat."

The pig looked up at her as if it understood exactly what she said, then it turned and hung its head.

"I said out." She pointed toward the open door.

The pig raised its eyes and looked at her, then, snorting in what almost sounded like a protest, it slowly meandered outside. But not before it stopped at the doorway and looked back with silly-looking sad eyes.

She shook her finger at the pig and it gave up and disappeared around the edge of the doorway. She was an odd little thing, living here in the woods, alone, except for animals that acted like her children.

She followed him as he moved, but he noticed that she still stood a good arm's length away, and she watched him with wary eyes.

"I wish I could reach those beams," she said with enough awe to make him look down at her. She sighed, like his sisters did when they were speaking of dream or a wish. "I have always wanted to be tall. Like the warrior maidens of old."

"So you can wear chain mail and . . ." He paused and swallowed at the dryness inside his throat, then added, ". . . wield a sword?"

"No. I do not wish to harm anything."

He thought to remind her of the pitchfork she had waved in front of his nose, but decided not to. That would involve reason. He had sisters. He knew better. Besides, there was nothing reasonable about a woman who threatened him with a pitchfork, but would not kill a fly.

"I would surely like to be able to reach the top berries without standing on a pile of stones. I cannot tell you how very many times I have fallen into the berry bushes because I was trying to reach the plumpest ones. The best fruit grows closest to the light of the sun, you know."

He found himself imagining her falling into the berry bushes, this small, pitchfork-wielding woman with all her false bravado and kind heart.

"If I were tall, I would have arms long enough to comb my hair without twisting about." She grabbed a handful of that incredible hair and brought the ends to her face and scowled down at it. Then she dropped it and looked at the east wall. "I would be able to reach the top shelves. Over there" She turned back to him. "And mount Horse more swiftly."

As he remembered it, she'd managed to mount the Arab swiftly enough. "Your size is as a woman should be."

"What a simple thing for you to say. You are tall."

"I am a man."

She looked at him and frowned. "What law of nature states that women should be small?"

"The same law that created men taller."

She wasn't wistful any longer. The fight was back in her. Her chin came up. "And why should men be taller?"

"To protect women. A man would not protect a giant woman."

She planted her hands on her hips and made a noise that suspiciously sounded like a snort. "She could protect herself."

"But then what would we knights do with no women or land to fight over?"

"You would still have your lands."

"Aye, but we find it much more amusing to bash our brains in over a woman." His voice cracked over the word "woman." And rough though the noise was, it had almost sounded as if he had truly spoken.

There was lapse of silence. He could feel her looking at him, measuring him with her eyes.

"You are making a jest, English." She seemed surprised, as if she were suddenly aware he had been baiting her. Then she smiled. With that smile, her cheeks grew warm and pink.

'Twas like a fist in his belly, that mouth. God in heaven, what a smile she had. It stopped him cold. Had he had a voice, he might have lost it.

He stared at her so long her smile waned and she looked uneasy. She reached up and touched her swollen eye, then tried to hide the small flinch she made.

He pointed to his own eye. "How?"

"When you were ill. You were fevered and tossing around. I did not duck my head quickly."

"I hit you?"

"Aye."

Her eye was horribly swollen and turning blue as the field on his coat of arms. "I am sorry."

She shrugged, as if it did not pain her, which was impossible. When he just continued to stare at her and say nothing she looked up at him. "That was why I had to tie you down."

He felt suddenly small inside. He reached out and gently touched one side of bluish mark. "I have never raised my hand to a woman."

"Never?"

He shook his head. "Never. 'Tis little wonder you threatened me with a pitchfork."

"I was afraid of you." She averted her eyes after she admitted that and chewed on her lower lip for a second. There was a small speck of the twine still stuck to the corner of her mouth.

He moved his hand slowly down the side of her cheek and touched her lip with one finger.

She pulled back swiftly, frowning.

"A bit of string." He pointed to the corner of his own mouth. "Stuck there."

She used the palm of her hand and scrubbed at her mouth, an action that made her lips redder and more full.

"Are you still afraid of me?"

"I do not think so."

Perhaps you should be, he thought, staring at her mouth again. Ah, little Welsh witch, you should run far, far away.

He looked up at the beams above them, because he did not like what he was feeling. His rasp of a voice seemed to have less of a hiss. It came to him, then, that the more he used his throat, the less strange it felt.

At first he thought it hurt to use it. But it was not pain he felt inside his neck. Instead he realized what he felt was just the odd flutter of his low voice. The words coming out and through. He touched his throat again and made a sound. He could feel those words against his fingers.

A moment later his gaze caught hers and he realized she had watching him.

"You did not answer me."

"What?"

"When was it that you first found you could speak?"

"I cannot speak."

She rolled her eyes and shook her head as if he were a silly child.

'Twas a simple truth. He could not speak. Could she not hear that? He could hiss like a snake and whisper like a coward, but he could not speak.

She said no more, but moved to the table and began emptying her basket of food.

"If I had been hanged and lost my voice," she said as if she were speaking of a Michaelmas festival, not a hanging, "the first time I could even manage a whisper I would be so happy I would most likely weep like a babe."

Knights do not weep, he almost said, but did not. He was a knight and yet he had wept over Elizabeth. He always seemed to weep whenever he thought of Elizabeth. Until then, the wound always felt fresh. However, his eyes did not moisten this time. He had no tears, yet the same old emotion came over him again, that hollow feeling of loss and regret, the one he could do nothing about.

Meanwhile she had crossed the room, and when he turned toward her she was lugging a water bucket which she swung onto the table with a loud thump. Humming a strange tune, she began washing off a pile of fresh vegetables, then took from the bottom of a basket the biggest cabbage he had ever seen. 'Twas almost the size of Tobin de Clare's head.

She did not look at him as she spoke. "Since you owe me for your life, English, the least you could do is answer my one question."

One question? It seemed to him as if she had a hundred questions. But from her expression he could see she was not going to drop this. She might be Welsh, but it seemed that women were the same everywhere. She reminded him of his little sister Margaret, who would always pester him until he finally gave in to her questions and told her what it was she wanted to know.

But this time, the answer to her question was that he had been talking to her animals. The ones in the cages. He refused to admit that to anyone, much less to her.

She was holding up the cabbage in both hands and looking at him expectantly.

"This morn." There. He gave her an answer.

That seemed to satisfy her somewhat, although she looked at him as if she wanted him to say more.

'Twas all she would pry from him with her words of his debt to her, words that were pointedly made to challenge his sense of honor. She had her answer.

Chapter

16

Roger mastered the use of his crutch rather keenly and found the more he walked with it, the more he could move with speed. He also discovered that his swollen ankle caused him not half the trouble that his bare feet did. If there was a stone anywhere nearby, Roger's bare foot found it.

By the time he left the yard to follow the savory scent of food coming from inside the cottage, the soles of his feet were well bruised.

But he was so hungry he cared about little else than sitting on a wobbling stool at the old trestle table and eating a strong stew of vegetables flavored with onions and garlic, herbs and flower petals. It tasted as good as something from the Queen's table.

There was no wine at this meal. No meat. No bread, thus, no trenchers. No bevy of courses. No plates of silver or pewter. They ate from roughly carved wooden bowls, those used by crofters, and used spoons made from the joints of slim willow twigs with the bark skimmed clean.

But the scent of the food was such it could stop an

advancing army in its tracks. After only a bite Roger found its flavor was as potent as its scent. He had not thought vegetables—a food he would never choose solely to eat—could taste so.

The cabbage was not bitter, and stank not at all. The turnips were drenched in the rich flavor of herbs and were soft and succulent. Huge pieces of dark mushrooms soaked up so much of the onion and garlic that for a brief moment he thought they were pieces of lamb or beef. And the carrots? They were so sweet he would have wagered his war horse that they had been sopped in Cyprus sugar.

Warm, solid food felt incredibly good in his empty belly. If the truth be told, the stew could have been dry and half-rotten and he would not have cared, for he was starved and felt as if he could eat a horse.

Unfortunately, he stupidly said as much.

Her spoon midair, she looked up at him for the first time since she had set down the bowls of food and joined him.

"Eat a horse?" A look of horror came over her face. She swallowed hard and all the color drained from her cheeks, suddenly turning her skin the pale color of the small amount of salt that sat in half of a walnut shell between their bowls. "You English eat *horses?*"

He had a sudden vision of her fleeing the table, leaping out the open window and running to hide the Arab deep in the woods before he could cannibalize it.

"No. We *English* do not eat horses."

She exhaled, but she still frowned at him.

"Such a comment is only a way we use words to state how hungry one is. One would have to be hungry, indeed, to eat a whole horse."

She stared down at her spoon, saying nothing.

He took a bite and added, "The Arab is safe."

She looked up at him then, her expression telling him without speaking that she found such use of words foolish and horrific.

So they ate in silence, one that seemed to stretch out

before them, and which after a time, seemed as taut as the muscles in his sore neck.

It came to him then, that between the two of them, one could not speak without offending the other. Coming from a family full of women, Roger was used to easily charming most women. It did not settle well with him that this one young woman could make him feel like a clod.

After a few moments she finally spoke. "Why do you call Horse 'the Arab'?"

"That horse came from the Arab lands in the East." He took a spoonful of his stew, then rested his arms on the table and glanced down at the empty bowl, surprised his food was gone so swiftly.

"You are staring down at that empty bowl with a lost and hungry look. You wish more to eat."

He cast a quick glance at her bowl, then back to his own.

Without a word she stood and took his empty bowl, then moved to the cook pot over the fire pit in the center of the room. As she was bending over the pot she said, "You only have to ask, English. I did not save your life so I could starve you."

She might be Welsh, but she was obviously a woman first. Through and through, for it seemed she would never let him forget his debt. She pointed it out to him almost as often as she reminded him that he gave his word of honor. For not the first nor probably the last time in his life, Roger wondered what was it about women that made them think men had no memory.

He looked about the cottage and saw what he had seen before. It was clean, but she had so little. The truth was that he did assume she had no more food and he did not want to eat both his share and hers.

He chose not to tell her of his mistake, even though she seemed determined to whip him with her sharp words. Her words came from a pride he understood.

And proud as she was, she lived poorly. He had not seen her change clothing. There was mud on her gown and she wore no shoes, not even the cheap wooden clogs of a farm girl. She had no convenience, not even a hearth and chimney, yet the place had a warmth about it that did not come from the puny fire pit in the middle of the room.

She turned about and walked toward him on bare and dirty feet, then set down a full bowl of steaming stew in front of him. He had downed three mouthfuls before she sat down on the stool opposite him, propped her elbow on the tabletop, and rested her cheek in her hand. Then she watched him.

After a moment, she said, "Tell me about my horse."

"That horse," he waved the spoon to accentuate his too quiet, raspy and whispered words, "belongs to Merrick de Beaucourt, Earl of Glamorgan."

She stiffened and her shoulders went straight, her lips thinned. He could see on her face the knowledge that she had stolen a horse from someone who had the power to see her die for it.

She gave him a sharp look. "I did not steal Horse. Think what you will, but I did not." She paused in thought. "He is not your horse, then?"

He shook his head.

"Yet you came after me?"

"Aye."

"There must be a reward for his return."

"No."

"Then perhaps the reward is for my head on a pike."

"No. Merrick would not harm a woman any more than I would. He would punish you for the theft, but not so cruelly."

"There was no theft."

"The horse is not yours."

"I have heard of this Earl Merrick."

It did not escape him that she had just changed the subject. "Then you should have heard he was fair and returned the horse to him."

"How was I to know Horse was his?"

"Most likely because you found the animal on Merrick's lands." He held up a hand to quiet her when she opened her mouth to argue. "I understand how you could take one look at the horse and want it. That Arab is the finest piece of horseflesh I have ever laid eyes upon. The breed comes from the Holy Land, where the horses need to be small, swift mounts with stamina. You can see the speed bred into their flanks." He ate some more, then looked up. "You have ridden the horse. You know of what I speak."

She said nothing, but he could see the knowledge in the stoic tightness of her expression, knowledge she tried to hide from him but could not.

"Earl Merrick was given the horse as a gift for saving the life of a Marionite leader when we were in the Holy Land, with Edward at Tunis." He paused, the spoon near his mouth. "Would that I had been the one to save the sheik, for from the moment I saw the horse I coveted that animal as I have never coveted anything." He chewed, then swallowed.

"Merrick knew it, too. I had been trying to wear him down for two years." He leveled a hard glance at her. "I had just about convinced him to sell me the beast when you came along and stole it."

"I did *not* steal Horse!"

"You did not steal him?" It did not take a prophet to point out that he did not believe her. His face and tone should have said as much.

"No." She shook her head adamantly.

"You rode away quickly enough in Glamorgan, that time when I almost caught you."

"I did not steal Horse. But I did ride away that day. I was a woman alone with a knight in full armor chasing me and his troops not far behind." She gave him that chin in the air look. "Pardon me for not standing still."

For someone who had been afraid of him earlier, she certainly did not seem fearful now, when it might serve her to be. She just gave him that square look in the eye

115

and said whatever she wished. He was not certain how he felt about it, either, though he probably should have been annoyed.

Her eyes narrowed at his silence and she added pointedly, "What a sorry thing it was that the river got in your way, English."

She had escaped him that time and was throwing his failure directly in his face—not a wise move. He knew he should do something to let her know he was not amused.

But he was amused. He found himself vastly amused at her fearlessness and the smug and daring look she blessed him with. 'Twas not a pleasing memory for a man of many wars to lay sprawled in a river, helpless under the weight of his armor while his quarry got away, but when he imagined the scene from her viewpoint, Roger supposed it was amusing. "I sank like stone and about drowned."

"Did you?" She did not sound the least contrite.

"Aye, chasing a horse thief."

"I did not steal Horse."

"I suppose like the Queen's lapdog he merely followed you home from Glamorgan."

"That is closer to the truth than you know."

Roger did not believe her. A horse was not a pet like a dog or kitten or that pig that seemed to nip at her heels every time she moved. He waited for her to admit the truth to him. But the stubborn woman looked as if she would remain silent until Michaelmas. "Tell me how the Arab followed you home."

She took in a long breath and wiggled atop her stool, as if settling in for a tale as long as the Bible, then she crossed her arms over her chest and stared at him. "I am not certain I shall tell you."

Jesu! She was as arrogant and stubborn as King Edward's beast of a mother.

"I do not have to tell you anything."

"No. You do not. I will simply know that you stole the horse."

She sighed. "This must be what you English call cross purposes."

"No. 'Tis what we call Welsh stubbornness."

She gave a small laugh, telling him without words that she considered stubbornness an attribute. She took a deep breath and began, "When I came across Horse he was drinking from the river."

"Which river?"

"River Neath."

Neath was miles from the woods outside Camrose. He studied her for signs of a lie, but saw no slyness in her eyes or her features. She was no liar. She was blunt-spoken to a fault. He thought about the possibilities for a moment. It was not impossible. The Arab could have run as far as the River Neath.

"I stood on the opposite bank and watched him. Admired him in truth, for I had never seen such a fine animal. He looked up for a brief instant, then his legs seemed to just give out, and he lay down on the river bank." She returned his look. "It was like someone had knocked his legs out from under him."

She stared down at the table, where she was absently playing with a splinter in the top. Her voice grew serious and as quiet as his whispered words. "I crossed the river and went to him."

Her chin went up higher, her eyes moist with the softest of emotions. "Horse had two arrows in his neck."

This time Roger's breath froze in his chest. Her story became suddenly very true.

"English arrows?"

"No. Welsh," she admitted quietly. "But Horse was covered in some black dye that smelled of walnut sap and was used to hide the white on his muzzle and legs. I took out the arrows and cleaned his wounds in the river. When I saw the white markings show through, I knew someone had tried to hide them. There was no reason to hide the marks unless Horse was stolen."

Roger remembered that day well enough. "He was

not stolen. Earl Merrick's betrothed, Lady Clio, had used the horse to escape from Camrose Castle in direct disobedience to his orders. She had disguised herself, so it makes sense she had tried to disguise the horse, too. Merrick's men would have stopped her at the gates had they recognized them."

She chewed her lip and said nothing, but he could see her thinking.

"All Merrick had known was that on a female lark, his lady had ridden outside the walls and the guarded gate. Outside his protection."

"Perhaps she had reason to leave him."

"No reason except he had forbid it."

"This tale you tell sounds as if he had locked her away in the castle."

"No." He looked at her, exasperated, then said simply, "He told her she could not leave."

She sniffed. "That is the same thing."

"No, 'tis not. There had been raids nearby from Welsh outlaws."

"Raids are what happens when you English come and build your castles on lands that do not belong to you."

"The land belongs to King Edward," he reminded her. "But that does not matter, for the woods were not safe."

"I would not like to have some man tell me I could not go into my woods."

Perhaps he should merely hobble outside and slam his head against the cottage wall. 'Twould be simpler and less painful than this conversation.

He counted in Latin and Arabic, then waited until she was looking at him again, then he gave her a long look and said pointedly, "Lady Clio is a good woman, but she was headstrong and did not like to be told what she could and could not do. A flaw in most females."

Her face creased into her own scowling look and she opened her mouth to speak.

"Once she had entered the woods," he continued swiftly, "she was attacked by outlaws. Luck was on her side for we were riding back to Camrose at the same time. Merrick took off after her and disposed of the outlaws, but not before Lady Clio had taken an arrow in the shoulder."

Now she did not look at him as if she still wished to speak, which was good. It showed some sign of sense about her. He looked down and saw his bowl was again empty.

She was watching him now, so he picked up the bowl. "I am still hungry."

She stood up, her eyes looking him up and down. "Where do you put it all?"

"I am tall. You said as much."

She shook her head and walked back to the cook pot.

He placed his palms on the tabletop and squared his shoulders. "Two bowls of this stew will only fill me to my knees," he told her with no little pride.

She muttered something about stuffing his mouth and grabbed her apron with both hands, then used it to hold onto the thick pot handle.

Before he could see what she was about, she unhooked the pot from its iron stand over the fire and lugged the swinging black iron pot toward him. She swung it up and it hit the table top with a loud *thud*.

She dropped her apron and stepped back. "There!" She picked up his spoon and stuck it in the pot and in that jaunty way she had, cocked her head at him and planted her hands on her hips. "That should fill you all the way up to your ears, English."

While he was still eating, and eating, and eating, Teleri went outside and hurried down to the brook, a clean shift and gown hugged to her chest. She ran past the bridge, following the small bank to a private spot downstream, where the brook widened into a shallow pool she used for bathing. She slipped out of her clothes, her eye on the small flickering light coming from the east window of her cottage. She figured with him eating his way down to the very bottom of her cook pot she had plenty of time to bathe.

The only person she had ever seen eat so much was Brother Dismas, the fat friar who ate a five-course meal as if it were the Last Supper. The man was her grandmother's favorite sport. Superstitious beyond ken, the brown cloaked man of the English church was forever crossing himself and praying whenever Old Gladdys was near. Gladdys loved it, too. She delighted in playing his fears and superstitions, winking at him as if she were giving him the evil eye, muttering false curses in Welsh that he could not understand, and flinging her cape about like batwings.

Her grandmother claimed that the only person she liked to play more for a fool was some handsome and cocky knight who played free with married ladies of the English court. Old Gladdys had told her a marvelous tale about how she had wickedly stolen the man's clothes and left him to walk naked as a babe all the way back to Camrose Castle.

Teleri shivered slightly, not because of the cold, for the air was still warm from the day's sun, but because from what the English had told her about Horse. She had Earl Merrick's Arab horse. Had she known, she would have returned him to the castle once Horse was well.

She sighed as she stepped into the middle of the pool where the water was cool to her feet. This was late in the summer, so the water level was barely deep enough to cover her. Teleri sat down in it and looked off in the distance, her stomach sinking to somewhere near the bottom of the pool.

She did not want to return Horse. She loved him. He was like family to her, that horse. But Earl Merrick had been good to her grandmother over the years. Old Gladdys had said as much. And she had never hinted or said a word about Horse belonging at Camrose.

But Teleri knew Old Gladdys well. Her grandmother

was sly enough to keep quiet if she had her reasons. Or perhaps she did not know or recognize Horse. She knew how Teleri loved him. She had helped her nurse him. Surely she had not known about his connection to Earl Merrick.

She whistled softly and within a moment or two Horse came prancing around the bend in the bank and followed her into the water, slurping up a drink and watching her from his sweet eyes. She reached out and stroked his muzzle, then cupped it in her hands. "Such a good and pretty lad you are, Horse. You are mine, are you not?"

She kissed his muzzle, and he stood still the way he always did when she talked softly to him. He was like her child, a big, gangly-legged child that was four times her size. But she did not care.

He tossed his head and splashed her playfully. She laughed softly and splashed back. But he soon bored with the game. He stepped back onto the bank, then began to poke around the ground for the perfect mouthful of grass, having no idea of the guilt Teleri was feeling.

She lay back and immersed her hair under the water line. She felt her whole body relax, felt her legs and arms and neck soften under the calm water as her feet and hands rose to the surface to float as if they weighed no more than the seeds of a dandelion.

But a heartbeat later she heard a sound and opened her eyes, looking at the opposite bank near the bridge.

A huge dark shape came at her.

She shrieked.

Water splashed everywhere. His weight sprawled atop her and sent her straight to the bottom the brook, where he pinned her on her back to the hard stones on the bed of the pool.

She kicked and bucked against him while her breath escaped her mouth in precious bubbles. She flung her arms about, fighting, then got her hands between their bodies and shoved him as hard as she could.

He grunted and lost his balance.

An instant later she managed to pry herself free.

She sat up swiftly in the shallow water, her head bursting through the surface. She gasped for breath and coughed and sputtered, then leaned back, her hands flat on the bottom of the rocky pool and supporting her as she glared at him.

He was sitting there next her, the whites of his eyes showing wide and innocent, as if he had not just about drowned her. Before he could see what she was about, she put her feet on his damp, hairy chest and pushed as hard as she could.

Chapter

17

❧

Pig sat back with a grunt of surprise. He gave her another doleful stare, his haunches in the water and his ears twitching with the need to play.

"You almost drowned me!" She cupped her hands flat and splashed water into his face the way he liked.

"Silly pig," she muttered, then she played with him, splashing and laughing at his antics. He snorted and grunted and finally got bored and began sniffing near the water's edge.

She sighed again and turned over in the water, floating on her belly and letting her arms rise out to her sides as if she were a bird gliding on the top of the water.

Before long, her skin began to suddenly prickle, the way it did when touched by a cool wind. But there was no wind. She put her knees to the bottom of the pond, sat back on her heels and glanced up.

A tall and familiar dark silhouette stood leaning on his crutch near the bridge. For the whole evening whenever he looked at her, her hands grew moist and her heart had sped up. She did not know why. It just did. He said nothing to make her feel that way, said nothing wrong. It was not what he said but what he didn't say that worried her.

She did not move, just knelt there in the pond, the surface water lapping at her ribs. "I thought you were eating."

"I finished." His rough whisper scraped through the evening stillness, sounding gruff and mysterious because it was only a sound. She could not see his face.

She said nothing, for there was nothing to say. She waited for him to leave, finally cupping water in her hands and pouring it over her shoulders. She felt an odd chill that had nothing to do with the coolness of the water and looked down, surprised when the tips of her breasts grew suddenly tight and puckered.

She was not cold. By instinct she touched them and heard him suck in a breath. She was thankful for the dark so he could not read her face.

But with that very thought, the moon came crawling over the tops of the very tallest trees. She did not take her gaze away from his shadow. Instead she sat there aware of each breath she took, aware of a buzzing sound that ran through her like swarms of bees, and aware for the very first time in her whole life of how truly loud silence could be.

"I'm bathing," she said.

His response took a long time. "Aye. You and everyone else."

"Pig likes the water," she said lamely.

When the English would pause before speaking like he just did, or when he remained so quiet, she did not know if it was because of his voice or because he truly had nothing to say.

Sometimes one paused like that because they were trying to think. But sometimes someone paused because they wished to choose their words carefully, to hide what they were really thinking about.

In the darkness, she could not read him visually. With only a rough whisper for a voice, she could not catch the tone that always hinted at the feeling behind one's words.

Certainly she could feel him looking at her. She could always feel him looking at her, when he was standing by the old hemlock tree, or when he was across the room, or even when he was standing near a bridge with half of the milky fall moon rising overhead.

She waited for him to leave, clearly something that was not going to happen.

He casually leaned on the crutch and pulled his shirt over his head.

"What are you doing?"

"The same thing you are." His whisper was low and she had to think hard to be certain of his words.

He tossed his tunic into the pool. "I cannot take my own smell any longer. Your pig smells sweeter than I."

"Pig is clean. He loves the water far too much, I think." She turned just as Pig scrabbled up onto the bank and trotted off after Horse. *Traitor.*

She sat up a little straighter and shifted back so she was sitting against the opposite bank, putting distance between them that strangely did not feel like any distance at all.

That waxing half moon chose to slip out from behind the treetops. Moonlight shone down, illuminating only one half of him, the way a mummer paints only half of his face.

But one half of this man was enough. She felt a sharp pain in her belly, low, as if it was somehow tied by a taut string to the hard tips of her breasts. Her hand went to her belly, her palm flat against it under the cool water. It was like living within the body of a stranger.

She shifted slightly, looking down, then looked up again, staring at him as if she were seeing him for the very first time. His chest was broad and covered with curly hair, thick and rough like the hair she had between her legs.

From bathing him during the fever, she knew well that the hair was red. She knew that he had the same color of hair at his groin and on his arms and legs. The rich color of a fox in the spring.

She was uncomfortable, fidgety, and lifted her arms to the bank and rested them on the tufts of damp grass that edged it. The moon seemed to brighten, and she watched his hands move to the ties on his hose.

Then the strangest thing happened: she forgot to breathe.

He was looking at her with an expression she could not read clearly. But her heart began that silly throbbing it did when she was around him. Before she had thought the speed of her heart was caused by fear, but that could not be what it was, because she knew she was not afraid of him.

When she finally did catch her breath, she realized her breathing was short and faster. She had to take two, three small breaths at a time, the way she had to when she had been running long and hard.

Yet for all the odd reactions, for all that she was feeling, there was not one thing in the world at that moment that could have coaxed her to tear her gaze away from him. She did not understand why, but really did not care because something stronger than her sense and thoughts made her need to stare at him.

She had seen him with little clothing on, had washed his fevered body and helped him with his functions. She had held the root of this man in her palm.

But that was not the same. Then there had been no thought of him in this lightheaded way. No heart beating like the wings of a hummingbird. No warming of her blood. She had done what was necessary only by rote and need to a man who was half dead, someone she was trying to save. Someone she did not know and had never spoken to.

He pulled his bad foot loose of his hose while still leaning on the crutch, then freed his other foot and tossed his chausses into the water. She watched them soak and sink with his shirt, felt them drift softly against her body. And all of this she did with a distant

126

unearthly feeling surrounding her, like the lifting spirit she had when she was in the middle of the stones.

Standing before her now as he was, tall, in the dark and the dim cast of moonlight, garbed in only the strings and soft leather of his loincloth, he was very much alive. And she was aware of who he was, how big he was.

Silly girl . . . He was not as tall as the old trees of the forest that formed a jagged shadow of black in the distance behind him. Not as big as the old oak deep in the forest.

But somehow he felt bigger. Perhaps it was because he was human and not some tall tree that only had a face in her imagination, something that could only be human because she fancied it was so.

She could feel his eyes on her, could hear him breathing because it was so quiet that evening.

Not even the crickets sang. It was as if they had abandoned her. Even the water was still and there was no wind in the air. No rustle in the tops of the trees. No leaves skipping along the grasses. No gnats or moths swarming in the air. Not even an old wood owl in the taller branches of the trees or a nightingale flitting from branch to branch, tree to tree, singing out at the half-moon.

In the quiet there should be no sound. But there was something other than sound, something that she felt intensely, an anticipation that was as if the whole world suddenly held its breath.

He slid into the water, which barely reached his hips. He did not take his crutch from the bank, but raised his arms and dove under in a long sleek line and surfaced in front of her, sitting on the bottom with his legs stretched out to one side of her, his hair sleek and swept back from his face by the water which dripped from his nose and eyelashes.

She shoved away from the bank and dove under as he had done, skimming along the water to the opposite side of the pool before she broke through the surface, her head tilted back from the wet weight of her hair, which was so long that part of it was still underwater. She could feel it brushing against her bottom. She stood up and turned around, only to find him beside her, looking at her and grinning.

She smiled sweetly, as if she were not surprised by his trick, then she sank into the water a little so her knees brushed the side of his hard thigh.

He looked down suddenly.

She laughed and splashed water at him with her hands, then moved away. She could trick, too.

But he moved so quickly she had not a chance to think. He came at her, his face huge before her and almost on her own.

She had just enough time to take in air before his arm snaked around her. He pulled her under with him to the bottom of the pool, her body held against his. She did not fight with him, but sank down, then let the water lift her up until they were floating body to body.

She opened her eyes under the water. As the bubbles of their motions floated away she saw a bright white half moon high above the waving surface of the water, which looked like a sheet of silver and limned the shape of his head over hers.

His hands shifted and gripped her bare waist and he lifted her from the water, pressed her back against the bank. It all happened so quickly that she grabbed his shoulders, then blinked back the water and his blurred face became clear.

He was not smiling. He was staring at her mouth, then his gaze went to her swollen eye. He looked as if he might flinch at the ugly sight of it.

But before she could say something tart and sharp, he raised his chin and touched her eye with his mouth, so softly she barely felt the kiss of his lips. She drew in a breath and froze. He looked down at her again, then his mouth touched hers just as softly as he had kissed her eye, lips pressed against hers in the most gentle and softest of touches.

The only men she knew were those of the village and they had never seemed gentle. Young boys threw stones at her and called her names. No man had ever treated her thus. She did not know a man could have such kindness of touch. And surely she had not expected this from a man of war, a knight.

She felt him kneeling between her legs, the touch of his muscled, male legs on her inner thighs, the crispness of the hair on his skin that felt so different from the silky feel of the water that surrounded them.

He cupped her face in his big hands and tilted her head so their lips and noses met as if they were made to touch that way. He licked at the seam of her mouth telling her he wanted more. And when she parted her lips, he sank his tongue deeply inside of her mouth, filling it, then retreating and drawing her tongue into his mouth with his, where they tangled together and moved and sent her throbbing blood to her breasts and between her legs.

It felt so good that she could not stop the tongue play and her hands moved over him and tangled in the hair on his chest to keep it from rubbing against her taut breasts, for she was certain she would go mad.

But she did not go mad when he placed her arms over his shoulders and pressed his chest against her, pressing her against his body and moving so his hands drifted down her neck and shoulders and arms to the sides of her breasts, drawing his fingers over the roundness of them, before moving his hands down past her waist to her bottom, where he pulled her legs wider. The water cooled the heat there until he brushed his fingertips between her legs over and over.

She moaned against his mouth and his lips left hers. He lifted her higher so he could draw her breast deeply into his mouth and flick it with his tongue and teeth. She gasped and her head fell back against the bank.

At the same moment his finger slipped inside of her. She gave a small cry.

"Hush, now—" He stopped. She heard his swallow,

as if he were drinking down a word. He cursed in a low half breath of a sound.

She opened her lazy eyes and saw his handsome profile in the moonlight.

He turned his head and stared at her strangely, as if she had suddenly grown horns. "Sweet Jesu, what am I trying to do to you?"

She had a good idea what he was doing. As far as she was concerned, he could do this all night long. "You are mating with me." She tried to pull his head back down to hers.

Before she could kiss him he said, "I do not even know your name."

"Teleri."

He stepped back away from her and drove a hand through his hair. "This is how I repay you for my life?"

She thought it a fine reward. Better than any she could have come up with. But he seemed angry. She did not understand why.

He looked out at the darkness beyond and whispered, "What am I?"

"Wonderful," she answered.

He whipped his head back around and scowled down at her.

"Your hands are wonderful, English. I like it when you touch me like you did."

He cursed.

She knew what that curse word meant. It was an old Saxon term for what she wanted to do.

She looked him squarely in the eyes and told him that was exactly what she wanted to do with him.

Chapter

18

Roger did not speak for a moment, because he could not think with her standing before him, a naked siren telling him what she wanted, which was the exact same thing his body wanted. He took a deep breath so he could try to think with some amount of sense.

God's eyes, but just an instant before he had almost called her by Elizabeth's name. That was what stopped him cold, had stopped him from taking her right there in the side of the bank.

In his mind he knew she was not Elizabeth. She was different, her taste, her smell, her mouth, the way she felt against his palms, her skin. And what ran through his blood was not love. He bedded women for lust and because they offered and he took.

But he loved Elizabeth.

This was neither lust nor love. This was a hot feeling he had not truthfully experienced for years. It was the kind of searing need a man gets to bury himself inside a woman only because it felt right, not because she was available or because it was forbidden.

He stood there in the water, aware that he no longer

knew who he was, unable to comprehend this stranger he had suddenly become. He shifted back in the water and put some more space between them. "I cannot do this to you."

"Why? Have you a wife?"

"No," he found her question sardonically amusing . . . and female. He answered with logic. "Were I married, I would not be in this pool with you."

"My grandmother has told me that the English do not always honor their marriage vows. She has told me of English knights who take married women to swive."

"I will amend my words. Were I married, I *should* not be in this pool with you."

She stood there lost in thought, then gave him that square look again. "You have never mated with a married woman?"

So much for logic. Suddenly this conversation was about his moral past. One moment ago he was lost in a hot and searing passion that surprised even him. Now he was looking at this Welsh woman with the lyrical name and being questioned about who he had slept with.

"You have," she said. There was no surprise to her voice, but there was censure in her tone, enough to annoy him. It was like talking to his mother and having to tell her the whole truth.

"I will not do this to you," he said, changing the direction of their talk back to the place it needed to be. "I might give you a child."

She seemed to chew that over in her mind for a moment or two. "I would like to have a child," she said in a decisive voice, then added more thoughtfully, "If we mated, the babe would have red hair, I think."

He did not know why he was surprised. She spoke exactly what she thought. It was almost as if whatever thought flew into her head came out her mouth.

"Come." She opened her arms, standing there

before him in all her lovely and enticing nakedness and unaffected by the awkwardness of the situation. "I would have your child." She paused, then added with complete seriousness, "Even though you are English."

Just nail me to the cross, he thought. No one who knew him would believe he would ever say no. But he stood there looking at her and seeing only passion and his needs. He took long and labored breaths, then looked past her, giving himself some time to think.

She was waiting for him, and he knew he would not do what she wished. But he wanted to. God's bones, but he wanted to.

There was some irony in the fact that he had a reputation for taking his sport where he pleased. He felt as if he were paying right then and there for every sin he had ever committed and probably ever would commit. This was Purgatory.

"You know, English, I have always wanted children." She was not looking at him now, but staring down at the water. "I would like a child, I think. I would like to teach children not to hurt people or to do things for sport that would harm an animal." She looked back up at him. "My children," she added in a fiercely determined voice, "will never throw stones or set iron traps."

"Animals are food. You think to make all of Christendom eat roots and berries?"

Her chin shot up in that way she had. "Believe me, English, I well understand about trying to survive."

He supposed she did, living alone as she did. But living in this isolated place was obviously her choice. She chose to hide herself away.

"My children will never hang people from trees. And they will teach others not to do such cruel things."

She had just taken her beliefs and twisted them to reflect his perspective. This small Welsh woman with wild hair, a woman who could hold out her hand and tame a deer or just as easily ignite a man's emotions. He decided then and there that she would make a fine diplomat.

"*My* children will change the world."

He looked at her and thought of his mother. Had his mother thought he would change the world? He hadn't yet. Oh, he had gone off to the East with Merrick and Edward. They had fought for control of some cities and had lost more than they had liked. But even had they won those battles, they would have changed little. By then, Crusade held little ideal and even less honor. There was in truth nothing to defend.

Once they realized that, they had all come home. Edward to rule England; Merrick to guard the borders of Glamorgan; and Roger to handle diplomacy with Rome and France, then to philander his way through the court until his Elizabeth had become suddenly widowed. Or so they thought. Edward's need for another border castle had come soon after Hugh Bigod's return from the Germans.

But until this very moment, until he listened to the honest words of a Welsh woman who spoke her heart and mind and of what she wanted from her children, Roger had never thought of his parents' desire for having children. He had never thought of the reasons.

He had not a clue of his mother's reason for wanting children, but he was certain of his father's. Baron Sander FitzAlan had only wanted children to control the way landlords controlled their serfs. To wallow in power.

"Come to me," she said to him again.

Roger looked up at her, tense with thoughts of his father.

Her arms were outstretched, her skin and breasts bare and glistening with water and the silver light of the moon.

Part of him wanted to walk into her arms and take

whatever she would give. There was something about her that soothed him, something about the way she stood there as if they were kindred in more than just human ways, in more than sex.

At that moment he thought he might understand why animals of the forest were unafraid of her. She had something he needed, not her body, not kisses and touches and burying himself deeply inside of her. It was something else, but he did not know what it was. He only knew whatever power it was it scared the hell out of him.

"Come to me," she repeated in a voice that he was certain was exactly as Eve's voice had been when she handed the apple to Adam.

From his mouth came that awful sound that was his laugh. There was little lightness in the harsh and ragged noise that came from his throat. "You do not even know who I am."

She dropped her arms to her sides. "Until a moment ago, you did not know my name. I am not a different person now that you do know what I am called. I am still the same Teleri I was when you were mating with me."

"I was not mating with you." Then he drove a hand through his hair. "Not yet I wasn't."

"Still." She placed her hand on her hips. "I have not changed, English."

With one comment, with merely the same amount of time it took to blink your eye, they were at odds again, a stone wall of ego and opinion between them and both of them butting at it like stubborn goats.

She shrugged as if nothing about him mattered to her, which annoyed him for a reason he didn't care to think about.

"I do not think your name will change my mind," she said. "What more do I need to know? You are English."

So she kept reminding him. "Then perhaps you

would like to know the name of the man you just asked to father your child." Though only whispered in his harsh voice, the words were meant to humiliate her and were angry and cruel.

She stiffened as if he had slapped her.

They both stood there silent and stubborn and proud.

She finally broke eye contact and looked away, chewing her lip before she averted her eyes. "Who are you, English?"

"I am Roger FitzAlan of Wells." And I am a selfish ass.

"FitzAlan?" She raised her face again and eyed him for a moment. "Your father did not wed your mother?"

"They are wed. My great, great grandfather was illegitimate. But now the FitzAlans would never have a bastard in the family. My father would not allow such a thing to happen." His tone was bitter and angry the way it was whenever he spoke of, or to, his father.

"You do not like your father?"

"No. I do not like my father."

She looked down at the water. "I do not know who my father was."

"I wish I did not," the words came from him without a thought.

The change in her face caught him by surprise. Her pride was gone. She stood there raw and open. The look she gave him was so empty he almost wished he had not spoken.

Her shoulders dropped and hunched a little, like the women who have lived so long they carried the pain of a whole lifetime on their age-weakened backs. "No." She shook her head slowly. "You are wrong."

She pushed herself up onto the bank then, a sudden stranger in spite of what had happened between them only moments before. She slipped into a shift that was folded on the grass, then put on a gown and silently bent down and picked up her dirty clothes. She hugged them to her chest so tightly and just stood there, staring off toward the eastern mountains high above the rim of the forest trees.

After a moment she turned and walked away, across the bridge, where she stopped and turned to face him, her hand on the fieldstones of the bridge, the moonlight behind her, her face little more than a dark shadow. "You would not truly wish such a thing, Roger FitzAlan of Wells," she said. "For I only know half of who I am."

Teleri was five years old the first time she asked her grandmother about her father. Old Gladdys hadn't answered her at first, just stood there instead as if frozen by the question, and she stared off into the past with an emptiness of mind and expression that was not lost on even a five year old.

Years later Teleri would come to understand the look Old Gladdys wore as that of a mother who lost her only child. But then, that first time, she was young and her world was small and insular, for children lived in immediate moments and saw only small snatches of the future, merely what was coming soon that very day. Because children have no past lessons to warn them, no what ifs to think upon, or mistakes to guide their actions.

Teleri knew only that she had no father or mother like the children in the village had. She had seen the villagers whisper. She had seen some of them look at her as if she were unclean. Some even crossed themselves when Teleri was nearby. When she asked Old Gladdys what she had done, she was told she did nothing.

At five she was no bigger than a summer lamb, her hair as thick and curly as spring fleece, her hands still pudgy with the plumpness of babies; she was still too innocent to know what hatred looked like. She did not understand. She only knew that she was different from them. And that they did not want her near.

Old Gladdys was her grandmother and the only

person with any answers to her paternity, but she would tell Teleri nothing. Her grandmother would just stare off in the distance toward the silent mountains, to the place where it was said that Annest disappeared, and sometimes she would cry. She would cry until those odd black eyes of hers were red as the autumn cranberries they gathered in the bogs.

Over time Teleri stopped asking Old Gladdys who her father was. But she never stopped wondering. And when she grew up and chanced one sunlit day when the world seemed right to ask about her father once more, her grandmother looked off to the eastern horizon, where the stone ring stood guard over the Brecon Valley.

Gladdys sat down on a hard flat rock near the edge of the woods and stared at her pale, veined feet. She stayed that way, with her head hung, for a long time. Her shoulders grew stooped and heavy-looking; they turned in a little, and even after she was done talking to Teleri, even after she went to Glamorgan, after many seasons had gone by, her shoulders never were straight again. From that day onward Old Gladdys walked with a stoop.

But on that very sunlit day, Old Gladdys told Teleri of her mother Annest, of how when her water broke and birth was immanent, Annest had run and stumbled all the way up to the plateau even though she was heavy with child and hurting with her birthing pains.

Annest had lain down in the stone ring to give birth to Teleri. It had taken a long, long time for Gladdys to find her daughter, and when she did, most of Annest's life had bled away and been soaked up into the brown dirt in the center of the ring.

Gladdys had handed Annest her newborn babe and asked the exact same question. Who was the man who fathered this babe?

Annest had taken a long breath that shook her body and sounded hollow and empty in her chest. "I swore on my love of him to never tell," she said as her eyes slipped closed ever so slowly.

Gladdys had cried and begged her for the name of the man.

Annest did not open her eyes, but she said, "The answer is in the stones." Then she died.

Chapter 19

Kent, England

It was almost dawn when a figure moved silently across the inner bailey at Leeds Castle, then edged along the wall where guards stood during the last tired hour of their night watch. Two guards with pike and crossbow passed each other along the upper walk of the wall and paused at a crenelate to speak of the troop of performers who had arrived at the castle that day, then of the castle's new laundress, a buxom young woman with flaming red hair and a hot look not one of the guardsmen had missed. The men laughed quietly over some bawdy jest, then moved on.

The dark figure hunkered down and ran along the wall to a stone arch that led to the outer bailey and the millworks and barbican. A dim torchlight burned in an iron socket in the wall and the nearby guard rested his boot on an oil barrel and sharpened his dagger, longing for time itself to pick up speed and his gate watch to be done.

There was a sudden scraping sound, metal against rock, like that of a sword against the castle wall. The guard looked up, his hand on the hilt in his scabbard.

He did not move, this guard. He did not breathe. He waited, listening.

But time moved silently by as if the noise had been a dream and he heard no more. Cautious still, he took the torch from the wall and moved to the archway, then searched the inner bailey. He saw nothing, and stood there watching for longer than need be.

Shaking his head, he turned and disappeared under the arch, only to reappear again when a small, childlike cry came from somewhere nearby. He moved into the bailey, his ears and eyes kept sharp.

There was movement in the yard. A shadow flickered near the opposite wall. He drew his sword and moved with caution, stopping when he heard the crinkle of hay and saw a motion in the bales stacked on the southeast corner.

He closed the distance as quietly as he could, the torch held high, his weapon drawn and ready. He rounded the hay bales and a pair of startled eyes looked up at him.

The guard stopped his sword mid-swing and cursed at the stupid goat that stared back at him. He dragged the goat back to the goat yard and put the wooden pin back in the gate, then he moved back to his post, where there was little to do until the next watch bell rang.

The guard sat on the barrel and went back to sharpening his knife, something, anything, to keep him busy from the boredom of his shift.

He did not see the figure in the outer bailey, the figure that had crept through the arch while he stalked the goat. No one saw the figure slip inside the door to the mill, or escape through a trap in the mill floor, where a set of old stone steps led to the moat and then to the river beyond.

The figure crossed the water, then disappeared into the woods where a horse was waiting. And a few minutes later, the figure disappeared, riding over the low hills of Kent toward the wild Welsh borders.

* * *

At that quiet time before sleep, when the mind wanders back over the experiences of the day, Teleri lay in the dark half-listening to Pig snore and she remembered something Old Gladdys had said when she was young.

She had told her Druid legend had it that fairies hide under the sycamore trees, and if she put her hand on the trunk she could feel the thrum of them dancing inside.

Teleri knew that was not true. Fairies did not live in sycamore trees; they lived in the hands and the lips and the eyes of the Englishman, for that was the only explanation she could fathom for how he made her feel, that thrumming feeling that happened whenever he looked at her or touched her.

It had to be fairies. It had to be.

Teleri was dreaming of kisses. Long, warm kisses that made her head feel as light as the winding of the wind and made her blood grow much too warm. She awoke with a start, feeling damp and sweaty. She blinked, startled for a moment, then realized she was staring up at the English.

He was standing over her.

She frowned for a moment, then wiped her eyes. It was still dark and the damp smell of rain was sifting in from the open window above her.

"Go to your bed," he told her.

She looked around. She was lying on her bed of straw, sleeping in the same spot she had been sleeping since she had found him. "I am in my bed."

"Go," he said again. "I put your tick back on the bedstead." He paused and nodded toward the back room. "In there."

She glanced to the corner where she had dragged the mattress. It was gone. She turned back to him. "Where will you sleep?"

"Here. On the straw. I am well enough now and will not drive you from your bed. Go."

She lay back down with her head on Pig, who was sound asleep and had not budged. She yawned, tucked her hands between her cheek and his coarse brown pighair, then closed her eyes. "I am fine here, English."

"You are sleeping with a pig."

"Aye," she said on a half-sigh.

Not more than a moment later she felt him kneel next to her. Stunned, she opened her eyes just in time to see his shoulder loom toward her.

"What are you doing!"

He grabbed her hand in an iron grip and pulled. Her breath fled her mouth with a grunt and he stood up with her flung upside-down over one broad shoulder.

"Put me down, English." She was speaking to his back.

"No." He reached out and grasped the crutch which was leaning against the wall, then jammed it under his arm.

She had two choices: she could fight him and he would still carry her to her bed, or she could accept it. Since the only reason she was not willing to walk to her bed was because she was too tired, a free ride seemed like a good enough substitute. He moved swiftly and easily with her bouncing over his shoulder.

"For a man who almost died by a noose and who has a badly swollen foot, you seem hearty enough, English." She looked down at her hair hanging in a curly fall that went almost to the dirt floor.

When he said nothing, only hobbled toward the back room as if he carried a feather, she muttered, "Must be borne from eating enough stew to feed a small village."

"Must be borne from having to deal with a stubborn Welsh woman," he said.

"I am not stubborn. You are stubborn. I was perfectly happy to stay and sleep where I was, but you, with some misguided sense of chivalry, feel you must see to my comfort."

He grunted something unintelligible.

"I was comfortable where I was."

"I was not."

"Put me down."

"I live only to serve you. . . ." He dumped her on the bed and made an exaggerated bow ". . . my lady of the woods." He straightened and gave her an arrogant male grin.

She frowned back at him, then crawled to the edge of the bed and gripping the sides of the tick in her hands, she leaned over and looked down at his bad foot. It was still swollen. "How did you do that so effortlessly? Does it not pain you terribly?"

He shrugged as if it took no strength at all to squat down on one leg, then lift himself and her so easily. "A warrior must be inventive. He must be able to think on his feet, even if he only has one good one."

Pig came trotting into the room, snorting and sniffing so fiercely they both looked down to stare at him. He stopped a few steps away and with something akin to porcine indigence looked up at her kneeling on the bed.

"Oh, no! I did not leave you, Pig." She straightened and pointed at the English. "Blame him."

Pig rolled his eyes toward the Englishman called Roger, then grunted and snorted a couple of times. Pig shifted back a few steps, paused, and with a running start he hoofed it across the room, then leapt on the bed next to her.

The English shook his head. "You are still sleeping with your cattle."

"Aye. I always sleep with Pig."

"Some of my men have said the same about me," he mumbled.

"What was that?"

"Nothing." He looked at her and shook his head. He stared thoughtfully at Pig. "He thinks he's a dog."

"No. But he likes to have his way." When he looked at her again, she added, "He is pig-headed."

He stared at her for a moment, just a pause that showed his surprise.

She grinned, and then he began to laugh, a silly

croaking kind of laugh like the night call of the pond frogs. After a minute their laughter faded and they looked at each other.

She was afraid of that look, and even in the dark she could read what passed between them, the flicker of that same strong feeling that overtook them in the water. She stared at his mouth, just the strong line of it, shadowed but still distinguishable in the darkness.

She had been dreaming of kisses. Kisses from that mouth. Kisses bewitched by fairies. She only wished that were so. She looked away for an awkward moment, then said, "You keep the blanket."

He started to protest, but she held up her hand. "Pig keeps me warm."

He did not say anything.

"I shall not sleep until you agree," she said with goodly stubbornness.

He smiled.

She could see the white of his teeth.

"Agreed." He turned and went toward the main room, but stopped and turned back.

She held her breath.

"Good night, Teleri."

She exhaled and smiled. "Good night, English."

Chapter

20

⤳

"Wake up, English!"

Roger sat up so fast he frightened that pet pig of hers away. It scurried across the room, snorting and whining. Roger shoved the hair from his eyes and stared up at Teleri's smile. 'Twas a good thing to first wake up to, that smile.

Leaning back on one elbow, he studied her at his leisure, from her eyes—one still bruised a bluish-yellow but no longer swollen—all the way down to her bare toes.

She was standing less than an arm's length away with her hands planted on her hips in that cocky way she had, one bare foot tapping impatiently on the floor. "You are sleeping away the best part of the day. Tell me, English. Do fierce warriors always fight battles after None? Is there an expressed time for brave knights to bash their brains in over rich lands and even richer ladies? After a leisurely meal of ten courses perhaps?"

"You are a saucy thing, so early in the morn," he grumbled, then locked his hands together and stretched them over his head. He cast a quick glance outside.

146

A soft autumn rain had been pattering on the ground outside for most of the night, but it had stopped. Sunlight was just breaking through and the sky was still colored with the pinks and blues of dawn. Frowning, he relaxed his arms and looked at her. "How long has it been light?"

"Not long." She stood there, still waiting.

He rubbed a hand over his eyes for a moment and yawned.

She took a few steps away and turned her back to him while she ladled something from a bucket into a wooden cup. She turned back. "Here." She held out the cup. "Drink this."

He took the cup and stared down at the clear liquid inside. "What is it?"

"Rainwater."

He sniffed it. It smelled like water.

"I told you before. I did not save your life so I could poison you."

"Perhaps not. But the last time you gave me something to drink, you drugged me senseless."

"Aye, that I did." She wore a small smile that said she had bested him and was proud of it. "At the time I thought you needed to be senseless."

He studied the clear liquid in the cup; it looked like water.

"I must need to remind you of the stew you ate. The *huge* pot of stew you ate."

"You tasted it first."

She shook her head at him and appeared to try to bite back a small smile. "You need not fear. I have no use for senseless knights this day. I have plans for us."

"What plans?"

"Drink the water."

"You first." He handed her the cup, crossed his arms over his chest and waited.

She sighed with exasperation, then, shaking her head, she raised the cup to her mouth and drained it in a couple of swallows. She started to hand it back to him.

He shook his head. "More."

Smirking a little, she turned and ladled more water into the cup from the bucket. She drank it down again. Then refilled it and handed it to him. "Now do you trust me, English?"

"No, but I'll drink it," he told her and did. He pulled the cup away from his mouth. "Why am I drinking this?"

"Rainwater is the clearest and cleanest water you can find. It comes from the heavens above, right from the clouds between the earth and sky. That makes it especially powerful. It will help your voice come back."

He grinned at her, then a moment later croaked out a laugh as he got to his feet, careful to keep his weight on his good foot.

"What is so amusing?"

"Why should I not just stand outside during the next rain and open my mouth? Or better yet, I could stand out there with my mouth wide open and my foot stuck out and then heal both."

"Since your foot is already in your mouth I do not think that would be necessary." She spun around, clearly angry at him.

"Teleri."

"What?" she snapped, her back to him as she pretended to be busy with something, but he could tell she just did not want to look at him.

"I was playing with you. Making a jest. I did not mean to hurt you."

"You did not hurt me, English." She turned to face him, her chin high and proud, her back to the shelf as she gripped the edge tightly. "I would have to care for your good opinion for you to have the power to hurt me."

He had done it again. He drove a hand through his hair and took a long, deep breath. "I am sorry."

She stood there and did not respond. She seemed to

be searching his face for something, some truth. Then she averted her eyes and stared at the floor, but not before he saw the hurt in them. "You laughed at me."

"Aye. I did laugh, and I am sorry for it."

"If I did not believe in the natural, godly magic of the earth and the sky and the air, I would not have believed that you would survive. It was my faith that made me believe I could help you. I believed you would live. You lived. Faith is part of who we are and who we become."

He thought about her words. All men had faith in something. Warriors had faith in their strength and ability. In their cause. Peasants had faith in their lord to keep them safe and most men had faith in their king the way priests had faith in God. He asked himself why women could not have as strong a faith in something as did men. It was not something he had thought of before. Women and faith. Not the way men thought of such.

She looked at him from such a wounded expression. "Surely you have beliefs that guide you?"

"Aye." He felt like a clod again for hurting her. 'Twas not well done of him, no matter how silly her Welsh cures and talk of magic rainwater sounded.

But he had apologized, not once, but twice. He would not do so again. He had four sisters and a mother who could milk an issue dry should he ever be foolish enough to act too contrite. He'd learned that early, when he'd made the mistake of bending to his sister Maud. And she went on and on and on *ad nauseum*.

He thought about that while he looked at her stiff, straight back and sour expression. He told himself with no little pride that he did not need to grovel.

She moved away toward the shelf on the opposite wall and picked up a basket, then hooked it over one arm.

He watched her stiff motions, silently, knowing if he told her he would not grovel, she might well fling that basket at his head. Any one of his sisters would have done so were he foolish enough to speak what he was thinking. So, he changed the direction of their talk. "You said you had plans for us today."

"Aye." She studied him from an unreadable expression, one hand resting on the twisted rim of the basket.

He waited, and when she said nothing he tried again. "There was excitement in your voice when you spoke. Tell me what it was that had you so pleased."

She gave him one of her direct looks, the kind that seemed to search for something in his eyes or in his expression. Whatever she saw made her tense, straight shoulders relax.

A truce again, he thought.

After a moment's pause, she said, "Since I've seen you eat, and eat, and eat, I have to believe that you like mushrooms?"

"Mushrooms?" he repeated blankly. "Aye. The castle cook used to serve a dish in the morn that could awaken you from a deep sleep by only the mouth-watering smell of it."

"What was it?"

"Mushrooms cooked with onions and bacon."

Her pig let out an ear-cracking squeal and suddenly scampered from the corner, right past them and into the back room, where he skidded to a halt, then cowered under the bed.

"What the hell . . . ?" Roger shook his head; his ears were ringing. 'Twas the worse sound he'd ever heard.

Teleri wore an understanding smile. "You cannot say that word around Pig."

"What word?" Roger frowned, tapping the heel of his hand against his ear. He looked up, thought about it, then repeated, "Bacon?"

Another horribly long and painful squeal came echoing out from the back room.

She flinched.

Roger was hunched over with his teeth gritted together. After the noise faded, he glanced at her.

"Aye, that's the word." she said with a nod.

He leaned to his left. From under the bed he could

see the whites of the pig's wary eyes staring at him. Could something so ear-cracking come from one plump and strange beast? Apparently so.

"Just ignore him. He'll come out later." She leaned closer and whispered as if the pig could truly understand their talk. "But try not to use that word again."

Use it again? God's ears. . . . Only if he wanted to deafen someone.

"Since you like mushrooms," she continued as if nothing odd had happened, "I thought we could go gather them together. With two of us, we would gather twice as many, I think."

He nodded as if he completely understood her. Yet in truth he understood little except he would not fall into a fool's trap again and say something she could use to make him feel stupid.

"Did you hear the thunder last night?"

"Aye."

"That means there will be mushrooms in the forest."

Thunder and mushrooms? Did she think lightning bolts split the earth and sent mushrooms up through the grass? Good God, and here he thought magic rainwater was worth jesting about. He stood there and stared out the window, where the sun had cracked through the clouds and the sky was beginning to clear to a bright blue. He turned to her and with great diplomacy said, "I know little of mushrooms. You will have to show me what to do."

A slow smile spread across her face and her body lost its stiffness. "I will teach you, English." She walked past him. "Grab your crutch and let's be off. Half the day is almost gone."

Half the day? He followed her outside, squinting into the gold sunlight. Hell, it was barely dawn. But Roger wisely kept quiet and walked beside her across the yard over the bridge, where her pig caught up with them and quietly trailed along behind.

As they moved into the meadow, neither spoke, but he looked down after a moment and watched her move beside him. She was a beautiful woman, but in an odd, wild way.

Roger was used to beautiful women, women who had skin like snow, hair that was artfully twisted up and decorated with jewels, and who wore the finest cloth in bold colors that flattered their eyes or skin color.

Her skin had a golden, tawny cast to it and her hair was free as the wind. But what he saw in her was a different kind of beauty, something primitive and un-controlled. When she moved she did so with a strange mix of innocence and urgency, and a kind of motion innate to her, one that made him feel as if life itself came from somewhere deep inside of her.

There were moments, brief snatches of time, when he caught her looking at him or when she smiled, and something more than life came from her. Whatever it was, this strange power he felt, seemed to be linked to him in some powerful but odd way. As if some part of her were also a part of him. A part he had never known existed until the past few days.

He continued to watch her. She typically walked with great fervor, but now she had slowed her pace to his, even though he moved well with the crutch and could have probably gone without it. Still she walked right beside him. No steps ahead and none behind. She was pacing him.

And he had to smile, for it took only a moment to see that as she moved with him, she, too, was limping. It was not obvious. He suspected she did not even realize she was doing it.

He said nothing, but looked ahead of him smiling slightly. Before him were all the colors of the woods, the green of the evergreen trees and the red and gold of the autumn leaves, which had fallen onto the path that started at the edge of the meadow and moved into the woods.

The signs of summer had all but disappeared. Gone in a matter of days. As he walked, looking around him, the thought came to him in such a clear way it stunned him for a moment. If the world around him could change in so little time—summer could switch so swiftly into autumn—it was not surprising that his life could change just as fast.

Here he was in this odd place where nothing was familiar. Yet he was comfortable. Here with this woman he did not truly know. Yet somehow he felt he knew her better than he knew himself.

He suddenly saw things he did not ever remember seeing. The small things around him that he never had noticed before. The color of the leaves and sky, the sounds of the rain and the wind, the way a young woman walked.

He was different. Changed. His mind. His perspective. It was as if he suddenly viewed the world with someone else's eyes.

And he wondered if life could truly be this simple.

Chapter

21

Near the edge of the woods, Teleri squatted down next to a clump of dark-colored goose grass sparkling with droplets of fresh rain. She set down the basket and rested her elbows on her bent knees, then searched around her, stopping when her eye caught a flash of white.

"Watch," she told him as she parted the grasses gently with one hand. A small cluster of white mushrooms lay hidden there with plump, round caps that looked like small moons. They were perfect and looked as if they had just popped right up from the dark earth.

He leaned his crutch against a tree and easily hunkered down next to her, his shoulder almost touching hers, the warmth from his body so very near. She saw then that he had put most of his weight on his good foot.

While he looked at the mushrooms, she stared at his bent legs. His thighs were covered with hose, but his leg muscles bulged tightly and ran over his legs in thick, strong ribbons. They were a warrior's legs, honed for power, the same kind of muscle and bone and sinew she could see in the strong flanks of a horse.

It was no wonder he had lifted her so swiftly and with such ease.

"Now what?" he said.

Startled, she looked up quickly, then felt the blood rush to her cheeks. She turned her face toward the new mushrooms and concentrated on those. "You hold them at the stem. Here. Like this. See? And lift gently."

She paused, then added, "I remember once when I found a hedgesparrow's nest that had tilted in the wind. One of the bright blue eggs had fallen out, but had not broken. They are so delicate—hedgesparrow eggs—and the shells so thin. I could not believe the egg had not cracked. But I knew the mother bird would never hatch that egg unless it was tucked back inside the nest. I had to be very gentle and carefully lift the egg and put it back." She laughed. "I remember, I think, that I held my breath the entire time."

She looked up at him and smiled. "Think of something fragile when you pick this kind of mushroom, English. What is the one thing you must handle with the softest hand?"

"A woman," he said without a pause and with complete seriousness.

Her breath caught for a second, then she quickly averted her eyes and continued. "You must be gentle with these white ones, field mushrooms, for they are the most fragile. But they are also the most delicious you will ever chance to taste." She picked one of the mushrooms, then looked up at him and nodded at the cluster in the grass. "You try."

He did as she suggested but he was awkward because his hands were large and the stems short and delicate.

"No, not that way." She placed her hand beneath his large one and guided his fingers. "Like this."

He was so close she could feel his breath next to her,

as warm as his body heat, and she saw the way it grew foggy in the morning air and mixed with hers. Their hands together were resting on the mushrooms, the damp grass cool and wet against her knuckles.

But she was hardly aware of the cool wet rainwater. His hand was very hard along the palm, where small calluses from the hilt of a weapon and the leather of reins turned his skin hard and slick.

She lifted her eyes and found him staring at her mouth. She returned his frank look. "You want to kiss me."

"Aye. I want to kiss you." But he did not move to do so.

She waited, but not long, then she slipped to her knees, an action that moved her even closer, so she was kneeling between his legs. She did not move her hand from his hand, there in the grass, but she slid her free hand behind his neck and drew his face down to hers.

The moment their lips touched she closed her eyes and parted her mouth with a soft sigh. He deepened the kiss so swiftly she almost fell over. But he did not kiss her hard or with command. He did not take the advantage, which clearly he could have.

He kissed her slowly and softly, a touch as gentle as lifting that hedgesparrow's egg. She opened her eyes to find his open and watching her. His look was intense and urgent, yet this kiss, this wonderful, warm kiss was so soft and tender. She wondered what it took for him to kiss her so gently when his eyes were so fiercely intent with something. She did not know what to call it, but felt it was the same, magical thing burning through her own veins.

Desire? Passion? An aching, aching want? Fairies dancing?

"Teleri," he whispered her name with a warm, sweet breath that touched her cheek and ear and ruffled the curls near her face. He moved his mouth and lips to her cheeks, then over her eyelids.

"I like your kisses, English."

He said something, but she did not hear. His hand had moved to her back and slid down to hold her bottom, to rub up and down and make the cloth of her gown and shift rasp against her skin.

She slipped both arms around his neck and their bodies touched from their lips downward. Her thighs were between his bent legs, her hips against his belly, the hard knot of him fitted into the dip at the top of her thighs.

He pressed her harder against him with the flat of his hand, then cupped her bottom with both hands and lifted her a little, separating her thighs and moving her against him in a earthy and slow rhythm.

His kisses grew insistent and became so deep and sensuous that she felt as if the two of them were nothing but mouths and tongues and wild, wicked licking sensations. It felt so good, these kisses, that she almost cried out when he slowed his tongue, then withdrew and touched only his mouth softly to hers.

He pulled back slowly, then kissed her on the tip of her nose and set her down and away from him.

She blinked in stunned surprise because he had stopped so swiftly. She wanted more kisses, but her pride would not let her ask.

Neither of them said a word, but their breathing was fast and harsh, their looks locked on each other.

Finally Teleri tore her gaze away and stared at her hands. Frowning, she opened her fist palm up between them. He did the same. There in each palm were the crushed remnants of two precious mushrooms.

A moment later they both burst out laughing.

"Fragile," he said with a grin.

"Fragile," she agreed, smiling back. "We might have just ruined our next meal."

He shook his head. "There will be more."

"You say that as if you know something, English."

"I know many things." From the way he looked at her, it was clear he was not talking about mushrooms.

His knowledge of this thing between the two of them frightened her, but at the same time made her want to know it for herself. What went on between men and women was not something she knew, but she wanted to know, at least with this Englishman named Roger.

After a pause he looked down at the grasses and pulled out a yellow mushroom which he held up for her to look at. "What kind is this? Are not some poisonous?"

"It is a chanterelle. And yes, some are poisonous. They are usually the ugliest ones."

"And this brown one?"

"A horse mushroom."

"And this?"

"A cep."

"Can we eat all of them?"

She nodded.

"Then I will find plenty of mushrooms," he boasted.

"Ah." She cocked her head and planted her hands on her hips. "Is that a challenge, English?"

With a quick nod, he winked at her. "Aye."

"Now, are we speaking of mushrooms?"

He did not answer but he was smirking when he looked down. A second later he pulled a beauty of a horse mushroom from between the grasses. He dropped it into the empty basket with a cocky grin. "One . . ."

He plucked another. "Two . . ."

She bent and scoured the grasses, then tossed two mushrooms in the basket herself. "Three and four."

"Five and six," he said, reaching out with his long arm.

She crawled away in the opposite direction. "Seven, eight, and nine!"

Now he was parting the grasses. "Ten! Eleven!"

"Twelve, thirteen, fourteen and . . . *fifteen!"* She laughed. She had never been a gracious winner.

They both crawled madly through the woods, this

way and that, throwing mushrooms at the basket and calling out numbers. It turned into a frantic race.

"Twenty-five!" she shouted.

Five more mushrooms flew through the air from his direction. "Twenty-six, twenty-seven, twenty-eight, twenty-nine, *thirty!*"

She began to fill the skirt of her gown, shouting out numbers and crawling around frantically, parting the grasses and tossing mushrooms into her skirt with little care. She broke the stems. She crushed the caps. She didn't care. She would win this race!

She turned, her skirt filled. He was just as far away from the basket as she was, his big hands piled high with a stack of mushrooms.

Their gazes met and a challenge passed between them.

"A race," he said in a voice too confident for her to ignore.

"Aye." She gave sharp nod. No English would best her.

"On our knees?" He asked, and like her, she could see he was gauging the distance to the basket.

"On our knees!" she agreed and lurched forward.

In an instant they were both scurrying on their knees toward the basket, each loaded down with mushrooms.

Her knees hit the ground in short rapid thuds. She saw that he moved more smoothly than she.

His head and chest did not bounce with each step as hers did.

Her breath came faster and harder.

Then suddenly he was ahead of her, moving on his knees more swiftly because he wore chausses.

"You have no skirt to hamper you!" she shouted at him when her hem caught on her heel.

Some of his mushrooms fell into the grasses and he had to stop and pick them up. "You mean I have no skirt to cheat and fill with mushrooms!"

"Cheat!" She laughed and hastened forward, crowing like a cock when she emptied her skirt into the basket.

In truth, they got there at the same time, both laughing before they collapsed on their backs in the soft grass, sprawled with their arms out and their chests heaving for breath.

After a minute he lifted his head and looked at her, grinning. "I won."

"I won."

"I won," he insisted.

"All right then, English. I give in." She sighed, still lying flat on her back and staring up at the blue sky. "You lost."

"Aye, a smart loser admits defeat. I—" he paused, then frowned. "Wait . . ." He turned and looked at her just as she doubled onto her side with more giggling laughter.

When her laughing faded away, she lay back, quiet as he was, thinking. She closed her eyes, resting. She sat up so suddenly she saw stars flicker before her eyes. "Your voice!"

He looked at her, his expression blank. Then he spoke, "What about it?"

"Your voice is no longer a whisper. It is clear, English! It does not rasp or crack."

His face suddenly blank, he touched his throat.

"I did not notice at first. But now that I think about it, when you called out the numbers your voice was clear." She raised her chin and straightened her shoulders smugly. "Perhaps now you will listen to me when I tell you to drink rainwater."

His eyes were closed and he lay very still.

Her smile faded, drained away at the sight of his expression. She studied his tight features, the thin line of his lips, trying to understand what he was feeling. It was a strong, strong emotion he was trying to control.

"You did not think your voice would return," she said quietly.

He said nothing.

"For a man who just gained back his lost voice you are very quiet."

He was still silent, fighting some inner demon.

She waited longer, plucking at the grass with her fingers. "Had I lost my voice and it returned, I would sing and shout to the sky."

She watched him swallow hard, as he had done when he first came awake from the fever. When his throat was swollen and rope-burned.

"If I were you, English, I would cry," she added. "I would not be afraid to show how I was feeling. I would freely shed my tears."

Finally he spoke without emotion and without looking at her, "You are a woman."

"What is that supposed to mean? I am a woman and therefore weak and sniveling? It is fine for me to sob and cry and no one will think me a coward?" She glared at him. "You insult me."

He lay there, then shook his head and gave a small bark of wry laughter. He turned his face toward her and said, "I usually do insult you somewhere in our talk. 'Tis nothing new, Teleri."

She searched his face for signs of what he was feeling. She saw no pain hidden away. She saw no tears in his eyes wanting to be shed, but she was certain he had felt something so strong it took all of his control not to show it. Whatever it was he experienced—joy, relief, pain—it had passed as suddenly as it came on, for he seemed at peace with himself as he lay there.

She, too, lay back on the grass and stared upward. "I am glad your voice is back, English. Even though you use it sometimes to say foolish things. The problem is in your head, I think, not in your throat."

He sat up on his elbows, turned and looked at her. "Do you always say whatever you are thinking?"

"No." She stubbornly stared at the blue sky. "I think much more than I ever say."

He laughed at her, then she heard him take a deep

breath. She did not know if he did so out of relief or comfort. But she was glad he was better. She was glad she baited him that way.

It had become quiet with neither of them speaking, only laying there in the damp grass with the sun rising overhead and peeking down through the tall crowns of the still trees. A few small birds chirruped around them and some wild geese flew in an arrow overhead, their honking as loud and piercing as the trumpet of a royal herald.

"Tell me what you are thinking," he asked her.

"I was thinking that I like the sounds of the woods. I like it when the sky is blue like this. Bluer than the cornflowers. I was looking up and thinking about the moon so high above us." She pointed up to where the faded outline of the moon still hung in the edges of the western sky. "It grows larger and fuller with each night that passes."

She paused for moment's thought, then folded her arms behind her head and stared upward. "You can hide from the stars during the day. But even though the moon shines brightest at night, you cannot hide from it. The moon is so stubborn that it comes out even during the bright light of day. Like now. Hanging there in the day-blue sky, not caring that the sun is still out. The moon just looks down at you as if to say, 'I see you. You cannot hide.'"

She cast him a glance. "And do you know why?"

He wore a soft and kind smile when he shook his head.

"You cannot hide because the moon is truly the eye of God. And when it is full, if you look very closely, you can even see his face in it."

She looked up and pointed. "There. See? It is daylight and you can only see half of it. The face is there, right there for us to look up toward." She sighed. "Is it not one of the most beautiful things you have ever seen?" She did not say much more but watched the moon drift down until not much of it was visible through the trees, then pulled her gaze away from the moon and looked at him.

He was not staring up to the sky. He was looking at her with the strangest, most pensive expression. "Aye. 'Tis one of the most beautiful things I have ever seen."

And she realized then that he was not speaking of the moon.

Chapter

22

❦

Leeds Castle, Kent, England

King Edward I of England was as tall and commanding a presence as his title indicated. His skin was golden from the recent hunting trip and his blond hair glinted in the sunlight that broke through a circular window filled with amber-colored, wavy glass.

"This is an odd message you would have me come home to. You say Sir Roger has disappeared somewhere in Brecon and claim Sir Tobin de Clare, Gloucester's son, is behind it?" Edward stood in his war room in the main castle with his back to a long, heavily-carved table of dark wood, his legs crossed casually at the ankles. But to anyone who truly knew the King well, he was actually anything but relaxed and indifferent.

"Those are strong accusations." Edward met the eyes of each man kneeling before him with an unreadable blue gaze. His left eye drooped slightly on one side, a trait of Plantagenet kings, his father in particular. But on Edward, no one would ever dare to think it a weakness or flaw. He was a man of one and forty whose mind was as whipcord sharp as his long and youthfully lean body.

Edward gestured for the men to rise. "Explain why you suspect this."

Payn Godart stepped forward. "First Sir Roger disappears in Brecon with no sign. He rides off after a woman on a horse and does not come back. One night and another day we waited, your grace, then we searched the countryside."

"You did not find any sign of him?"

Payn shook his head. "But de Clare was gone searching alone for longer than anyone else. He returned with no explanation for taking a day longer than the others. When I suggested we ride to Earl Merrick for aid, he refused, even though he knew Glamorgan was closer and could give us aid in the search."

"You think he had reason to harm Sir Roger?"

"They did not get along. That is no secret. And there is de Clare's sister, the Lady Elizabeth."

"We all know of the Lady Elizabeth and FitzAlan, but I think Hugh Bigod is more of a threat to him than de Clare."

"But even more damning, Sire, is the fact that de Clare has disappeared from here while we were awaiting your return." Payn paused, then added, "Innocent men do not choose to hide information and do not sneak away at night."

"What information is that?"

"Riding to Glamorgan to get help from Earl Merrick, who does not know of what has happened to his friend. He is close to Sir Roger."

"As am I," Edward said pointedly. "And someone saw de Clare sneak out of here?"

"No. But he told no one he was leaving. I did not find out he was gone until this morn," Payn Godart complained.

"In Brecon there were no tracks from Sir Roger's mount?"

"De Clare claimed they disappeared at a river north of Brecon Wood," John Carteret explained, then bowed his dark head again in deference to his king.

"I see," Edward rubbed his pointed beard thoughtfully.

"We searched the area for two days and the nearby village. Bleddig, I think 'tis called." Payn Godart turned for confirmation to the men standing weaponless behind him, their swords placed along the outer wall of the hall and helms tucked under their arms.

"'Twas Bleddig," John Carteret agreed. "No one there had seen him, Your Grace. I know it is impossible, but it was as if FitzAlan and his horse just disappeared."

Edward began to pace in front of them, his big beringed hands clasped behind his back as he walked, his pointed shoes with their fine leather soles tapping his impatience over the tiles of the floor. "There has been no ransom. No sign that someone captured him." He turned swiftly and faced the men. "Someone should notify his family."

"I'll send a man to Wells, Sire," Payn told him. "Should one of us go to Camrose? Earl Merrick will want to know."

Edward crossed to a side door that led to a private chamber. He opened it, then turned to Payn Godart. "No. I'll make certain Earl Merrick is notified." And Edward disappeared through the door leaving Sir Roger's men-at-arms standing there. Dismissed.

About the same time King Edward closed that door, a black-haired man rode over the Welsh Marchlands. He rode alone, no squire or servant behind him. He rode with only his sword in its silver hilt at his side.

He had already ridden over the Black Mountains, through a pass at Mawr, where last winter's run-off water still fell over the rocks into streams, where salmon swam and wild brown geese stood on one leg in the shallow edges of the water. He stopped there and filled a flask with fresh water, staring off toward the southwest, apprehensive about what he had to do.

But before he could think on it overlong, he swung

back up into the saddle and moved down to the valley below. His mount cantered swiftly up and over the rolling hills and across deserted moorlands where sheep grazed and the hawks flew overhead, and where an occasional single tree on a distant hill aimed the same way the wind blew.

He was headed toward Brecon.

Roger and Teleri ate the mushrooms they had found that same day, along with more vegetables from the cottage garden, but as Roger lay on his straw bed that night, he thought about how Teleri carefully measured what she used from her small larder and from the garden. She had so little, yet she shared it with him, asking only that when he left he did not take the Arab with him.

He had never known hunger. He was the only son of a wealthy baron, maternal grandson of one of the oldest and most formidable families in the land. He had been fostered to a powerful earl, and friend to the crown prince who then became King of England. Even in battle and under siege, Roger was still nobility and a knight. For them, food was always plentiful. When he was on Crusade, where on earlier campaigns plenty of men had almost starved, Roger had fought at Edward's side.

Kings did not go hungry, even on the battlefield.

Chapter
23

Roger left the cottage the next afternoon and disappeared into the forest. His mission did not take him long, and when he moved back along the path toward the clearing, he was whistling a tune and keeping time with the rushing sound of the wind high in the trees around him. He looked up and around him and watched the orange leaves float to the ground and felt them crackle under his bare feet.

He stopped just out of sight, not far from the clearing near the west end of the cottage yard. He saw Teleri and he just stood there watching her. He had watched women before. Watched them walk and talk and move. But the women he knew were alike in so many ways. Even Elizabeth could get lost in a crowd at a fair or a feast. He would have to look for her dark hair to separate her from most.

But with Teleri he was certain he would have known her even in the most crowded street of London. He would know her by the way she moved, by her swift steps, almost as if she were walking with the wind. Her small feet moved with the swiftness of a forest animal and when she stood in one place, which wasn't often, she would cock her head the way a bird or deer listens for danger. It was almost as if she felt she had to be ready to run.

She was moving along the south side of the cottage, looking this way and that. She stopped in the cabbage garden and raised her hands to cup around her mouth, then she called out, "Pig! Pi-ig!"

She waited, then planted her fists on her hips and scanned the yard, obviously frustrated and looking for the fat rascal of a pig that she treated the same way the Queen treated her pet dogs.

Roger looked past her, searching for the pig, but he could not see the thing anywhere.

"Is everyone gone this day?" she muttered and hurried across the yard to the brook where some wild ducks quacked loudly and flapped their wings. "Pig!" She clapped her hands together. "Come now!"

But there was no pig. No snorting. No trotting of hooves. No loud squeal.

He thought about shouting out "bacon," but thought his ears could not take the noise if the pig was anywhere nearby.

She stood there for a moment, her finger tapping against her lip. She sighed, then turned her face up to the sun and raised her arms out. She began to slowly turn 'round and 'round. Faster and faster. Her hair moved outward and the skirt of her gown filled with air.

A moment later she began to chant,

"Oh Sun so high, so warm, so gay
Help me, please, I cannot delay
I'm out here spinning 'round and 'round,
Something is lost and cannot be found."

The oddest thing happened. Suddenly the sunlight grew brighter, then brighter still, the way it would in battle or joust when it reflected off the shining metal of a knight's helm. The light blinded him so quickly that he forgot to breathe.

He stepped to the side and the sunlight seemed to widen so it was still bright and shining directly above him. He stepped right and the sunlight continued to beat down in the same manner. He had a odd and eerie feeling that should he go clear to London, the sunlight would move right along with him.

Those bright rays warmed the top of his head and shoulders, and he began to sweat as if it were midsummer in Wells. He blinked, his eyes tearing from the intensity of the light, but still could not see anything. He raised a hand to shield the light from his eyes.

She still stood where she had been moments before, but she was looking to her right, across the meadow to another section of bushes where the sunlight was shining down as sharply as it did on him. He wiped his eyes and shaded them again just as that odd pig came trotting out from the bushes, sniffing the ground until he got to her bare feet, where he plopped down like a huge platter of ham.

She scolded him but even Roger could see she was not truly angry, only worried. She knelt down and laughed at the pig when she scratched his ears and he rolled over, his hooves straight up in the air.

She laughed again and Roger just stood there listening to the sound. There was a joy and freedom to her laughter that he seldom heard. When they were young, his sisters had laughed that freely, but it had been a long time since he had been home. Women of the court did not laugh without motive.

She stood and looked up then, toward him, and she froze, her eyes on him and the light that still felt as if it surrounded him. She frowned. "English?"

"Aye."

"There you are," she said and sounded relieved, which made him feel good. He liked it that she had been thinking of him.

Roger moved out of the bushes and the strange

sunlight then faded almost as quickly as it had come. He glanced up at the sky and saw that a cloud had just passed over the sun.

A logical reason for sunlight to wane, he told himself. A logical reason. Aye.

"I was wondering where you were," she said.

Roger stepped through the low scrubby bushes and firs which caught on his hose, scratched against his calves, and almost knocked the dead hare from his hand.

He left the protection of the waist-high brush and moved into the clearing.

She stood there not moving, her eyes pinned on the rabbit hanging limply from his fist. The first sound she made was almost like a cry of someone who is wounded. Her face grew taut with a look of horror. "What have you done?"

Her voice was so quiet he had to pause and think about what she had just said.

"I've brought a meal." He held up the hare, his gift to their table that night. His means of partially repaying his debt to her. "I could not find much else, but rabbit will make for a fine meal this eve and a good stew tomorrow."

"You killed it."

"For you." He held up the hare for her to see, proud that it had taken him little time to snare a meal for them, especially when it was not simple to catch the thing with no weapon or trap.

"For me?" She looked up at him, her mouth open. "To eat?"

"Aye."

Her eyes filled with shock and he could see them suddenly turn teary. She covered her mouth with her hands the way women did when they saw something they could not stomach.

He had sisters. He knew a look of female horror when he saw it. Something was very wrong.

She dropped her hands but those tears continued to

stream down her cheeks and she whispered, "Did I not feed you enough?"

His chest felt like it was somewhere near his ankles. "I wanted to supply food for us. A way to repay you for all you have done for me."

"So you killed a rabbit. An animal that is a thousand times smaller than you?"

"I have brought meat."

She began to cry harder and he stood there feeling like the village idiot.

"You killed that rabbit *for* me? How could you do that?"

"I do not know," he said sarcastically. "It seemed like a fine idea. Meat *is* food."

"Not to me. Have you seen me serve any meat for our meals?"

He assumed she didn't have the skill to kill an animal for meat. He thought to surprise her with something good and filling.

"Do you not see that I would never want something like that? Do you not look at who and what I am? How can you live here for even one day and not see that I would never kill an animal!"

Roger looked at the hare. He didn't know if he should cook it or say Mass over it.

"You do not pay attention to what is there before your very eyes. You did not notice the most important thing about me. I could never eat that poor dead thing. *Never.*" She raised her eyes to his, the tears pouring down her red cheeks as she swiped at them with the back of one hand.

He did not know what to say and just stood there feeling worse than someone who had just kicked a kitten.

She kept crying and her shoulders shook.

"We eat meat for food, Teleri. It is not a sin."

"I understand that some people eat animals for food. Here, where I live, where I grow cabbages and turnips, onions and carrots, where the berries are sweet and the mushrooms grow after a rain, I have more food than I could ever need. I choose not to eat meat. The animals are my friends. They are the only friends I have, Roger." Her voice cracked. "They are all I have."

He thought about the food they'd eaten, stew and berries, about the soft eggs from the wild geese and the soup she'd fed him. He had not seen her eat meat. But until now, he had not noticed.

She faced him again, her expression serious. "I could never eat anything that has a face." She turned and ran into the cottage, the pig following right behind her.

Roger sat near the bridge, his back against a thick tree that arched over the roof of the cottage and the small pond. In front of him was a smoldering fire. But the fire was not the only thing that was smoldering.

She had not come out of her cottage.

He had not sought her out or gone back inside.

The rabbit was spitted on two green oak twigs and cooking slowly over the fire. He had rolled a weathered round of oak over from a stack of cut wood and used it as a stool.

Now, he was sitting there swatting mosquitoes and gnats and watching the meat cook. He rested his wrists on his bent knees and leaned forward as he occasionally turned the meat.

The quickly cooling night air filled with the scent of roasting cony. Every so often, just often enough to make him stare blankly at the spit, the meat would drip into the fire and sizzle and smoke.

There was a telling silence between those sizzles and spits that managed to annoy the hell out of him. So he picked up a stick and poked at the wood coals, wondering with complete bewilderment how he could be so wrong. So completely wrong.

In that silence he heard her words again and again. The accusation that he had not bothered to try to understand a kind and gentle woman whose only friends were animals that were broken or maimed, a woman who had saved his life.

For the first time he thought about her existence here. He wondered what it would be like to live with no other people around you. He had come from a large family where privacy had been scarce and treasured.

Not so for her, he thought. Her whole life was private, protected. Empty. Lonely. There was true pain in her words when she cried that the animals were her only friends.

He took the rabbit off the spit and pulled off a piece. He raised it to his mouth and stopped. It no longer smelled good. He stared at the meat in his hand and muttered, "Eat it you fool. Eat it."

But he could not put it into his mouth. All he could see before him was a fuzzy black nose and two big brown eyes. Whiskers that twitched and long, long ears. He dropped the meat into the orange coals of the fire where it sparked for a moment as if the last of its life just burned right out of it.

Then he sat there, unable to eat it because all he could see was a rabbit's face.

Sometime that night, the air grew cold and the wind picked up. Soon it blew so hard that the trees leaned and creaked and branches broke off and cracked into pieces. That sudden, harsh and unexpected wind got colder and colder, turned into the kind that can drive clear through one's skin and muscle and freeze a person's very bones.

The shutters banged against the cottage wall and Teleri sat up on her bed, disoriented and feeling frightened from a deep sleep. She realized she was shivering from the bite of the wind that was whistling and blowing something fierce outside. She quickly slid from the bed and walked into the main room.

No fire smoldered in the pit. The straw in the corner

was empty, and the blanket lay nearby, still folded as it was every morning.

"Roger?"

There was no answer. He was not there.

She crossed the room and pulled open the door, then walked outside. The wind was wild and cold and it tossed big pieces of tree branches and bushes across the front of the yard as easily as a juggler tosses his wooden pins.

"Roger!"

There was nothing but the noise of the wind.

She walked close to the cottage walls so the eaves would help block some of the gusts and she rounded the corner just as a blast blew so hard it made her eyes tear. The ground against the soles of her bare feet was cold even though the sun had shone brightly that day.

She moved along, stepping over split pieces of wood and twigs that had tumbled into her garden. Nowhere could she find him. Had he left her? He had the opportunity to take Horse and leave as he had done before.

She rushed toward the bridge and whistled for Horse, but the wind swallowed the sound. She tried again and heard the piercing sound of her whistle ride high with the wind.

A moment later Horse trotted across the bridge and over to where she was standing. "So he did not take you," she said in relief.

Hawk was hanging from his mane by his beak. When Horse stopped in front of her, he moved up and perched on Horse's head, where he squawked and rocked the way he did when he was trying to get attention.

"I see you, Hawk. Come home, now. Both of you." She stroked Horse's muzzle and led him toward the cottage door and inside. During a freeze like this one, the animals would help warm the inside.

She hurried back around the corner and past the

garden, looking for the English. It was dark, but the moon had risen and turned the ground from black to gray. She scanned the yard, the view from the bridge to the cottage, past the spreading tree that hung and swayed over the brook, its long branches snapping in the gusts like whips. And there, lying in a lump beneath the tree, she spotted him.

Chapter
24

~

He could feel himself shaking. All over. And he awoke from a strange, listless kind of sleep.

"Roger!"

It was so cold. There was no heat. He had made a fire. It was gone. He needed to light it again, he thought. But he could not open his eyes. He could not feel his hand to raise it to wipe his eyes. To move.

"Roger! Get up!"

"Why are you shouting at me?" He murmured. "I did not eat the rabbit."

She did not move or speak for just an instant.

"English!"

"Sorry," he whispered, then sighed heavily. "Truly sorry."

"English!" She grabbed his shoulder and shook him hard.

He could feel that. "I am awake."

"Get up!"

"No," he said, his mouth dry and cracked feeling, especially when he took a breath, which the wind seemed to steal right from his lips. "I cannot."

"Open your eyes, English."

"I cannot."

"Come. There is a freeze. You must open your eyes and come inside the cottage."

He wanted to sleep. It was not cold when he slept.

She pinched him.

"Ouch! Damn you, woman!"

"Good. See? You can open your eyes."

"You pinched me."

"Aye. It is a good thing you can feel a pinch. It means you are not frozen. Now get up while you can still feel your limbs. I do not want to freeze out here with you because you are too lazy to move."

He sat up. His teeth were chattering. His lips would not stop moving. His shoulders, too. "'Tis cold," he told himself vaguely and he looked around, strangely disoriented the way he was when he awoke from a long nightmare he thought was real.

It was dark and the moon was white and cold looking. A huge round ball of snow high up in the sky. The stars glittered brightly. Small chips of ice in the black night sky. The wind was howling like wolves; it was icy cold and bitter, and he could only feel it touch on certain parts of his body.

He looked at Teleri and through chattering teeth said, "I thought you were not talking to me."

"Stand up." She stood up next to him and tugged on his numb hand.

He pulled his hand away and moved onto his hands and knees. He could still feel those, his knees and the base of his palms. He shifted and stood up, but his legs felt deadened and weak, and all he could feel of his feet were the brittle bones deep inside. The bottoms of his feet had no feeling; it was as if there was no skin or meat on them.

He knew the signs: disoriented, sleepy, numbness. She was right. He was freezing.

She grabbed his hands with both of hers and pulled

him with her. It was hard to move because he was shaking so. She was running and it hurt his feet and legs.

He made a sound, he thought. Every time his foot hit the ground a grunt escaped his lips. The air he tried to take in hurt his chest; it was so cold and thin he had to breathe in quickly to get a small bit of air.

He moved with her; she was pulling him along like a puppet at a fair. She shoved him inside the cottage and slammed the door, then ran around the room closing the shutters which he realized vaguely that the wind was battering and slamming against the walls.

He moved to help her, but she was there before him. "I will do it." She handed him the blanket. "Use this and move over to the fire pit."

He did as she said, but turned back to her as she was dragging the tick from her bed toward him. "There is no wood to light," he told her.

"I have wood. Lie down. There. By Pig. He will help warm you."

Roger did as she said, but only because his hands and feet hurt so badly. He lay down and pulled the blanket over him. He had trouble using his hands. It took him some time to get the blanket over his feet. He realized then that he was not certain he could have helped, that he could even have picked up a piece of wood or struck a flint to light it.

She dropped an armload of dry wood into the fire pit and added some squares of peat, then lit it.

The flames sparked and grew and glowed in the center of the room. She had not moved, but stood staring down at him. "Your lips are still blue."

He did not say anything. They felt blue.

She looked over her shoulder and moved to the cages where her broken animals were. She lifted each, one by one from the cages, and brought them over to lay on the mattress.

He was surprised that they did not move away from him, even though they were lame. They were still wild. But they did not seem to be aware of that fact, because they just curled up against his back and legs with their fur-warmed bodies.

Then she was standing over him. She knelt down and crawled onto the mattress between him and the surprisingly intense warmth of her pet pig. She squirmed and wiggled and pressed her back and buttocks against the front of his body.

There was some irony in that, for he was so cold and numb except where she squirmed her bottom against him.

Her bare feet brushed his legs and even through his hose he could feel that they were like ice.

"You are freezing, too."

"I am fine." She pulled his arm over her shoulder and rubbed his hands between hers. "We, all of us, will use each other to keep warm." She wiggled again and again until she was comfortable.

And he was not.

He pulled his hand away to grab a corner of the blanket.

She turned and looked at him from over her shoulder, frowning in that way she had whenever she did not understand him.

"Here." He pulled the corner and twisted so the blanket covered her. "Tuck that side under you. There is enough so we can both use it. I do not sleep in a quiet manner and could toss and turn and easily pull it off you during the night."

She faced the other way and pulled the blanket over her. He could smell her scent in her hair. She smelled of things green and alive, of fresh, clean air and lush leaves. A true and natural scent of the wild. No perfumed oils with their strong smells and aphrodisiac claims. No patchouli or frangipani, even attar of roses. Just Teleri.

He took a deep breath and slipped one arm over her waist, then shifted more closely against her. His hands were beginning to throb and prickle and so did his feet. It was as if his toes and fingers were being stuck with sharp pins.

She took his hand in hers and rubbed it slowly. "Can you feel your fingers?"

"Aye," he said. "They hurt like bloody hell."

"That is good. Your feet, too?"

"Aye. My feet hurt, too."

They both lay there still and quiet, while the wind roared outside and whipped and whistled over the thatch roof above them, every so often sending pieces of straw floating down onto the floor or the fire, where they sparked and disappeared. He could feel the warmth of the fire on his face and the warmth of the animals at his back. One of them stirred and he turned just enough to look at it.

It was the hare with only three legs. The one she said had chewed off its own leg to escape a trap. It nuzzled its warm fur against the cold skin of his neck in a way that was anything but wild. He lay still as a rock. The hare sighed and fell asleep against him.

A moment later Roger's stomach growled. But the odd thing was, he did not care.

Teleri awoke in the middle of the night with the sense that something was not right. She remained still and tried to keep her breath even. Then she realized his hand was holding her breast.

She lay there almost afraid to breathe, but closed her eyes and feigned sleep.

"You feel so good," he whispered in her ear.

She opened her eyes in a flash.

He was kissing her ear, teasing it with his tongue and lips while his hand rubbed her breast ever so slowly. His hand slid down her ribs and slowly over her belly and lower. His mouth moved to her neck and his fingers began to draw up the cloth of her gown. She could feel the hem of it slipping up her legs, higher and higher, to her thighs and more.

She turned her head to look at him. It was still so very dark inside but the fire had burned down to a warm glow and cast a red light over his features. She could see his hair falling slightly over his brow, his eyes open and looking at her. His hawklike nose and his wide, serious mouth, which moved closer and closer, then took hers in a deep and passionate kiss. It went on for the longest time, their lips and mouths and tongues together. Then he pulled back from her and slid his fingers between her legs to touch her in the intimate way he had before.

She sighed and her legs fell open a bit. He was watching her and she him. Her breath sped up and caught in her throat, then sped up again and again. His hand cupped her and his fingers played more, so she slid her hand down to him and rubbed him through his hose the way he was doing to her.

His eyes grew darker and his lids slid half-closed, but he was still watching her. His hand explored her with fervor and she mimicked him. Then he took his hand away and untied his hose, then pulled them down and placed her bare hand on him.

The moment she moved her hand up and down him he closed his eyes, then touched her there again. His breathing quickened and matched hers. Their hands moved together on each other, giving pleasure and sensation and wonderful, wild touches.

She moved her chest against him because there was some kind of ache in her that made her need to rub against him the way his hand was rubbing her and making her body sweat there and grow wet.

He was hard and long against her palm and the more she rubbed her hand against him, the larger and harder he grew.

She lifted her hips, going higher and higher from the play of fingers, and by instinct she rubbed him harder.

He fingered her deeper and faster, almost going inside of her. She was slick now and moving with his hand, a deep rhythm, like Celtic drums.

She gasped and closed her eyes. "If you stop, I'll die. I'll die."

"I won't stop," he whispered into her ear. "My love, I swear." Then one finger slipped deeply inside of her while his knuckles pressed against that place she needed him to touch. His finger went in and out and his knuckles moved in a circle. She raised her hips higher and higher. Her hand closed around him and slid up and down. Up and down in the same rhythm.

"More . . ." He breathed in her ear and she pressed against his hand, unable to catch her breath it was coming so fast. His hips pushed against her hand and moved the way hers were, 'round and 'round.

Then something happened. Something burst, as if the sky above her just broke right in two. Stars flashed in front of her eyes and even inside her body, then flowed like fiery, shooting stars from the center of her outward to her feet and hands and head.

She felt her heart pulsing right between her legs, as if it suddenly grew bigger and moved from her chest to that place between her legs, where it was beating and beating and beating.

From a far-off place she heard his groan, long and low, and felt him throb wetly against her hand, which she moved and moved with every pulse beat. When her heart finally slowed, so did her hand.

They lay spent and breathing hard, the animals quietly sleeping around them as if nothing wonderful had happened at all. She watched his breathing calm down the way hers was and waited until he opened his eyes.

"We did not mate," she told him.

He looked at her, his expression showing he was surprised by her words.

She looked down, then patted him on his root. "You have to put that thing in me to mate, English."

He stared at her so strangely that she had another thought. She frowned up at him. "Am I wrong? Do you English mate with your hands instead?"

There was long pause, then he burst out laughing.

Chapter
25

~

Teleri looked past the fire pit to the mattress, where Roger was still asleep, surrounded by all her equally lazy animals. All except Horse. She had gotten up with the light and let him outside. And now he was in the frosty meadow happily chomping on frozen grass.

She mashed some berries into a mush and added water, then some oats she had been saving for the colder weather. She poured it into the cook pot and stoked the fire a little so it would thicken faster.

As she poked at the firewood, Roger opened his eyes and gave her a look that made her warmer than any burning wood could ever do.

She jabbed at the coals a few times, then said, "Good morning, English. Still wasting away the best part of the day, I see." She smiled at him, then dropped the stick into the fire.

He gave her a long and unreadable look and propped his head on his hand. He just watched her as if he had all the time to do so. "I would argue about which part of the day is the best. I rather like the middle of the night."

She could feel her skin flushing and she raised her chin and said, "I like mornings."

"So do I. Come here, and let me teach you about staying in bed in the morning."

She laughed, but before she could speak his arm snaked out and grabbed her ankle, then pulled her toward him. "Roger! Stop. I shall fall!"

A moment later she tumbled across his chest and heard him grunt, then felt the air rush from his mouth and past her ear. She was sprawled on top of him, their bodies pressed together, her palms on either side of his head.

He was looking up at her with that look she knew. His hands moved from her back to her head and pulled her mouth down to his. He drove his tongue inside and kissed her senseless.

He turned with her and she was on her back on the mattress, his arm across her breast and his head just above hers. He moved one hand to touch her eye, which was not swollen any longer, but even yesterday was still gray and yellow from where he had hit her.

He started to say something but she raised her finger to his lips to stop him from speaking. "It does not matter. My eye is fine. I have seen how you feel about it. You were not even conscious. How can anyone blame you?"

"I blame me."

"Well, I do not." Then to distract him she ran her finger slowly over his mouth, along the lines of it and down his chin. "You have not let your beard grow back."

"No," he answered as she rubbed his jaw and cheek, which were rough with stubble he had shaved off every morning with her knife.

"It scratches when you kiss me," she told him. "But I like it." She touched his cheeks and brows, ran her fingers along his eyes and over his ears where his hair had grown longer and was shaggy at the ends.

He stopped her fingers with his big hand and turned

her palm to his mouth and kissed it. It was one of those tender things he did to her that never ceased to surprise her. And every time he did so, she lost a little more of her heart to this man.

He sucked one of her fingers into his mouth, which was so unexpected it completely caught her off guard.

"Why do you do that?" she asked, truly curious.

He frowned at her and pulled her finger out of his mouth. "What?"

"Suckle my finger."

He laughed a little. "Men and women touch each other in many ways. You do not like it?"

She shrugged. "I like it better when you suckle my breasts."

He laughed again.

"Or my neck." She paused thoughtfully. "But I like it best when you call me your love."

He stopped laughing.

"No one has ever called me that, Roger. Not ever."

He was giving her the strangest look. But before she could ask what was wrong, the porridge boiled up and over and began to splatter and sizzle into the fire.

"Oh, no!" She pushed away from him and scrambled up, then used her skirt to lift the pot from the fire and move it over to the table. "I cannot ruin our meal because I'm laying in bed with you. Get you up, so we can eat this."

He stood and was adjusting his clothes, then he folded the blanket neatly the way he did every morn.

"The wash water in the corner is warmer now," she told him over one shoulder. "You are fortunate. When I first awakened the bucket had a crust of ice on it."

While he washed in silence, she moved around the room gathering the bowls and spoons and setting things on the table. She poured the porridge into the bowls and pushed his over toward him. Then they ate.

She wondered why he was so quiet, then noticed he had finished eating. He had set down his spoon and did not ask for more. He seldom did ask, even though she told him to. She always had to fill his dish for him.

She wondered why that was, why he did not just ask her for another serving instead of sitting there. She did not understand people who did not just say what they were thinking. How was she supposed to know what he wanted if he never asked?

She wondered about what his life was like, where he had come from. Who his family was and the father he claimed to hate. How could someone hate their own father? She looked up at him, but he wasn't looking at her. He looked as though his thoughts were miles away.

She thought about that and decided that he seemed to want his silence. She stood to get him more to eat and ladled it into his bowl.

In the center of the table she had placed a small basket filled with some of her favorite things: round flat stones she had plucked from the sea, and whole shells, the kind she found along the beach haphazardly strewn among weaker shells that cracked and crumbled when they were tossed by the tide.

Sometimes when it was late at night and too lonely, she would put a few of the seashells under her pillow so she could hear the sound of them talking to her all night. It was a soothing sound that made her feel less alone.

He was holding one that was shaped like a cornucopia and had brown stripes and small blue spots on it. He was turning it over and over in his hands and staring at it.

"They say that if you put your ear to a seashell you will hear the sea call out to you, you can hear the tide rise and fall as if all the seas in the whole wide world are inside that one seashell."

He looked up at her and she smiled at him. "Put it to your ear and listen."

"What?"

"The shell you are holding. Put it to your ear and listen."

He did. "What am I listening for?"

"The roar of the sea. Now be quiet. You cannot hear it if you are talking." She waited. "Can you hear it now?"

"No. I cannot hear it if you are talking."

She shook her head. "Then take it outside and listen where there is little noise. The wind has stopped and the sun has come out. It might warm the air enough to be pleasant."

He stood and looked down at the shell in his hand, then glanced up at her with a look that was somehow sad. She paused as she began to clean up the table and she wondered, for just a brief moment, why he looked at her that way.

When in the hell had he told her he loved her? Roger drove a hand through his hair and paced the yard, trying to remember what he had said last night. He did not remember saying the words. He had never, not once, done something so foolish.

He did not lie to women. He prided himself on that. And he had been with plenty of women over the years, but had only said I love you to one.

Elizabeth.

There was some irony in the fact that Teleri was the woman to whom he owed a huge debt and the one single woman he should never have touched. She saved his life. Freely gave him succor from a still unknown enemy.

Yet he was having trouble keeping his hands from touching her. She was an innocent, not the kind of woman he chose to sport with. So he asked himself why he was doing so now. No answer came to him. No logical answer.

The shutters were cracked open and he heard her moving around inside. He stepped back a few paces and stood in a spot in the yard where he could look in.

She began to hum to herself while she worked, and he

wondered if she even knew she was doing it. The sound was lovely. Clear and clean and perfectly on key.

He watched her move, the lightness of her step, the smile on her face. It seemed so natural that music would come from her that way, the way he imagined heavenly songs came from angels.

He looked down, because he felt as if he were looking where he should not. Spying on her, when he already felt immensely guilty. He stared at the melting frost on the ground, at nothing really, until he opened his palm and there was the seashell he had been holding.

A seashell. Something so simple and small and ordinary that he might ride right by it, or worse yet, trample over it. Yet she had saved the shell and laid it in a basket full of more shells and rocks, then proudly set them out as if they were her dower gifts.

He touched the shell and ran his rough fingers over it. He felt its smoothness and fragility. He remembered what she had said about the hedgesparrow's egg and the way she had helped him with the mushrooms he could not pick without breaking into pieces.

Curious, he lifted the shell to his ear and listened. There was sound; it was distant, soft, and it sounded like the waves of the sea.

He frowned and kept listening, wondering if he was imagining it, the way he had imagined the sun was shining down on him that day she chanted to it or when he imagined that she had brought a dead pheasant back to life.

For reasons as unknown to him as the workings of heaven, he looked up and in the window. She was across the cottage wiping her hands on a cloth and looking back at him as he held the shell against his ear.

Teleri smiled, and he heard the sea.

I leaned my back against an oak
   Thinking it was a trusty tree.
      But first it bent,
      And then it broke
And let me down as my love did me.

—"The Water Is Wide,"
traditional folk song

Chapter

26

❧

Later that day, after the sun had come out and melted all the frost away, Roger was walking back to the cottage when he stopped in his tracks. He swore so viciously that he startled the birds in a nearby chestnut tree.

He was staring at his worst nightmare—Old Gladdys, the Druid witch from Camrose Castle. He could not believe his eyes, but there she was in all her hellish glory: the chalk white hair that stuck out like a dandelion, a skinny, chicken neck, her body size indeterminate because it was always swathed in layers of black cloth.

It was Gladdys.

Instinctively his right hand went for his sword, which wasn't there. So he did the next best thing. He hid behind a tree.

She was standing next to what looked to be a stack of supplies: a sack of flour, oats and other such things piled near the cottage door. Teleri was talking to her. It was clear they knew each other well.

Old Gladdys reached out and placed her gnarled

hand upon Teleri's cheek, tilted her face up and studied her. Teleri said something but he was too far away to hear. The old woman appeared to listen, then they made a few more exchanges, before Gladdys nodded and bade her farewell in a voice that wasn't cackling for a change. She swung around in a flurry of black clothing and walked toward the path nearest him, the one that led around the back of the cottage and to the east.

Roger was a brave knight of the realm who had faced many enemies, but he ducked down lower.

Even time had not healed his pride where Old Gladdys was concerned. The last time he had been stuck alone with her, the old witch had stolen his clothes. He'd had to walk back to Camrose as bare as a plucked chicken.

He peered through the bushes.

What was Old Gladdys to Teleri?

She was surely not the one who tried to kill him. He'd been in Old Gladdys' gnarled clutches before. She would ravish him to death, not hang him. She was a lecherous old witch, but no murderess. He suspected she wasn't even much of a witch, even for all of her bonfires on the hillsides, her chants and that winking evil eye. She only liked to cause trouble.

Roger had faced wild Turks and Welsh outlaws, had faced an unknown murderer, but not even for a guarantee to heaven did he want to face that Druid again, charlatan or not.

He waited until he could no longer hear her footsteps, then he straightened and came out from behind the tree.

Teleri looked at him, her face puzzled.

He heard the jangle of a harness and spun around.

A small wagon came rumbling out from behind the other side of the cottage, Old Gladdys at the reins. She jerked the cart to a halt the moment she spotted him and her eyes narrowed to wicked slits. " 'Tis *you?*"

She looked at Teleri. "This is the man you found?"

"Aye, grandmama. Do you know him?"

Grandmama? Roger cursed under his breath.

Gladdys never answered Teleri. She flew down from the wagon seat like an angry bat. She landed with a dull sound and whipped around before he could say witch. She grabbed something from the wagon bed.

A moment later she spun around and came at him, waving a long willow broom. "Ye hulking brute! You brought yer huge hand against my sweet girl and smite her in the eye! I'll smite you, you young cock!"

"Wait!" Roger shouted and ducked.

But there was no time for an answer. Old Gladdys came at him, swinging that willow broom like it was a battle axe.

Roger ducked and tried to speak, to explain.

"I'll smite *ye* in the eye!" The broom swiped the air above his head, then her other fist came at him. He stepped back, and with her next swing he grabbed the broom.

She was strong and she jerked the broom back, right out of his hands, then whacked him a good one.

"Grandmama! Stop it! You'll hurt him!"

"Aye! I will hurt him! I want to hurt him!" the old woman shrieked, whipping the broom around like she was some kind of barbarian warrior fighting off the Roman Empire.

Roger raised his hand high and turned his face away. "Stop that!" The broom just missed his face and struck him on the shoulder.

She came at him in a flurry. So he used his hands to cover his head and tried to get away from her. The broom whacked him a few more times and one really good clout in the ear.

"God's teeth! Will you cease, woman!" He bellowed and his hand shot out and gripped the broom handle.

She wouldn't let go, even with Teleri behind her, begging her. She shrugged off Teleri's hand and said, "You have no idea who this is, girlie!"

"He is Roger FitzAlan of Wells!" Teleri said. "He

was ill. He did not know he struck me. He did not mean to hurt me. He is kind, Grandmama! Please. He is a kind man!"

Gladdys glowered back at her, then her eyes darted back and forth between them. He tried to pry the broom from her and pulled as hard as he could.

She was as strong as a team oxen. Only uglier.

The two of them tugged back and forth on the broom, each one glaring at the other, Teleri hopping around them in a circle, trying to get them to stop while Gladdys pummeled him with foul names and evil curses in both Welsh and English.

"Grandmama, please! I beg you. Let go. He is not dangerous."

"Ha!" Gladdys spat. "Not dangerous? You do not understand his kind of danger. I do."

Roger jerked the broom from the old woman's strong hands and held it in front of him the way men of God held up the cross before the Devil's own.

Gladdys pointed a gnarled finger at him, her hand shaking slightly. "He, this man, he is the rogue I told you about!"

"Sir Randy?" Teleri asked in a shocked voice.

Sir Randy? He turned and looked at her. Who called him Sir Randy?

Teleri was standing so still she looked like one of those doomed deer that sometimes become stuck in a winter snow drift and freeze to death. "You are the Englishman who mates with all the married women?"

Roger turned from Teleri and glared at Gladdys from narrowed and angry eyes, wanting to whack her one with the broom for telling Teleri anything of his past.

"Grandmama says you mated with *all* of the women in the English court."

"I did not mate with *all* the women at court," Roger said with more patience than he felt.

The old witch gave a loud snort as if he were lying. "I have seen you, meself . . . with that black-haired woman."

"I loved Elizabeth de Clare. I have always loved Elizabeth!"

Teleri made a small sound, one he could barely hear, but enough for him to pull his glare away from her witch of a grandmother and look to her.

Her face was tight with a look of betrayal. She shook her head as if she could not believe what she heard. As if she never knew him.

He did not mean to hurt her and felt suddenly worse even than he had when he found out it was he who had hit her. He dropped the broom.

"Teleri," he said, lifting out a hand to her and trying to think of some way to explain.

She backed away from him, her face frozen, her hands pressed to her cheeks which were flushed and red with shame and embarrassment.

She looked at him from eyes that were filled with tears. She shook her head, then turned and ran away.

Teleri ran through the woods, tears pouring down her cheeks and the sobs echoing behind her like people calling out, "Fool! Fool!"

As she burst through a narrow, overgrown path, her breath caught painfully in her tight throat. Spindly willow and beech branches with bare twigs clawed at her face and shoulders.

If they caught on the hem of her gown or her sleeves, she twisted this way and that. She raised her arms and pushed the branches out of her way, but when some of them cracked and splintered, they made a terrible sound, just like that of a heart breaking.

She ran on, ran and ran, because she had to get away, far, far away from her horrible shame. But shame was like her shadow, something she could not get rid of no matter how far and fast she ran.

She did not know how long she ran, but she stumbled finally and stopped running, because her legs were heavy and sad, and they could not run any longer. She was panting, her body damp with sweat and tears.

There was a strong odor that seemed to be coming from her skin; it reeked of betrayal.

She stood there in the middle of the dark woods, because she felt as if there was nothing left inside her. Nothing, not a heart, not even a soul.

The old oak tree at the fork in the paths stood just in front of her and she stared blankly at the tangled knot in the trunk that had always looked like the wizard's face.

Her breath caught in her chest over and over because she could not seem to suck in any air. She wiped her eyes with the back of her hand and looked at the tree trunk more closely.

But all she could see was a huge knot in the wrinkled trunk. There was no wise wizard's face to tell her how to stop the hurt. There was only the gnarled growth of an old oak tree.

She reached out and touched the tree trunk, wanting so badly to see that face again. But it was not there. Nothing was there but the things that truly existed: old bark and rippled wood.

Teleri hung her head and cried, cried awful, aching sounds that had never come from her before. She sagged back against the tree, then slid down to the ground. All she wanted was to disappear into the spiked leaves and briars of the ugly weeds around the tree's tangled roots.

She hugged her knees to her chest and laid her head on them, then cried so very hard her shoulders shook with it, the same way people for hundreds of years had cried hard for the things they had lost.

But Teleri did not cry for what she had lost. She cried for something she never even had.

Old Gladdys hit him with the broom again, then she tossed it back into the wagon and turned to glare at him. "You hurt her. She saved your life and all you do is hurt her?"

Her jaw jutted out and she narrowed her eyes. "Hear

me. You'll not get in my wagon. You'll not ride back with me!"

"I would never get in a wagon with you again, old woman. You think me a fool?"

"I know you for a fool!" She spun around before he could say more and climbed onto the seat. "Go away from here, Roger of Wells. Go far away from my girl, or I swear that I will call down so many curses on you, even your great-grandchildren will have snakes for heads!"

She snapped the reins and took off.

"Go with her," Roger muttered. As if he would. "Get you lost, old woman!" he shouted after her, shaking his fist even though she had already disappeared, because it felt good to shout at something when he was so damn angry at himself.

He stood there for moment, looking around him, and he asked himself what was he doing here. He was well enough to walk home. He could have left before now.

His hand went to his throat. He touched the ragged and puckered skin that ran across the burn marks on his neck. He saw them there every morning when he looked at his reflection in the water of the pool.

He heard that haunting and fearsome sound again: the laughter of the man who wanted him dead. The memory of it was all around him, just as if it were happening all over again.

Sweat broke out on his forehead and the back of his neck. His hands began to shake. He could not stop them. He stared down at them, watching hands he could not control, shaking hands that must belong to someone else.

Cowardice was an ugly thing. He saw it for the first time in himself. It was live and squirming inside of him like an apple that shrivels and rots from a worm. He could try to hide it, from everyone, even from himself. But he could not. It was there in everything he did, each decision he made, a part of him that he could not get rid of any more than he could get rid of his past.

A sound made him jump, and he spun around suddenly.

Teleri came from the woods, dragging his mail coat behind her. She dropped it in the grass and turned to him, her face stiff, her lips drawn into a thin line. "Here is your armor, English. Take it when you leave this day."

"Teleri. Let me talk to you," he said.

She stepped back as if she couldn't be too close to him. "I will lead you to the edge of the woods," she told him as if she had not heard what he said. She spun around and walked into the bushes again, then dragged out the last of his chain mail. She went back once more, then came and tossed a prick spur on the lot of it. "I could only find one spur." She walked past him.

"Teleri. . . ." He reached out to touch her.

She sidestepped him, holding her hands up as if to ward him off. "Do not! Do not touch me again." Then she turned and walked away so fast she was almost running toward the cottage.

Chapter

27

❧

After Teleri tied up Pig so he would not follow her and gave water and food to the animals in the cages, she went into the back room and headed straight for a wide-planked chest that sat in one corner. She slipped the latch up and lifted the lid.

The rusty iron hinges creaked, proof she had little reason or desire to open this chest. She leaned over and pushed aside some of her old clothing. Beneath was the leather saddle that had been on Horse when she'd found him.

Teleri had never ridden him saddled and had thought she would never put the saddle back on him again. She touched the slick brown leather, aged darker in spots from the imprint of all the people who had used it.

Near the pommel there were some even darker spots the color of spilt wine. One of the Welsh arrows had hit Horse near the saddle, for she remembered wiping the blood from it all those years ago.

She closed her eyes, and a second later the tears came. Burying her face in her hands, she sank down on the corner of the chest and just sobbed until she had no tears left. She did not truly know who she was crying for, herself or Horse. Nor was she certain what hurt the most, losing the animal she had come to believe was hers or the heart she had almost unknowingly given to a knight who had no heart to give back.

Rubbing her eyes and nose, she stood, then took a deep breath and lifted the heavy saddle out from the chest. She staggered a little under the weight of the saddle the same way one can stagger under the weight of life.

Then she dropped it on the bed and quickly pulled her hands back almost as if she could not stand to touch it any longer. She turned and closed the chest, then took the bridle off a peg in the wall and draped it over the saddle.

A few moments later she was outside, lugging the saddle past the north side of the cottage and heading for the large tree by the brook. She had a purpose in taking the back route; she did not want to see Roger.

When she was near the brook and partially hidden by the low and dripping branches of the tree, she whistled. The sound of Horse's hooves clapping over the stone bridge followed a moment later. Horse turned and she could see Hawk perched easily between his perked ears as if he belonged there.

Within minutes she had Horse bridled and saddled. She tightened the girth strap and straightened just as Hawk squawked and jumped down from Horse's head onto hers, then he slid down her hair and hung off the back of it, swinging back and forth, back and forth. She grabbed a huge handful of her hair and lifted it over her shoulder, then set her hand in front of Hawk so he would perch on it.

"Come, now, Hawk. Come." She looked at him as he stepped onto her hand. "Will you stay here with me? Or shall you leave and go back where you came from?"

He squawked and flapped those worthless wings he had never used to fly, then rocked from one foot to another, and cawed and squeaked and cooed as if he were talking to her and telling her something vital.

Teleri had always talked to her animals, but she talked to them because they were all she had to break the silent loneliness of her existence. They were her only friends, because they were all she had to make into friends. They were the closest thing to life she saw.

Trees and flowers did not have hearts or souls. The stones on the hill, the rocks in the brook or the brook itself did not have minds or the ability to speak. Animals did. She could talk and talk and they would make noises back to her, perch on her head, follow her, sleep with her or answer her whistle.

But in truth, even for all the imagining in the world, and all the wishful thinking and pretending, they could not understand her words, any more than she could truly understand them.

She looked at Horse, at Hawk, who had leapt back to the saddle and was waddling across it, then she leaned down and picked up a sack already packed with food and water and slung it over the pommel. She grabbed the reins and walked Horse toward the front side of the cottage.

She rounded the corner, Horse trailing behind. Roger stood clad in his chain mail, looking taller and leaner and nothing like the kind of man who had kissed her, laughed with her and touched her, nothing like the man who had made her body and mind burn, and everything like the kind of man who then lied to her and called her his love.

He was buckling a wide belt at his waist, then he glanced up. His expression changed from a look that gave nothing away to a frown. "What are you doing with the Arab?"

Without answering him, she mounted Horse, then looked down at Roger. "Follow me. I will show you the way out of the woods." The sooner he was gone, the sooner she could get on with things, like her lonely life, like crying on her bed until she could cry no more. Like trying to forget he had ever existed.

She prodded Horse forward with a tap of her heels and led him to the northernmost trail, where she had to duck through and around low branches before the trail became visible and widened at the spot where the beech trees and their branches grew together and looked like forbidden lovers.

She moved slowly, since Roger was following silently on foot. She did not speak, and never once did she look back.

By the time they reached the north edge of Brecon Wood, it was late afternoon. In the distance she saw the ridge and the plateau where the blue stones were, where this all started.

She reined in Horse, then dismounted. She drew her hand slowly over his flanks and up to his neck. His neck and flanks showed deep patterns of muscle and bone, finely honed as if to prove God's perfect hand in all of nature. She slid her arms around his sleek equine neck and rubbed her cheek against his muzzle with its white marking.

When she pulled her cheek away she looked into his huge dark eyes and rubbed her hand over his forelock.

Goodbye.

She turned, took the reins, and held them out to Roger. "Take Horse back where he belongs."

He looked at her for what seemed like forever, searched her face like it was the most important thing he had to do, like he was searching for truths in her features or lies in her eyes.

To stand there without a single tear in her eye was the hardest thing she had done in a long, long time. But she did it.

"I thought we had made a pact. As I remember it, I had to swear not to take the Arab back, under threat of dying by pitchfork."

"I did not know he belonged to the Earl of Glamorgan. The Earl has been good to my grandmother. It would be poor of me to take his prized horse. Had I known before, I would have returned Horse long ago."

"I do not want to leave without talking. You and I. You gave me back my life, Teleri. I shall always be indebted to you."

It was not payment for a debt that she wanted. What she had wanted was for him to feel what she felt. She wanted someone to love her.

He loved someone named Elizabeth.

She looked at him and shrugged. "There is no debt, English. I did the same for you as I have always done for any animal that was hurt. It is no different. A weasel, or an Englishman."

Her comparison was not lost on him, for his features tightened with some hard emotion.

"You make your point well, Teleri," he said, then added in a quiet tone, "for a girl who hides in the woods."

Perhaps it was a good thing that animals did not speak, she thought, staring at her hands, for words could sting as much as thrown stones.

He mounted Horse and Hawk squawked at him, then leapt onto her shoulder, his wings flapping as if he wanted to suddenly fly. She cooed at her bird, then stroked his feathers. He calmed down and quit squawking.

"There is food and water in the sack," she said to Roger, then she reached inside her gown and pulled out a long and heavy knife. "Here. I do not need this." She handed it up to him.

He stared at her for a long time, saying nothing, not looking at the knife, only at her.

"Take it." She stepped closer.

He took the knife and slid it into his belt. He looked off toward the east, toward the hills that rolled on and on and led back to the eastern Marches and England.

"Goodbye, English," She stepped back a few feet, then turned and ran into the woods, stopping near a chestnut tree with branches low enough to climb and thick enough to hide her. The outskirts of Bleddig were not too far from this end of the woods.

She pulled herself up on a low limb, then climbed higher and higher, until she found a place where she could clearly watch him ride away.

He moved slowly at first and reined in once as if he did not know where exactly to ride. She saw him look toward the stones; he appeared to stare at them for a long time, then he and Horse took off toward the Marches, riding hard and fast.

Her heart caught in her throat when she watched them moving across the rolling hills, Horse stretching his legs out to run like the wind. They looked like one beast that was half-man and half-horse, and moved so swiftly that from her spot in the tree it looked as if they did not even touch the ground. As if they were carried by the wind.

She closed her eyes and imagined it was she who was riding. She who was feeling the thunder of hooves across the grasslands, feeling the wind pulling hair away from her face and the air cool and crisp against her warm cheeks.

Tears began to burn the corners of her eyes, for she knew she would never ride Horse again. She would never see Roger again. Yet she could not hide behind closed eyes forever, so she opened them and stared up at the blue sky, blurred by that nagging moisture she could not seem to control. She swallowed hard and squeezed her eyes shut, trying to wring those tears from her eyes the way she tried to wring water from cloth.

How much time passed she did not know, but when she finally looked off into the distant horizon, Roger and Horse had shrunk into a small black outline that looked like nothing more than a lone tree bending into the wind.

Above them the moon was already rising in the eastern sky, chasing after a sun that had not even started to set. Teleri leaned her head back against the tree trunk, her hands still gripping the fat branch overhead.

Perhaps she was like that rising moon, she thought, and the love she longed for was like the setting sun. She looked off into the distance, holding on to that tree and knowing in her heart that no matter what happened, neither of them would ever catch up with the other.

Chapter

28

Roger was to ride home. An easy thing, he told himself. Just put your heels to the horse, man, and take off in that direction.

But at merely the thought of returning, his hands started shaking again. His breathing picked up speed, but the more he tried to inhale, the less air he got in his chest.

For some odd reason he could not breathe. It was as if his throat had suddenly closed up, clogged with a huge lump of fear and cowardice.

He did not dare look back to the woods. If he did, he might not leave. He might turn and ride back into the forest where his enemy could not find him, where he would not have to live with the thought that his killer could be standing right behind him.

The moment he returned home whoever wanted him dead would know he had failed. And the truth was, Roger was frightened that his enemy might try again and succeed.

He had always thought himself invincible. A youthful thought, he supposed, but now that he had faced death down, he was smarter. Smart enough to be scared.

He tried tightening his hands on the reins, but they felt clammy. Sweat beaded along his hairline and he could feel it drip down his temples.

He thought of his duty to Edward, but it did no good. He thought of his friends, like Merrick, who did not know where he was. But that did not help either. He thought of his mother and sisters, but they lived on his father's land, under his father's ruling thumb.

The image of his father flashed before his eyes. His father who had once, when Roger was a youth, accused him of running away from trouble instead of facing it.

Those words still struck him deeply, made him angry enough to kick the horse into a run. The Arab took off toward the rolling hills, running open and free. The wind whipped across his face and made his eyes tear. The horse moved so flawlessly it was as if he were riding a dream horse, an animal that knew just by the mere press of his leg or heel exactly what he wanted.

There was a sudden sense of freedom, something he had thought he'd lost. He found there was plenty of air to breathe, as if the air had come to him. He glanced down and the hands that held the reins were his again, calm and sure; they did not shake.

He leaned low and gave the Arab the lead, letting it run, open and free, not running away, but running toward home, toward his father, and toward his unknown enemy.

Teleri jumped down from the bottom branch and landed with a jarring thud. Her feet slipped and she fell hard. A shriek of surprise escaped her lips and she covered her mouth with her hand, then gave a small laugh. Hawk squawked once, flapping his wings, but then he settled down on her shoulder once again.

"That landing held no grace, did it, Hawk?" Teleri gave him a quick stroke, then turned and moved along the path that led back to her sanctuary in the middle of the woods.

She had walked not more than a few lengths when she heard footsteps. Running footsteps.

"Look! The witch of the woods! I told you I heard her! See? 'Tis her!"

Teleri spun around.

"Get her!"

An instant later the first stone hit her hard in the chest. Another hit her on the shoulder, making Hawk squawk and flap his wings in front of her face.

She held up her hands and faced the boys. "No! I am not a witch!" she cried. "Please! Stop, please!"

"Get her! Hurry! If she looks at us we will turn to stone!" shouted a boy with hair the color of a new coin.

She turned to run, to run away as fast as she could. Off she went into the trees and bushes. Hawk squawked and suddenly he was gone.

She looked up. "Hawk! Hawk!" But leaves slapped her face and scratched her arms. She could not see him and dared not stop to look. She had to run. She had to escape.

Her heartbeat was hard and rapid. Her bare feet moved swiftly over the ground. One after the other, faster and faster. She whipped through brush and brambles. But they were following fast behind her.

Stones flew past and rustled the leaves around her. She ducked, then sidestepped, and the stones bounced against trunks and pattered to the ground.

But some of them struck her feet and legs. Some of them stung her skin and bruised her bones. Some of them hit her back.

She cut back to the north and burst through the brush at the edge of the forest and ran across the grasses toward the hills, away from the private place she called home and off toward the stones where the villagers were afraid to go.

"Get her! Hurry!" they shouted, running right behind her. "Get her!"

A stone struck her sharply in the ear. She cried out. Another struck her so hard in the head that the pain made her sink to the ground on her knees.

She could not see. Just flashes of light. Like falling stars before her eyes. She put her hands to her head and her ear and groaned, because they hurt. Hurt so badly the pain shot across her head and down her neck.

The moment she touched her skin she could feel the warm blood trickling down her hand and face. She blinked once, then looked down at her bloody hand.

Something warm and wet dripped into her eyes. She thought she heard Hawk cawing in the distance and looked up.

Then there was nothing but a black void.

Roger had just ridden over a hill when some crazed bird dove down from the sky and pecked him in the head.

"Damn you cursed thing!" he shouted, swinging one hand at it as it flew up. He watched it circle and dive down a second time. He waved his arm furiously, but the bird flew past and lit on his shoulder, squawking.

"God's teeth, where did you come from?" He recognized it. It was that goshawk, the one that only made squawking noises. The one that never flew.

He looked at the bird, half expecting it to peck his eyes out. It didn't. It cooed a slew of odd sounds into the air as if it expected him to understand.

Roger shook his head and kept riding forward. "I suppose you want a ride back to Camrose," he muttered as if he expected the bird to understand him. As if it could any more than he could understand it. Foolishness, he thought with a shake of his head. That is what this was.

The bird began to squawk something fierce.

Roger ignored it.

It pecked at his neck. Hard.

"Damn! Stop!"

But whenever Roger tried to ride ahead, the bird

would peck at him or nip his ear or pull out a beakful of his hair. And whenever he would swat at it, it took off and flew in a circle over his head, cawing and diving and flapping its wings frantically.

Roger threw up his hands. "You fly at me like that one more time and I swear it shall be your last!"

The bird flew 'round and 'round and 'round, then went high until it was only a speck against a dove gray sky.

"Good riddance," Roger muttered and prodded the Arab forward.

A moment later the bird dove past him in a flash of brown and pecked the horse's rump.

The Arab reared.

Roger slammed to the ground so hard he almost bit off his tongue. By the time he stopped seeing stars, the hawk had lit on the ground next to him and was hopping from foot to foot, waddling its way back toward the woods, then it would stop and look back at him, then squawk and move on.

He stared at the bird, puzzled, then looked off in the distance. The hawk hopped over and grabbed the cuff of his glove and began pulling on it and hopping.

"You want me to go back," he said to the bird.

The hawk hopped and squawked and cawed and kept hopping back toward the south and the woods where he had left Teleri.

Roger got up and dusted himself off, then remounted and reined the Arab around and rode off back toward the woods, the hawk flying just ahead of him.

He asked himself what he was doing riding back, talking to birds. He wondered if this was another excuse for him not to ride home where he belonged.

So he was feeling the fool when he came over a grassy hill and reined in so hard that the Arab reared up, then shifted back in protest for his stupid sawing of the reins.

"Sorry," he said, then stroked the horse's long neck as he scanned the valley below.

Then he saw her, saw her running from the woods as if she were being chased by the hounds of hell. A moment later a pack of boys came after her.

He saw a stone fly and his anger became a live thing; it turned the edges of his vision red as blood.

"A FitzAlan!" he cried, his battle cry frightening and powerful, echoing down the valley as if it came from the Devil himself. Roger raised his fist high and spurred the horse forward.

Then he saw her fall.

Chapter
29

❧

The moment Roger rode down from the hilltop, the cowards chasing her scattered like rats scurrying from a flame. He leaned low and rode straight toward her, then reined in and dismounted in one swift motion. He knelt next to her, the knife drawn in his hand.

She lay so very still.

"Teleri?"

He leaned over her, watching.

She did not move.

"Teleri? 'Tis I." He searched for some motion, something that would indicate she was not harmed. "'Tis Roger." He paused. "The hard-headed English."

He brushed aside the thick curly hair that was covering her face. Blood from the cuts on her creamy skin made strands stick to her cheeks and jaw.

One look and his fist tightened on the knife hilt so hard his knuckles turned white. The urge to go after those who had stoned her was so powerful he had to remind himself she needed care more than he needed vengeance.

He stared down at her lying there, unmoving. Something he had never experienced rose like bile in his throat. He could not breathe. He could not speak. He did not move for an empty and helpless moment.

Then he saw her take a breath, short and soft. An unconscious kind of breathing.

He relaxed only long enough to slide his hands gently under her limp body and lift her in his arms. He held her to him and pressed his cheek to her chest.

He could feel her breath. He heard her heartbeat. He felt the warmth of her life against his skin and muttered thanks to his God.

He stood up with her and moved to the horse, then coaxed the Arab to kneel for him. He mounted, then settled her against his body with one arm around hers, holding her tightly. "I have you, Teleri. You are safe now. I have you. Hold on, my love."

Then Roger rode straight for the cottage.

Miles away, at the southern end of Brecon Wood, a dark-haired man rode up to a place where the woods and brambles were so thick they looked impregnable. He dismounted and knelt at the ground, studying the grass and dirt.

He found no trail here. No sign of anything. He moved closer, but still saw nothing. He eyed the brush suspiciously, then looked under the tangled bushes where the wild, knotted branches sheltered the ground from wind and rain—the things that stole away the tracks of man or horse.

He spotted a light impression and looked closer. One bare foot? Aye. He saw the toe prints and the deeper mark of a heel. Small, like that of a female or youth.

He crawled deeper into the small hole in the twisted bushes until his shoulders were inside and snagged on the branches which were full of sharp thorns. He did not care.

He searched the grass and carefully moved aside some fallen leaves. He found what he was looking for. He found hoof marks.

He straightened to his knees and shoved aside the branches. There was an opening. He drew his sword and sliced angrily through the brambles and branches until he was in an opening. He sliced away at the thorn wall over and over, his sword hitting the roots of the bushes and cracking them in two.

Before long he could stand in the opening and he knew his mount could fit through. Sword held high, he grabbed the reins of his horse and they moved into the woods, following the tracks that had been hidden by the leaves.

She still was not awake.

Roger dipped a cloth in a wooden mazer of cool water from the brook. He wrung out the cloth, then sat on her mattress and lay the cool cloth across the wounds on her brow and cheeks. They were swelling and starting to color. The cool water would help the swelling as well as soothe her. Perhaps awaken her.

"Teleri." He studied her face for some sign of consciousness. There was none. "Teleri?"

Nothing.

The warrior in him wanted badly to find those who did this to her. She was but an innocent young woman. One who had a heart as big as the woods. A woman he knew would not even hurt a fly, yet people stoned her as if she were a demon to be feared.

He looked at the cuts on her cheeks and the wound near her eyebrow, which was a gash that was deeper than the others. It must have hurt her badly when the stone that made it hit her skin. The wound was coloring into an impression of the rock and was still bleeding in a thin line of red that would drip into her hair if he didn't press the cloth to it.

It worried him, that bleeding did, but not as much as the wound on her ear, which was the worst of the lot. That was the wound which truly frightened him. He had seen that kind of wound before, on his friend Merrick.

Five years before, Camrose Castle had been seized by Welsh outlaws. Roger, Merrick and his men had to tunnel under Camrose to rescue Merrick's wife, Lady Clio, and take the castle again. They had been successful, had broken the siege by tunneling.

All had looked like victory, until the tunnel had collapsed on Merrick. He'd had head wounds not unlike Teleri's. His lips had been white and chalky as hers were.

He had not awakened. For days and weeks. The King's physicians had claimed his mind was dead, but his body lived.

"Teleri," Roger repeated her name over and over. "Wake up, sweet. Wake up."

But she did not awaken. He could do nothing but look at her and feel completely helpless. It was not a good feeling for a man who liked to see results. A man who had thought he could do almost anything.

"Teleri! Wake up."

She did not move. Her breathing remained even and soft, so easy it was as if she were sleeping with angels.

Merrick had not awakened for months. Roger and Clio were the only ones who did not give up. People said the Earl was dead and his lady wife and good friend were mad with their grief.

But it was not grief that drove either of them.

If the truth be known, had it not been for Clio's absolute faith and stubborness, even Roger might have given up. But he could not. He loved Merrick like a brother.

Instead he had helped her move Merrick and wash him. He had talked to him, day after day, as if Merrick were merely sleeping and could hear every word he had said to him.

In the end, Merrick did awaken.

Now, as Roger sat there next to Teleri, he thought about that time, and he remembered something important. At the time he had believed that Clio's faith and perseverance had really been what brought Merrick back.

With that thought came the sharp and recent memory of Teleri's words to him.

It was my faith that made me believe I could help you. I believed you would live. You lived. Faith is part of who we are and who we become.

He had not thought further of what she said to him then, or of what her words had meant. He just knew that Teleri had saved his miserable life.

But now he realized the similarities, that she had done so on faith, like Clio had done for Merrick. He had never once doubted that Clio and Merrick loved each other as much as any man and woman could love.

He looked at Teleri, frowning. Then he asked himself if anyone but her would have acted as she had.

His mother would, he knew. But he was not certain any other woman would have believed in him so strongly or cared enough to fight for his life on a level that took sheer faith and will.

No woman from the court would. Not even Elizabeth, for he was the one who initiated their meetings. He was the one who chased her, who had been chasing her and longing for her ever since their youth.

It was a hard thing to look at himself and see what he saw, to see that he was not the man he wished to be. That he was very close to being the blind and selfishly youthful man his father had accused him of being.

And he was ashamed.

He looked at Teleri for a long time, this rare woman who gave him a gift he could not repay. Her face was pale and her lips frosted with pain.

A grunt came from next to her where her silly pig had wedged its way between them. It was lying next to her, the way it did when she slept, its fat back pressed against her to keep her warm. The pig snorted in a whiny and pleading kind of way, as if it sensed something was wrong. The hawk just stood perched on the bed, waiting.

But Teleri still did not move.

Roger felt something stinging and painful rise to the backs of his eyes, something that felt exactly like tears. He looked away for an instant, then as if he were afraid not to keep watch over her, he turned back, waiting and wondering if she would open her eyes.

As softly and gently as he could he brushed some more hair back from her forehead, then ran his fingertips along her hairline, where the bruises and swelling showed the worst. He traced his hand lightly over her small straight nose and her lips and that stubborn jaw of hers.

A long hank of her curly golden-brown hair spilled over the back of his hand, which he raised closer to the light. He stared at that lock of hair, at the gold strands running through it, then at the red and copper colors that were there too.

Such simple things he had not noticed before. Things that were right there before his very eyes.

He looked at her hair and it was as if all the colors of the sunset were there in that one single hank of hair. He looked around, a foolish and self-conscious kind of action, the kind of thing he did without thinking. Then he lifted that lock of hair to his face and breathed in the scent of her.

A few moments later he began to cry.

Someone was crying. She could hear them. It was a man, something that made it seem even sadder to her because men tried to be brave, as if in their minds crying and hurt was somehow tied to honor and bravery. She understood pain and hurt, yet she cried.

But the sound she was hearing held more sorrow than she thought a single sound could ever hold.

Do not cry, she wanted to say.

He called her name.

Teleri?

It came from somewhere far, far away.

It sounded like Roger. He was far away. So very far

away that he was gone. She saw him ride away. Saw him disappear over the wild Welsh hills. Gone. He was gone.

She wanted to speak. Her lips were dry and cracked and felt like the ground under the summer sun. Her head hurt. Places on her skin burned as if they had been touched by fire. And she was so tired.

When she slept, it did not hurt. Her skin did not ache or burn. She did not have to think or remember.

The man had stopped crying now.

Why were you crying? she wanted to ask him, but she could feel the warmth of sleep tugging hard on her, pulling her back into its protective arms, where there was no more pain. Where she did not have to run away from anyone or anything. Where there were no stonings or broken hearts. Where people did not cry.

The wind howled over the roof and blew some of the smoke from the fire hole back into the cottage. The shutters on the windows rattled from the random gusts of air that hit them.

The animals in the cages must have felt the storm coming for they paced and shifted in their cages and some of them made odd noises that sounded like the chittering of birds.

Roger lit a few of Teleri's small candle nubs, one in the main room of the cottage and one in the back room. They were so small and had so little wick left that they cast shallow and dim light that flickered constantly, threatening to go out completely.

Roger talked to her, over and over, told her stories of the Crusade and tournament. He tried telling her jests and laughing, but it was a forced laugh because nothing seemed amusing when he had to look down into her bruised and cut face.

Finally frustrated, he stood and went over to the corner where the supplies Old Gladdys brought had been stacked. He bent down and dug through them until he found a box of tallow candles, which he opened and brought into the back room. He lit twenty candles, then ten more, until there was so much light he thought it looked like daylight and hoped that the light might make her wake up.

"Teleri. Open your eyes."

Nothing.

"Teleri! You are sleeping the morning away!" He paused when it looked as if her head moved a little. "Wake up, you!"

A moment later she did.

She opened her eyes and stared up at him blankly, as if she did not know him.

"Teleri? 'Tis I, Roger."

She frowned, then closed her eyes and whispered, "No. He is gone."

"I am here. See?" He took her hand when she opened her eyes again and pressed her palm against his cheek and rubbed. "That is my naked chin. The one you shaved."

She looked at him as if she expected him to disappear.

"Come, now, my love."

She flinched, then turned her head away and murmured, "No love."

My love, my love, he thought. God in heaven, how many times had he called her that? Words spoken without thought to their meaning. Except to her.

He looked away, then took the cloth and dipped it in water again and placed it on her cheek and ear. "The cool water will help."

"They stoned me." She still did not look at him. He did not know if she could not because of the way he hurt her or because she was ashamed.

"They will pay for hurting you."

She took a deep breath, one that did not hold anger, but only puzzlement. "I am no witch." She faced him then. "I tried to tell them. I am no witch. They just threw bigger stones."

"They will never hurt you again. I swear it."

Her lips thinned and began to quiver as if she were going to cry. He leaned down and touched his lips to hers. "I swear on my honor I will protect you."

She shook her head and looked away, closing her eyes as if they were just too heavy to keep open.

He sat in a chair by the bed and placed his hand on hers while she slept. His own eyes began to burn with the need for sleep and he lay his head down on their hands.

He did not know how long he slept, even if he had slept. But the candles flickered as if the wind was inside and a couple of them went out.

Roger sat up and looked around the room. The shutters were still closed. Overhead the wind was still howling and he could hear a tree branch cracking outside. The animals were sleeping now and the cottage was warm. He reached out to relight the candles, but a shadow drifted over the wall.

Roger froze for an instant, then looked up.

Standing in the doorway was the tall and dark silhouette of a man. With his sword drawn.

Chapter

30

❧

"I ride all over Brecon looking for you. Your king, your men-at-arms and friends are in an uproar over your disappearance, and here I find you hidden away with a woman. 'Twould serve you right if I used this sword on you."

"Merrick!" Roger shot to his feet. "Jesu! You almost got my blade thrown straight through your throat." He slid the knife back into his belt.

"There was a time when I would have never made it through the front door without a knife at my throat." Merrick sheathed his sword. "You must be growing old and slow, and your instincts puny."

Roger felt Merrick's words of jest cut too close to the bone. Not only had he lost his courage, he had lost his focus as a warrior. He drove a hand through his hair in frustration, then looked down at Teleri, knowing that from the moment he found her lying in the grass, unconscious and bleeding, he had not been aware of anything but this one small and battered woman with hair as wild as the wind.

Merrick began to walk around the bedstead and Roger went to meet him halfway.

"'Tis good to find you well, my friend." Merrick clasped Roger's arms and shook them in greeting.

"How did you find me?"

"I found a trail through the south end of the woods, a section that appears impassable."

"I remember it."

"Not far inside there were prints that led to an even darker section of the woods. There were drag marks of some kind that led here."

The image of Teleri, still angry and dragging his mail out of the woods flashed before Roger's mind.

"I also found this."

Roger stared at the spur in Merrick's hand. He glanced to the bed. "She said she could not find it."

Merrick looked down at Teleri. "What happened to her?"

"The villagers stoned her. They think she is some kind of witch."

Merrick moved closer. His disgusted expression showed that he could not understand this kind of cruelty any more than Roger could. "Superstitious fools."

"Her grandmother is Old Gladdys."

"Good God . . ." Merrick's eyes narrowed and he leaned in for an even closer look at her, then turned back to Roger. "Are you certain?"

"Aye."

"Not much resemblance there." Merrick studied her for a long time, then sat on the bed next to her and picked up a strand of her long hair that fell over the side of the mattress, looked at it, then dropped it again. "Well," he added. "Someday perhaps the hair."

Roger did not think so. Teleri's hair was like no one else's, in the same way she was like no one else he had ever known.

"Is that a pig next to her?"

"Aye." Roger looked at the pig, still sound asleep. "Her pet."

"And here I complain to Clio over a one-eyed cat in the bed," Merrick murmured as he stood up, then he turned toward Roger and started to take a step. He stopped as if suddenly rooted to the ground.

Roger glanced at Merrick, whose expression changed to a puzzled frown, then to clear and livid anger.

He was staring at Roger's neck. "Who did that to you?"

"I do not know." Roger turned away and walked past him to the bed, where he took the cloth from Teleri's head and dipped it in the water again. Something. Anything to keep his hands busy. To keep them hidden.

"I thought your voice was different."

"I did not even have a voice for a long time. At least I no longer sound like a frog." Roger laughed, but it had a hollow and forced sound.

Merrick was not laughing.

"Whoever did it attacked me from behind. Knocked me out." Roger placed the cool, clean cloth back on Teleri's cheek and ear, then glanced up at Merrick. "When I awoke, I was blindfolded on horseback and there was a noose around my neck." He looked down, staring at nothing really, but he could not look Merrick in the eye just then, not when he could feel his brow and his back begin to sweat again.

Merrick swore and looked away, his hands in tight fists and his neck growing as red as the lion on his pennant.

"I saw nothing. I only heard a strange and eerie kind of laughter before I blacked out." Roger nodded at the bed, his gaze on Teleri. "She found me, apparently about as good as dead. She thinks my mail and weight broke the branch." He paused, because it was still difficult to talk about, even to the one man who knew him better than anyone, someone he always thought he could tell anything.

But Roger could almost feel the rope again, could almost feel it tightening on his neck. It was hard to breathe. It was hard to talk. The air in the room seemed to disappear.

"English?"

Roger looked at Teleri and his mind snapped back to the present. "You are awake again." He sat down on the mattress. "Is your mouth dry? You want some water? Here." Before she could even answer he slid his arm under her shoulders and lifted her up, then tilted a small cup of water to her mouth. She drank a little, then waved it away. He lay her back down on the bed and saw that she was very still, her dark green eyes wide and staring at Merrick.

"This is my friend, the Earl of Glamorgan."

Merrick stepped closer and into the candlelight that spilt over the bedstead.

She gave him a wary look, then said quietly, "I have your horse, my lord."

"And I have your grandmother."

Teleri nodded, her face still serious. "You have been good to her and I thank you."

"From the looks of that horse in the meadow I'd say you have been good to the Arab as well."

"I would have returned him had I known he was yours."

"Ah, but then I would have had to return your grandmother and I don't think either she, or my lady wife would want that."

"No," she looked down, her voice so quiet Roger needed to lean closer to hear her. "Grandmother needs to stay at Camrose."

Roger frowned then asked, "Why?"

"Clio has spoken of it to me. Something about her husband dying there. The old woman won't leave because of it." Merrick nodded at Teleri. "Look. She can barely keep her eyes open."

Roger turned back and Teleri's eyes slid closed and almost an instant later she was sound asleep.

"Come," Merrick said, walking toward the doorway.

Roger put out all but one of the thick tallow candles, then stopped in the doorway, because for his peace of mind he needed to take one last look at her.

Outside the wind died down once the rain came. It pattered on the thatched roof and fell through the smoke hole and lightly into the fire pit making the fire sputter. Roger and Merrick were eating bread and cheese from Merrick's pack and sharing a wineskin between them.

"Bigod did not take the news of you and Elizabeth well."

Roger chewed on a hunk of bread and stared at the fire. "You think he is the one who did this." His hand went to his neck, his fingers rubbing over the rough and scarred skin.

"There are those who have sworn they heard him vow to kill you." Merrick took the wineskin from Roger and drank.

"I have disliked Hugh Bigod from the moment he wed Elizabeth, but never did I think him so much a coward that he would not fight a man fairly. I thought he had honor."

"He also has a reason."

Roger grew angry then and jabbed at the fire with another log. "Elizabeth would never have come to me if she thought her husband was still alive."

Sparks flew out from the fire pit and Merrick held up his hand. "I know that. Give me that thing before you catch us both on fire." He grabbed the log from Roger and threw it into the flames, then turned back to him. "Think how it must seem to him. If you were Bigod, what would you do?"

"I would never have left Elizabeth," Roger said stubbornly.

Merrick shook his head. "De Clare thinks Bigod has had no opportunity to come after you."

Roger was taking a swig of wine and he choked on it,

then swiped at his mouth. "De Clare? What does that green knight know of this?"

"He is careful, not green."

Roger snorted. He did not like de Clare any more than he liked Bigod.

"Edward trusted him to come to me and tell me you were missing. If not for de Clare I still might be at Camrose. I am here because of Tobin de Clare."

"And de Clare thinks Bigod is not suspect?"

"Aye, and Edward agrees with de Clare."

"Why?"

Merrick gave him a square look. "It was Edward who has kept Bigod tied up with Pembroke in Northumberland."

Roger frowned. Northumberland was about as far north as one could get and still be in England. He looked over and studied Merrick. "Edward sent me to Brecon."

"Aye."

Brecon was too far from Northumberland to make an attack easy. "I smell something foul, like the kind of plot Edward concocts when he is caught between politics and what he truly wants."

Merrick did not say anything. That silence said it all.

Roger shook his head, then buried his tired eyes in the heels of his hands and just sat there. He knew what had happened without asking. Edward had sent him here to put distance between him and Bigod.

"I did not think you would be happy once you saw through this."

"I am not." Roger dropped his hands to rest on his knees and stared at the blue flames of the fire. He took a deep breath and looked at Merrick. "Did you know this mission of mine was a mockery?"

"It was not a mockery. Edward does want a castle built on the site. A castle in Brecon was in his plans years ago when he gave me the license to crenellate Camrose. Granville was to have the job of it."

"Edward has always sent me on diplomatic missions,

not to establish strongholds. I should have seen through this play of his."

"Your thoughts were elsewhere. You have not been easy since Elizabeth sent you away."

Roger did not say anything.

"I need some sleep." Merrick stood and stretched. "You are also not an easy man to find, my friend." He crossed the room and took a blanket from his things, then made a pallet near the fire.

Roger put out the candles and lay down in the straw. Before long he could hear Merrick's even breathing. But as tired as he was, Roger could not sleep. All he could do was think about what Merrick had told him.

He knew it was all true. He had not been easy. In the months since he'd last seen Elizabeth, he had driven his men hard, and himself even harder. Although he hated to admit it, there had been truth to de Clare's angry comment about his treatment of his men the day he rode them so hard to get to the stones.

He had been driven by emotion, not sense, something that was a death knell for a warrior. Perhaps it was not his cowardice that took him down. Perhaps it was his stupidity.

Chapter

31

~~~~

The next day the men arose and went through the supplies. Among them, Roger found sacks of stone ground flour and a jar of bubbling stuff that, after both men sniffed it a few times, they agreed was most likely yeast. While Merrick went outside to feed his horse, Roger looked from the flour sack to the jar. He supposed he could mix them with water to make bread, but he was not certain exactly how one made bread, so he looked for something else to make for Teleri to eat.

Fortunately behind the flour there was a sack of grain meal, barley and oats, the kind of food knights carried in their saddle packs. He mixed it with water and honey and set it to boil over the fire.

When it was moist and thick he dumped some in a bowl and went into the back room where he sat on the mattress.

Teleri looked at the bowl, then frowned.

He tried to put the spoon to her mouth, but she grunted something, then twisted her head away.

"Teleri. You must eat. Come, sweet."

She crossed her arms stubbornly and looked at him. "You would not make it easy for me, English."

"This is not the same."

"You think not?"

"Aye."

"I think it is exactly the same."

"Fine." He stood and put one knee on the mattress. "I will sit behind your head and pinch your chin until you open your mouth, then I shall call you a hard-headed Welsh."

"I can do it," she told him, then she tried to sit up and what little color she had completely disappeared. She moaned and grabbed her ear, wincing.

"Let me help you." He slid his arm under her and lifted her so she was leaning against his chest.

"I want to do it," she insisted.

"Still stubborn as ever, I see."

"Hand me the spoon."

He held it out to her.

She reached for it and missed it by a good foot. She stared at her empty hand as if she expected the spoon to be there.

"Here." He placed the spoon handle in her palm and held up the bowl in front of her.

She stuck the spoon in his elbow.

"Want to try again?"

"No." She handed him the spoon and almost poked his eye out.

"The wound near your ear has you befuddled." He fed her some gruel, which she ate and looked surprised.

She swallowed. "Tastes good."

"You think I cannot cook a meal? 'Tis simple," he boasted, as if he did so every day.

He kept feeding her and talking. Every so often she would hold out her hand and stare at it as if she expected it to be closer to her. She had no judgment of distance.

"Do not frown so. 'Tis common to misjudge distance

and depth if you are hit in the head. Knights suffer from the same affliction. It will not last long. Sometimes one day. Sometimes longer. I was unseated at a joust once in Brittany and couldn't find my feet for a week."

He told her about the joust and managed to get her to eat and drink most of what he fed her. When he was done, he set the bowl down.

Pig was snoring peacefully at her other side and she reached out and tried to stroke him, but her hand missed. He took her hand in his and helped her.

She stared up at him. "Why are you here?"

"To take care of you. Remember? I have a debt to repay."

Her eyes narrowed and he knew instantly that he'd said the wrong thing.

She looked away, her lips thinned and her jaw set. "You do not need to repay me. I can care for myself."

"No you cannot."

"I have been alone for a long time. You think this is the first time I have been stoned?"

He had not thought of this happening to her before.

She raised her finger in the air, then looked at it as if it did not belong there. She dropped her hand to the bed, then said, "The mark on my cheek near my eye is from rock."

"I did not know this or I would not have left."

"I threw you out, remember?"

"Aye."

"You can leave."

He shook his head. "I am here because I want to be here."

"Why?" The look she gave him told him how important his answer would be. But he was not certain he would say the right thing. So often he said the one thing that made her angry. He could not tell her exactly why he was there. He just knew he was there because he needed to be there.

So he leaned forward and kissed her. He could feel

her surprise, the small gasp of a breath that filled his mouth. But she did not push him away. He did not touch her with his hands. Only his mouth.

He just kissed her in a lazy and soft manner that said he had all the time in the world. He traced her lips with his tongue and deepened the kiss. Next to his hand on the mattress he felt her fingers tighten into a fist.

He could stay there kissing her like that for half the day. She tasted sweet, a natural flavor that was her and had nothing to do with the honeyed gruel she had just eaten. She always tasted this way to him. Different and necessary.

But he broke off the kiss when she made a small sound, a moan. He could feel the tension running through her. A passion as strong as his, but because of experience, he was able to hold back. She could not, and he knew that was unfair.

He pulled back and stood up, looking down at her.

She sagged back against the mattress, her eyes wide and even more befuddled looking than before.

"I am here for a number of reasons. To protect you. To make you well. Because I want to be here. Go to sleep. We will talk later."

"Why can we not talk now?"

He studied her for a moment, then he held up two fingers. "How many fingers do you see?"

She squinted at his hand. "On which hand?"

"You see both hands."

"Aye."

"Then you will remain in bed." He pulled the blanket over her and the pig, then walked to the doorway. "I was only holding up one hand."

Teleri sat with her back against the mud wall and her hand somewhere in the vicinity of Pig's back—at least she hoped that was where her hand was. She gave him a stroke and he lifted his head off his front hooves and looked up at her.

Her sight was still so skewed that he had two snouts

and many, many eyes, all of which were looking right at her.

"Oh, Pig," she whispered. "What am I to do?"

He gave a couple of sympathetic grunts, then nuzzled her elbow. She stared at him and his heads for a long and pensive moment.

Animals did not hide their feelings. Pig always wanted to be with her and made that perfectly clear. He followed her everywhere and snorted and whined when she tied him up. And Horse lumbered along behind her almost dogging her steps and nudged her in the back until she played with him in the meadow. Hawk paced and squawked and carried on if she did not pay attention to him.

Not one of the animals she had in the cottage hid how they felt. When she entered the room, their ears and noses perked up. Some of them stood and watched her with eager and adoring gazes.

Even the wild doe and her fawns showed so clearly that they trusted her, for they walked right up to her and put their heads to rest in her lap. All she had to do was look into their faces to know how they felt. It was all there for anyone to see.

But she did not know what Roger was feeling. His actions did not reveal what was in his head and certainly not what was in his heart.

In turn she tried to hide what she felt for him. She tried to protect herself, but it was so very hard to do. And when he kissed her like he just had, so slowly and with such easy control, as if he had done this hundreds of times, she could almost hear her heart breaking.

Roger and Merrick stood outside near the bridge, where they watched the horses drink from the brook running below. The afternoon was cool and cloudy, and the air had that damp and metallic taste that always came with fall weather.

Roger noticed that Merrick stood there and searched

the trees and then turned and looked around the clearing. "This place must be near the center of the woods. If I hadn't found those drag marks and followed their trail, I doubt I would have ever found you."

"I know. Had Teleri not just led me out one of those paths, I would not have been able to find the place myself, though God knows after seeing her stoned I would have tried. And I do think the Arab knows the way back here."

"Did you see who stoned her?"

"Only from a distance. They looked to be lads. One of them was tall enough to be called a man. She told me she had been stoned before. I do not know why she did not leave here." He paused in thought.

"She probably felt safer here."

"Aye," Roger nodded. "These woods are tight and tricky. There are paths that appear wide and easily traveled, but lead nowhere. Many places look so much alike that 'tis all too easy to get lost in these woods."

Merrick was silent for a while, then he said, "We need to talk about what you intend to do."

"I do not know." Roger stared down at the water spilling over the stones in the brook more heavily than before the recent rain. It went down to the wide pool below and he saw that the water level was higher than before. There was less bank, showing the water was closer to the long grass that fell over the edges. "If I go back, things will be complicated. I will have to find out who wanted me dead."

"Aye. You sound as if you do not want to avenge this."

Roger was quiet. "I do. But I am not ready to go back yet." He tossed a stone into the water and watched the rings move out and disappear. Every time he looked at that pool, every morning when he had shaved, every time he had bathed, he remembered that night they had almost made love in it. And for the hundredth time he called himself a fool. He bent down and picked up another stone, then threw it into the pool. He rested his arms on the bridge and locked his hands together. "When did you know you were in love with Clio?"

Merrick glanced at him rather sharply.

Roger could feel his friend studying him.

Finally Merrick looked away and said, "You mean other than our first meeting?"

"Aye," Roger laughed quietly. "Other than that time. As I remember it, Clio said you had a fat head, then asked if you would throw any female children she gave you into the moat."

"Aye. The woman is a constant test of my patience." Merrick shook his head. "She is unlike any woman I have ever known. Stubborn and willful." He was smiling when he said that. It was a contented and happy smile, one that he'd had ever since his marriage five years ago.

"And beautiful and she loves you."

"Aye. I am a lucky man." He paused, then said, "In truth, I think I knew I was in love with her the moment I saw that Welsh arrow in her back." Merrick paused as if he were re-creating the memory in his mind. He stared off into the woods. "I remember thinking that I had finally found the woman I truly loved, and here she was going to die. Scared me more than any battle I'd ever fought. More than anything in my life."

Merrick turned and looked back at him, a question in his expression as he studied Roger.

Roger looked away, down at the horses. "She has taken good care of the Arab."

"Aye." Merrick still was looking at him.

"That horse follows her like a pet dog sometimes. I have watched them together. God, but that one small woman can ride." He paused and neither of them spoke.

There was no sound but the night birds and insects and the quiet trickle of the water over the rocks in the brook.

"I wonder what would have happened had I caught her those years ago."

"But you did not."

"No. I had no idea that rider was a woman until I saw her at the stones." Roger looked up. "Before the horse turned up missing, you were willing to sell him."

"Aye." Merrick grinned at him. "You are still willing to pay dearly for the horse?"

"Aye."

Merrick clapped him on the back. "You do not have to pay me, my friend. As soon as that young woman is better, I will give you the horse for a wedding gift."

Chapter

32

~❧~

By late that afternoon Roger and Merrick were both standing in front of the trestle table with a stack of vegetables before them and two of Teleri's huge cabbages. Merrick had three more wineskins stuffed in his saddle pack and they had shared one before they decided it was time to make something to eat.

The vegetables—turnips and onions, cabbages and some mushrooms Roger found after the rain—were all lined up as straight as candles on an altar.

Merrick looked at Roger. "Stand back from the table."

"Why."

"Wait. First give me some more wine."

Roger tossed him the wineskin and Merrick took a deep drink, then set it aside and drew out his sword. He stepped back a step, sword high in the air, then suddenly he moved down the table with the speed of a lightning bolt.

Whack! Whack! Whack!

He brought the sword down with methodical precision and when he reached the end of the table all the vegetables lay scattered across the table. Massacred.

"Well done! Particularly the cabbage heads." Roger clapped him on the shoulder, then took a drink of the wine and handed the skin to Merrick. "Let me try."

Roger took the sword from Merrick, then stood at the end of the table and whacked the hell out of the vegetables until they were completely chopped, then he used the sword to scrape most of the vegetables, except those that fell on the ground, into a pot of water, which he hung over the fire.

"We need bread," Merrick said casually, and by the time Roger turned back around, Merrick had sliced open a sack of flour and was looking around the table. "Where is a bowl?"

"There was a bowl over there." Roger waved his hand toward the shelves. "Do you know how to make bread?"

"Fetch that jar of yeast for me," Merrick said without answering him. Instead he just looked around the room. Then he set down the flour sack. "How difficult can it be? I have never had one whit of trouble finding a castle cook and all of them know how to make bread." He grabbed a bowl off the table and dumped out the useless rocks and seashells, which clattered onto the table.

Roger looked up. "Jesu, Merrick, stop! Those are Teleri's shells!" He set the yeast jar down and elbowed his way in front of Merrick, then he carefully picked up the rocks and shells one by one and put them back into the bowl, which he set in the center of the table.

He glanced up.

Merrick was looking at him as if he were daft.

"They are special to her."

"Rocks and seashells?" Merrick shook his head.

"There are bowls over there," Roger told him. "Near the eastern window where the herbs are hanging."

Merrick fetched a large wooden bowl and set it on

the table, then he turned the sack over and filled the bowl with flour, which came tumbling out of the sack in great creamy puffs that dusted everything nearby.

Roger waved away the flour dust. "That looks like too much flour."

"You think so?" Merrick gripped the sides of the table and squatted down until he was eye-level with the rim of the bowl. He sized it up as if he were sighting the distance to a target. "No. I think 'tis fine. Here." He pushed the bowl across the table toward Roger. "Put some of the yeast in with it."

Roger looked into the jar as if he were hoping it would magically make itself into bread. "I do not think this is a good idea."

"Of course it is. Just pour some in."

"How much?"

Merrick shrugged. "What do you think?"

Roger stuck his hand into the jar and held up a huge handful of the stuff.

Merrick nodded and Roger dropped it into the flour. "There."

"Put another one in just for good measure. I remember watching the cook as a lad. She always mixed it with her hands." Merrick stuck his hammy hands into the dry flour. "Needs water."

Roger wiped off his hands and grabbed a ewer of water, then dumped half of it into the bowl; it spilt over the edges, onto the table, and beaded into hand-sized puddles in the dry flour.

"Damn! 'Tis too much."

"Sorry. I shall fix it." Roger scooped out some of the water, turned and scanned the room, then he dropped it into a slop bucket in the corner.

He came back to the table and Merrick was up to his wrists in sticky flour dough. "Add some more flour," he told Roger.

Roger dumped flour into the bowl and almost everywhere else.

"I am kneading the dough," Merrick told him.

"Kneading it?"

"Aye."

"How?"

"See here?" Merrick showed him. "Pretend 'tis a woman's soft and naked breast and just gently squeeze."

"Let me try," Roger waited, then he stuck his hands into the huge bowl of dough. After a few silent moments of squeezing, he looked up at Merrick and said, "Feels more like a bottom than breasts."

Teleri woke up to the smell of food cooking. She sat up and did not feel so light-headed. She held up one hand and stared at it. One hand and five fingers. Just for good measure she held up her other hand and stared at both of them.

Ten fingers. Two hands. Her sight was back. She tossed the blanket aside and slowly got up. There was some water nearby and she washed her hands and used the cloth to gently wipe off her face and her ear. She could hear the men talking in the other room and she quickly got a clean gown and changed, then she walked back to the bed where she lit a few candles.

When she turned back, Roger and Merrick were standing in the doorway.

Roger had a bowl in his hands and he looked surprised, then he scowled at her. "You should be in bed."

"I have been in bed. I feel much better."

"We made you something to eat."

She bit back a smile. "I can see that."

"How is your sight?" Roger asked her.

"I felt fine until a moment ago. I think there is something still wrong with my eyes, though."

"Why?"

She crossed her arms. "You are both covered in flour."

They looked down at themselves then looked back at her. "We made bread."

"I can see that." She nodded, then asked. "If you look this bad, what does it look like in there?"

Both men leaned back as if they were joined at the shoulder and they peered back into the main room of the cottage. They winced in unison.

Teleri moved to the doorway, which the two large men had blocked. She elbowed her way through them and stood there stunned.

The room looked like her supply sacks had exploded. There was a thin film of flour on almost everything, including Hawk and even the windows. Chunks of vegetables were scattered all over the dirt floor and Pig was underneath the table munching the bits of cabbage that were there. Every bowl and pot and utensil she owned was stacked on the table and had been somehow used to hold the huge mounds of rising bread dough that covered every surface.

"Were you planning on feeding bread to all of Wales?"

"Just us."

She shook her head. It would take a long time to clean this up.

"'Twas my idea," Merrick said. "I will clean up."

"No. I shall do it." Teleri started to walk into the room, but Roger stopped her.

"No, wait. Are you certain you feel better?"

"Aye." She held up her hand. "See. Only one hand."

Roger set down the bowl and the hunk of half-burnt bread he had in his hands. "Come. Let Merrick clean this up. I want to talk to you." He took her arm and led her outside.

It felt good to be out of the cottage. It was dark, but there was still a glow of sunset in the sky above the western trees and they walked silently toward the bridge, then Roger stopped her when they were beneath the huge tree near the brook.

"How do you truly feel? And tell me the truth."

"My face hurts some and my ear, but I am not light-headed and my sight is good. I feel well enough."

He reached out and ran a finger over her cheek, then down to her jaw and chin. "Does that hurt?"

She shook her head and wondered what he was about.

He touched her lips. "Does this hurt?"

"No."

"Good."

The next thing she knew she was in his arms and he was kissing her. He did not hold her too tightly or press his lips too hard against hers. He kissed her as if she might break if he was not gentle.

So she slid her hands up to the sides of his head and she pressed herself against him. It worked, for his hands slipped under her bottom and he lifted her up.

Her hands gripped his head and she ran her tongue along his mouth and slipped it inside. She always loved the taste of him, but this time he tasted of sweet, rich wine, so she swept her tongue through his mouth again and again.

He groaned and kissed her back, kissed her until her head felt light again. He moved his mouth to her cheeks and then to her neck. "I want you, Teleri. I want you so much I ache with it."

She whispered his name and he was kissing her again, he slid to his knees and took her with him. He shifted and moved one hand down, then pulled up her gown so he could touch her thighs and in between. The moment his fingers touched her intimately, she moaned and gasped into his mouth.

He leaned back against the tree trunk and pulled her on top of him. Their bodies touched from their mouths to their feet. He took her hand and moved it down to the front of his chausses and she felt him the way they had touched each other before. Their hands played until their breath was fast and hard and their kisses desperate.

He shifted, then pulled off his tunic and spread it on

the ground. He lifted her into his lap and undid her gown, then tossed it aside before he lay her down on his tunic and pressed his bare chest against hers.

She arched up to meet him, the tips of her breasts growing hard when they touched the thick curly hair on his chest. He moved down her neck, kissing her, and then he suckled her as he had before. She clasped his head to her breast and held it there, loving what his mouth and lips did to her.

His hand was between her legs and touching her there where she was damp and crying for him. It felt so good there, when he pushed his fingers inside and moved them slowly, so good that she begged him not to stop.

She moved her own hands to the ties on his hose and opened them so she could touch him without the cloth between them.

When her hand closed around him and slid up and down the way he had shown her before, he looked down at her. "Feel how hard I am for you. Feel it. You do that to me. Just you." He moved and pushed her legs apart, then settled between them. He slid his hand back down to touch her and rub her there, then he put his root against her and shifted his hips up and down, sliding against the place where she ached.

"That is how much I want you. I want you in every way a man can want a woman, my love."

She froze and forced herself to open her eyes and look up into his face. "Do not say that. You do not have to lie to me and call me your love."

"I am not lying. You are, Teleri. You are. I want everything from you. Everything you have. Your heart, your love. I want it all."

She stared at him long and hard because she was not certain she understood.

"I want to give you myself, Teleri." Roger slid his hand to her cheek and cupped it gently as he looked at her. "I want to give you my protection. I want to give you children. I want to give you my name."

She could not speak. She said nothing, because she was afraid if she spoke, if she made even a single sound, she would wake up and see that this was not really happening at all, that she was dreaming.

"Will you have me? Say you will. Will you have my children? Will you take all I want to give you?" He kissed her deeply and passionately. "Will you wed me and take my name, my sweet love. Say you will, Teleri. Say you will."

"Roger," she whispered his name.

"Say it."

"Aye. I will take your name and your children. I will take it all."

He kissed her and slowly pressed into her, pausing when she gasped or made a motion or sound. "Easy, love."

He was filling her, stretching her so tightly she held her breath. He lifted up enough to put a finger between them and he moved it slowly over the place that sent her flying. He kept rubbing her there and pressing forward so slowly, stretching her while his finger flicked against her and made her want to shift her hips higher and higher.

His tongue was deep in her mouth. His root slipping deeply inside her. It hurt, but she wanted him there and his finger was moving faster and faster.

She could feel it coming, that feeling she craved. Just one more touch. One more flick of his finger.

He touched her in the perfect place.

She pulsed hard.

At the same time he sank deeply inside of her, tearing something that made her grip his shoulders harder and hurt for only an instant. He was completely in her, seated fully, and she throbbed around him again and again.

He was whispering, "Come, come, come . . ." And he began to move each time he said it. Slowly, almost moving completely out of her body, then he sank slowly back inside. Again. Again and again.

"You are so tight, so hot," he told her. "You feel so good, Teleri. So good. God . . ." He sank deeply and stopped for a moment, his head buried in her neck. His breath came faster than hers and his hands were twisted into her hair. He lay there, filling her, not moving, his breath in her ear. Then when his breathing was more even and controlled, he moved again and again, slowly, in and almost out, and made her feel things she did not know she could feel.

His hand was not between them, now, but she could feel that wonderful thing coming again, closer and closer, each time he moved inside of her.

Soon she was pressing her legs up and pushing against him, moving with him, and telling him, faster and faster and faster, calling it out until she throbbed again, throbbed hard around him.

He stopped moving suddenly, stiffened and groaned so deeply she knew he was as much a victim of their passion and their bodies as she was. A moment later she felt the warmth come from him—his life, his love.

Chapter

33

Roger and Teleri walked in the door of the cottage and stopped. Even Roger was amazed, for the whole place was clean, and even more orderly than before. Each wooden bowl was stacked neatly on the shelves according to size. The wooden cups were clean and rearranged in straight rows with their rims turned upside-down. There was not a lick of flour dust on anything in the room. Even the floor had been swept clean.

In fact the main room looked as if no bread had ever been made there. Until Roger looked in the corner, where Teleri's pig was eating the remnants of two half-burnt and very hollow loaves and the hawk was picking at crumbs.

Merrick was sitting at the table, his chin resting in one hand while he was intently stacking the rocks and shells from the bowl into something that looked like a mock battlefield—the seashells on one side and the rocks on the other.

"Merrick!" Roger bellowed.

His friend glanced up, looked at both of them, then

turned on the stool. He leaned back against the edge of the table with his arms crossed, eyeing them.

"We are to wed." Roger slid an arm 'round Teleri and pulled her closer to him.

Merrick looked from him to Teleri and then back to him. He appeared to be fighting back a knowing grin. "I would say from the look of you both that a speedy wedding would be a good thing."

Teleri glanced down, then quickly shook out the skirt of her gown. Grass and leaves fell to the floor. Chewing her lip, she glanced up at Roger with a look that was somewhat embarrassed, but mostly proud and happy.

Roger took that look, her green eyes so trusting and clear, and felt it take root and grow inside of him as if at that moment, with that one look, she became part of him. And for the life of him he could do nothing then but smile back at her.

She reached out and affectionately brushed some grass from his clothes, then stood up on her toes and flicked away bits of bark and leaves from his hair.

Roger liked the way she stretched up to touch him, for her breasts moved just enough to capture his attention. He knew underneath her gown, they were a soft, pink color and they tasted like honey and Teleri.

"Were I overlord in this part of Brecon," Merrick told them. "I think I would have to impose a fine, a legerwrite, for 'tis obvious you have anticipated the marriage bed long before your vows."

"But we shall not wait long, my lord." Teleri told him. "These woodlands are deep within Wales. Here a fine for loving early is the rarity, not the usual. Women are more often with child before they wed to prove their fertility."

Roger was certain there was a wry word or two and a few bawdy thoughts running through Merrick's mind, for Roger had had a few of his own, but he would not poke fun at her beliefs again. He had learnt that lesson well. Besides which, he rather thought the Welsh had the better idea.

"Priests are scarce," Teleri continued, "and deemed unnecessary. Here handfast is the custom, and the most convenient."

"I know of this handfasting. 'Tis an old tradition, Saxon and Pict as well as Druid and Welsh, but I have heard that it binds together for merely a year and one day."

Teleri shook her head. "It can be for a year and a day, for three and ten years, or for a lifetime. The couple state the length they have chosen when they speak their vows." Teleri looked up at Roger and slid her arm through his. "We have talked and decided to wed here in Brecon, tomorrow. At a special place in the woods." She gave Roger a look so full of eagerness and hope that he closed his hand around hers. She turned around and looked back at his friend. "We would be so very grateful, my lord, if you would act as witness."

Merrick stood and crossed the room, then took her hand from Roger, bowed, and placed a kiss on her palm the way Roger always did with Clio. Merrick even mimicked Roger's manner and kept his lips on her skin overly long. And even though Roger knew he did this for his benefit, seeing Merrick's lips on Teleri's hand still annoyed him. He scowled down at Merrick's black head and quelled the urge to clout him a good one.

Merrick straightened, gave Roger an equally annoying wink, then said, "Come. We will drink to your betrothal" He raised the wineskin. "To you, Teleri, I am now only Merrick. My lady wife claims too much my-lording will go to my head and make me unbearably difficult to live with."

He handed Roger the wineskin and when he raised it to his mouth and drank deeply, Merrick grasped his shoulder and squeezed hard. "This man is like my brother. I will think of you as a sister as well as the woman who could bring my closest friend to his knees." Merrick laughed, then said to her, "Tell me. Surely he did the honorable thing and begged for your hand on bended knee, did he not?"

Teleri looked at Roger with eyes that were misty with memory and lips that had the softest bit of a smile. "I would say you were on your knees, English. Aye?"

The truth was his knees were bent and between her legs at the time. "Aye. I did the deed proper." Roger agreed heartily and threw his head back to take one more drink of the wine. "My knees were on the ground."

The night before her wedding Teleri dreamed of her mother. It was an odd thing to dream of someone she did not know. Someone she had never seen.

But still that was what she dreamed. Her mother was standing before her amidst the green rolling hills of Wales, the jagged ridge of mountains and a dark and deep cave in the distance behind her.

Annest was there, beautiful, magically alive, looking half-human and half-myth with a eerie swirl of silver mist hovering over her golden head. She had familiar, slanted green eyes like Teleri's own, but they were under a slash of straight brows that were much darker than Annest's pale and wildly curly blond hair.

The scent of heather was all around, almost as if it came from her fair skin. She had cheeks of rose, and her wide lips were moving with words Teleri could truly hear, quiet and certain words that told her all those secret things that mothers must try to pass on to their daughters:

It is good to be wild and to owe no one. Never be ashamed of what you feel or of your tears. Remember that the way to hold your man close to you is to keep him in your arms. Teach your sons as well as your daughters that to love is to be free. You are good, you are kind, you are Teleri. Do not ever change into what you think you should be. Stay Teleri, for your name is great.

What name is great? Tell me! Teleri wanted to say, but her mother only held out her hand to her. A reach. A touch. The hand was so much like hers that Teleri thought it was her own.

But it was Mother's.

She had her mother's hands. The same oval nails and long fingers. Part of her wanted to know if the pattern of lines and creases on their palms were the same.

Love long and well, my daughter, for you and the children you bear are all there will be left of your father and me.

In a flash of light that was as swift as a shooting star, a tall and formidable looking knight was standing next to her. His mail shone silver like the moon, but his face was hidden by a golden helm with Celtic lines and markings etched on the visor. There was an eye slit, and she could feel that he looked at her intently.

The sword hanging at his side was huge; it shone as brilliant as the summer sun and the hilt, too, was etched with Celtic symbols. He raised his large hand in greeting. Or perhaps in farewell.

Who are you? Why do you hide from me? She wanted to ask him.

He did not speak to her as her mother had. He only took Annest's hand in his, and together they turned and walked toward the dark outline of a cave scored in the stone of the mountains.

Teleri awoke the next morning to the songs of the birds that nested in the thatch of the roof overhead and to the soft and buttery color of the fall sunrise slanting inside the cracks between the wooden shutters.

In that first breath of morning, the quiet time before she even moved other than to open her eyes, she lay there and all around her was the faint scent of heather.

Come live with me and be my love,
And we will all the pleasures prove
That valleys, groves, hills and fields,
Woods or sleepy mountains yield.

And I will make thee beds of roses
And a thousand fragrant posies,
A cap of flowers, and a kirtle
Embroidered all with leaves of myrtle.

—"The Passionate Shepherd to His Love,"
Christopher Marlowe

Come live with me and be my love,
And we will all the pleasures prove
That valleys, groves, hills and fields,
Woods or steepy mountain yields.

And I will make thee beds of roses
And a thousand fragrant posies,
A cap of flowers, and a kirtle
Embroidered all with leaves of myrtle;

The Passionate Shepherd to His Love
Christopher Marlowe

Chapter
34

❧

Roger and Merrick were deep in Brecon Wood, in front of the giant, old, wrinkled oak tree from which shadowy forest paths fanned outward in different directions. Fall sunlight filtered through the breaks in the thick clusters of the tree's leaves, and dragonflies and gnats flitted through the streams of warm autumn light.

Roger stood there waiting for Teleri and smiling to himself, for he knew this felt good and right, as if he were finally in the one place in his life where he should be.

It was not all that long ago that he had seen these green and richly dark woods as a prison. He had seen Teleri as a fey creature who had saved his life, and had thought he should leave her to her world, her green, lush little world where she was safe and where the only things that died were the leaves on the trees that protected her.

But he found when he did leave her that he had felt as if he left part of himself behind, and he cried for her because she was the best part of him. He did not want to lose her. She was the one thing he had sought for so long. But until then, he had not known she was there right before his very eyes.

Aye, he cried for her. He would live for her, and he would die for her.

Teleri was his destiny. Not Elizabeth. He understood that now. After he had made love to Teleri under the tree and the stars and the moon, she had asked him about Elizabeth. He told her their story and had felt none of the loss and ache he had before he met Teleri.

That horrible night when Elizabeth told him they were through was now months past, and yet it seemed like it had been years. Now, as he stood there, Elizabeth seemed to him to be from another lifetime.

She had been right. He knew that now. They did not have love, not the kind he had found with Teleri. Not strong love, the kind that brings happiness and peace and contentment. What he had had with Elizabeth was emptiness and obsession and anger. It was an odd thing to find out that at his age he had not known what love truly was.

The soft sound of rustling leaves came from Roger's left. Merrick jabbed an elbow into his ribs to get his attention, then nodded at one of the northern paths.

Teleri was walking toward him, her heart in the incredible smile she gave him. The power of that smile was something to see. If he could see that smile every day for the rest of his life he would die a happy man.

Long and wild curls flowed around her shoulders and face, down her arms and back, where they looked like twisted ribbons of gold and brown and copper, the colors of the earth itself, colors that were solid and alive and honest.

She wore a woolen gown of a faded green, lighter than her eyes, and around her hips was a loose belt of woven myrtle leaves and ivy. She carried a basket of guelder roses and as she approached Roger, she tossed a handful of soft white petals at their feet. She handed him an ivy wreath woven with yarrow and marjoram, then knelt at his feet and bowed, waiting for him to set the ivy circlet on her head.

He placed it on her, then gently cupped her face in his hands and tilted it upward. She smiled as he brought her to her feet and placed a swift kiss on her solemn lips.

She reached into the basket and took out a wreath of holly. He went down on one knee at her feet, then stared at the soft earth, at the tips of her bare toes that peeked out from beneath the hem of her gown. He felt her place the wreath on his head.

He stood, then, and raised his hands before him. She placed her hands flat against his, palm to palm. They were warm and soft and so much smaller than his. Together they threaded their fingers, holding fast and tight to one another.

He took a moment to think, for he had pondered all night and morn searching for each word he would use to wed with her, this woman of his heart and mind and soul.

He took a deep breath and began, " 'Tis she, Teleri, I have set my heart upon. I shall know no other love but hers, and if not hers, then no other love at all.

"For she has surpassed all, so fair, so noble, so true, that I should love, and not until I be dead, love or be loved ever again.

"From this moment onward she has my heart and my name, FitzAlan, and I share with her all in this world that is valuable to me—my title and my property and wealth," he paused. "And I give to her for her own, an Arab horse."

Her eyes grew wide and he could hear Merrick quietly laughing nearby.

She smiled and her eyes were misty with emotion, the same thing Roger was feeling.

She lifted her chin as if she were talking to the whole

world. "For it is to you, Roger, that I give my body and soul. I shall love no other, for longer than a year and a day, for longer than three and ten years. I honor and love you, my husband, for my lifetime, and I swear that for me, forever, there will be no other love.

"I share with you all I have in this world, my home and my possessions, and," she smiled, "my animals. I shall take your pain as mine. Your wounds as my own wounds. I give to you my body. My woman's eyes so you can see the world in a new way. I give you my lips and voice to speak in your defense. I give you my womb to bear your sons and daughters, and my heart and mind.

"I have no name to forfeit as a sign of my respect and love, but gladly I take your English name of FitzAlan. I take it with pride and honor. I will cherish it deeply in my heart. From this moment onward, I am Teleri FitzAlan, wife to Roger."

They lowered their hands, but Roger lifted hers to his mouth and kissed both her palms, then placed her hands around his neck and gave his wife a real kiss, all lips and mouth and tongues. It lasted so long that Merrick began to clear his throat, then hum and finally he punched Roger in the arm and said, "Save something for later."

Roger and Teleri broke apart, but they still stood there looking at each other, neither one of them willing to speak first.

Merrick spoke. "As the Earl of Glamorgan, Tydfyl and Severn, as Lord of Camrose and Dreighmore, I stand as witness that you two are wed." He paused, then clapped Roger on the back and picked up Teleri. He swung her around and she shrieked, then he laughed and gave her a huge and all-too-familiar kiss on the mouth.

Roger pulled Teleri away from Merrick and back to his side. "Enough kissing of my wife. You are not her kin."

Merrick laughed, but poor Teleri just looked shaken and somewhat embarrassed.

"You have to forgive Merrick. He only did that because Clio is not here. She will have his ears when I tell her what he did."

"Aye, that she will," Merrick said, truly looking not the least bit worried. "However," he said after some thought, "I would hate to think of what she might put in my ale were I ever to cast my eyes on a woman other than her."

Teleri and Roger locked hands and walked back through the woods, while Merrick talked and told jests and stories of his wife to Teleri, who laughed and every so often looked up at Roger.

He would smile at her, then watch her move, the steps she took, which were light and carefree, the excited look on her face, as if she expected something wild and wonderful to happen.

But to Roger, it already had.

Inside the cottage, while Teleri cooked, Roger and Merrick told her stories of their years together, of court antics and Crusade, of friendship, jests, and tourneys. Roger helped her whenever she would allow him to and they all decided that Merrick was best at cleaning up.

That afternoon they dined on a feast of pumpkin soup, mushroom and turnip pie, cabbage with honeyed carrots, walnut and raisin pudding and a special wedding cake of flour, ginger, honey, coriander and rose petals.

Afterward they had gone for a walk in the meadows, where Pig had followed them and snorted at Merrick's heels as if they were plump and juicy cabbages. They came back and played a mock game of chess using Teleri's shells and rocks. Teleri, who had never played, paired off with Roger, and they were pitted against Merrick who was the victor.

But now when the sun was beginning to set and the caddisflies were flitting through the air, Roger was outside with Merrick, while Teleri was in the back room, where she had just lit candles and put them in the rush holders on the wall.

She placed some squat tallow candles that gave off soft golden light atop the trunk, then spread rose petals over the bed, as was the Welsh custom to ignite passion for all their wedded years.

She looked at the bed and smiled, though her heart beat a little faster than it should and her steps were more nervous than usual.

She took a yarrow cluster tied with ivy and ribbons and climbed atop the mattress so she could hang it over the bed. She stepped back and eyed it, then adjusted the licorice stems and elder flowers that were mixed in. When it was straight, she stepped back and studied the cluster.

Aye, she thought. It was perfect. She turned to find her husband leaning against the wall, watching her with a soft look that made her belly flutter inside.

"What is that posy for?" He nodded at the flowers.

"The ivy is a female plant. It symbolizes the woman and her fertility."

He grinned at that.

"The elder flowers," she continued, "bring luck to those who have handfasted. Licorice brings fidelity and passion to the marriage."

"You think we need more passion, love?"

She smiled. "Can you have too much passion? I do not know these things."

"No, I suppose not. If it works the bed might burn up." He paused. "But what a way to die."

She turned back to the flowers, smiling. She touched the misty green stems with the white clusters that some called Lady's Mantle. "And this is yarrow, which is supposed to ward off the Devil."

"Aye, that one worked. Merrick has gone off to the village. Finally."

"Roger." She turned. "That is unkind. I like him. He is a good man."

"I like him too, love, but not enough to have him here on the night of my wedding."

"He has gone to the village?"

"Aye." Roger grinned. " 'Twas good of you to give him the direction of Bleddig. I would think three in this bed might be much."

"Three in a bed?" Her expression was confused.

"Never mind that." Roger pushed away from the wall and set some cheese and wine near the bed. "He gave us these. He said he can buy more food in the village. I think what he truly wants is meat, fish or some kind of fowl."

"Was there not enough food?"

"There was plenty. But Merrick, like most, wants his meat, love."

She made a face and shivered.

"Come down, now."

"Just let me fix this one side. 'Tis drooping a bit." She reached for the ribbons and found she had to retie them. "Is his wife as amusing as he claims?"

"Aye. Perhaps more so. Merrick and Clio are good together. But not as good as we shall be." Roger knelt on the mattress and grabbed Teleri's ankle. "Hallo, wife."

She looked down as he lifted her gown. "What are you doing?"

He gave her a wicked grin, then slid his head beneath her hem and began kissing her calves.

"Roger?"

He moved his lips to her knees while his hands held her ankles apart.

"Roger!" She gripped his head. "What are you about?"

"I am kissing you, love," he said, his voice muffled from beneath her clothes.

Teleri placed one flat hand on the wall and closed her eyes. Her other hand still gripped the back of his head.

His lips moved up to the insides of her thighs, licking and kissing softly, then nibbling on her skin the way one nibbled on a special treat they wanted to last and last. A moan escaped her lips and her knees went weak and quivery.

His mouth moved higher and higher, then he almost kissed her between her legs. His mouth was right there. She could feel his breath on that place where his fingers had played, where she always became dewy for him.

Then he kissed her.

"Roger!" She grabbed his head and lost her balance, taking them both down on the bed in a tangle of legs and arms.

He was laughing at her under her gown, with his face pressed to her bare belly. He kept laughing.

She shoved at his shoulders and scrambled up the bed, until her back was against the wall and her feet out in front of her, her ankles pressed together.

He looked up from her feet and grinned at her, then grabbed her ankles again and slowly ran his hands up her legs, then down again, up, then down, until she gave up watching him and closed her eyes.

She let her head fall back against the wall. He stroked her legs, then slowly pulled her toward him, an act that made her gown slide up her body while he pulled her down and closer, lifting her legs out on either side of his shoulders.

He touched her then, with his fingers, so gently, stroking her again and again, then he stopped and untied his hose and pulled himself free. She opened her eyes and looked at him, at his root, which was swollen and resting against her nether lips.

He used it to stroke her there, used his hardness to slide over her, flexing up and down and moving against her.

She watched what he did to her, watched him move himself over her. Their eyes met once, twice and the look he gave her almost burned her up.

He reached out with his hands and threaded them with hers and pulled her up until she was kneeling in front of him, face to face. He pressed her solidly against his naked body, his hands on her bottom, and he kissed her over and over until her eyes drifted closed.

She moaned, then he stopped kissing her and lay her back down, with his hands still under her. The look in his eyes was so intense that her breath caught and he took advantage and lifted her to his mouth. An instant later, he gave the most intimate kiss of all.

"Roger . . ." she called his name again and again, but he wouldn't stop, and she did not want him to. This was a wicked and wonderful kiss.

He used his tongue and lips and sucked her into his mouth. She throbbed from it, again and again and again, but still he went on, as if he were so hungry for her he had to taste her more and more.

She called out his name when it happened again and shifted away, then looked at him, at his half-closed lids, at the passion she could see in him.

She had no idea of this thing, that you used your mouth to love someone like this. But she liked the way it made her feel. She loved the pleasure of it.

So she tried to do the same for him. She kissed his legs, rubbed her palms down them and her fingers along the insides. Then her mouth followed, as he had done to her and she licked the inside of his thighs, moved slowly up and down, until she was so close to him she touched the tip of him with her finger and then her lips.

He groaned, "Teleri, Teleri, Teleri. . . ."

She licked him and he groaned again, the same kind of sound he gave when he throbbed inside of her. She played him a little longer, then suckled him, took the tip of him in her mouth and pulled at him with her lips.

He moved so swiftly she hardly knew what happened. He flipped her over him, so he could kiss her while she sucked on him. It was like flying and soaring, the mutual touch of their tongues and lips.

She changed the motion and slowed, then scored her teeth lightly down the length of him. She rested her cheek on his belly and glanced up to where his head was between her legs. Then she closed her eyes for the just the moment it took for her to peak.

She came hard and fast. It went on a long time and her breath was rapid and shallow, but the love she felt for this man and what he was giving her was anything but shallow. It was deep and forever.

He pulled his head away and set her hips down near his shoulder, so she was alongside of him, her head still resting on his belly. He raised his head up off the bed and looked down at her, a wicked smile on his mouth.

She sat up, smiling too. He started to sit up. She placed her palms on his chest and shoved him back down, enjoying the power she had, the ability she had to render this man, this huge and strong warrior, helpless at her command. To make him moan and quiver and beg her not to stop.

She did not stop. Instead she bent down and kissed his belly and lower, slid her tongue over the length of him and dipped her lips down deeply and took all of him in her mouth. A moment later, when he called her name, cried it out as if she were his whole world, she tasted the sea, his substance, his life.

He moaned and throbbed, saying, "I love you. God in heaven, how I love you." Then he moved his mouth and did the same for her again.

A few minutes later they lay there on the bed, ragged and spent, sweaty and damp, their breathing finally slowing. Teleri had her cheek resting on his thigh. She was looking at the random swirls of red hair on his legs and near his root, the arrow of curly hair that ran up his body and spread over his belly and chest like curls of bright fire.

"You liked that," he said, stroking her arm. His voice sounded surprised.

"Aye," she said softly, for she was thinking and tracing one fingernail down to the inside of his knee because it made him flinch. She liked that he had no control when she did it. "I did not know such a thing could be done, this mating with your mouths."

" 'Tis one of the many ways to love for a husband and wife."

"How do you know of this? Who taught you?"

He groaned and covered his eyes with one hand, then lay there.

"Tell me."

He gave a huge sigh, then said, "I heard my father's men speaking of mouth-mating. Then I tried it and found out what all the talk was about."

"Who did you try this with?"

"The first time it was with one of my mother's maids."

She was quiet then, not knowing how she felt about his words: the first time.

He sat up and pulled her into his lap. He lifted her twisted and skewed gown off and tossed it aside. His hose had been gone for a long time and were nowhere on the mattress.

He sat up and pulled his tunic over his head, then cradled her in his lap, so they were both naked and clasped together, holding each other, and settling in the midst of those fragrant rose petals.

"I can taste the roses on your skin and your shoulder."

"Hmmm."

He pulled his head away and stared at her. "You look deep in thought."

"Aye." She looked at him. "Tell me this."

"What?"

"If we mate that way and I become with child, will the babe come out my mouth?"

He did not speak for a moment, did not move. He frowned, then threw back his head and laughed and laughed, holding her almost too tightly. Laughing and rocking with her in his arms, his chin on her head.

"Teleri, my Teleri," he said. "I do love the way your mind works."

"Why is this so amusing? Does that not make sense to you?"

"Aye, love, but I have never thought of it in that way." He brushed some hair away from her face and said, "You cannot become with child when we love that way."

"Oh." She looked at him. "I cannot?"

He shook his head.

She frowned.

"You did not like it?"

"I liked it. I loved the way you made me feel."

"I sense there is a *but* coming."

She nodded, then looked up into those blue, blue eyes of his. "I want a child, Roger. Your child. Our child."

He gave her such a look then, when he opened his arms to her and said, "Come to me, love."

She did.

He bent then and kissed her again, kissed her slowly and passionately. His hands went to her ribs and then her breasts. He shifted and lay her down on the bed as his hands and mouth made wonderful, sweet love to her.

And in a while, when she was damp for him and wanting him, he slid deeply inside of her, filling her and loving her and stroking her for the longest time.

He told her how she felt inside, that she was warm and tight.

She touched his throat, placed small kisses over the rope marks there, the same way he kissed the marks made by the stones and the bruises that still stained her left brow and temple.

"I love you, Roger," she said. "I do so love you." It

was the last thing she said before she gave herself up to this man who, that very day, had given her his name and his property, had given her Horse.

And a few moments later, perhaps thanks to the ivy that hung over their heads, he gave her something more. Something neither of them even knew of yet. He gave her a child.

Chapter
35

❧

The days were growing shorter, which was fine with Roger, because when a man was just married, it was the nights that were the best part of the day.

Merrick came back three days after he left, loaded with supplies and gifts for both of them. Laughing heartily, he burst through the door of the cottage carrying in a huge wedge of cheese and balancing two small jugs of cider and a third jug of wine vinegar. With vinegar, Teleri could pickle the vegetables she grew and eat them throughout the winter.

Like the king's magician, Merrick pulled small bags of spices, nutmeg and cinnamon, turmeric and saffron, from his saddlebags. He gave Roger a sword, belt and hilt, and Teleri a shining silver bowl in which she could keep her shells and stones.

But what truly had Roger fascinated was watching Teleri's reaction when Merrick gave her a small carved wooden box with a brass latch and pin.

"This gift," he told her, "is from both my lady wife and I."

"But you have given us so much, my lord."

"Who?" Merrick scowled at her.

Teleri smiled. "Merrick." She already seemed overwhelmed by the few things Merrick had given them.

"Clio would want you to have something like this."

Teleri unlatched the small box and looked inside. Her mouth dropped open.

Inside were steel pins, which were stuck in a small violet silk cushion along with three shining, golden needles. There were two slim wooden spools of thread, one brown and one black, and last, she pulled out small silver scissors shaped like swans, which hung from a long silver chain so she could wear them around her neck.

She touched them almost reverently, then swallowed hard while she stared at the box.

Roger realized that because she had so little, she did not know of gifts such as these, casual everyday things owned by his mother and each of his sisters and almost every other lady he knew.

Teleri looked to Merrick. "Thank you. And thank the Lady Clio for me. This is the loveliest gift. I shall cherish it, always."

Merrick grinned. "Good!" He slapped his thighs and said, "I think I would like to teach you both to play chess again."

Roger looked to Teleri, who was still staring at the sewing box.

She looked up at him and smiled.

"Merrick wins one game and he is suddenly the expert. Come, my friend," Roger said to Merrick. "Teleri and I shall teach you how this game is truly played."

This time Roger's mind was on the game and he and Teleri, who was learning most quickly, took Merrick's queen in eight moves.

It was dark when Teleri rose from the bed, that time between night and morning when everything was still as snow. She moved as quietly as she could. Roger was sleeping. His breathing was even and quiet, that shallow kind of breathing of someone who was completely asleep, the kind of sleep that is almost too deep to dream.

She moved around the bed and the small room by instinct, then went to the small window near the trunk and opened the shutters. She sat on top of the trunk, resting her chin in her hand and looked outside. It was so very still. Everything in the world must have been sleeping at that moment.

The night sky was clear and there were stars overhead, bright, flickering stars. She loved the night sky, because every time she looked up, she felt almost as if she were seeing those stars for the very first time.

She had wanted to do something for Roger, something special. That was what had kept her awake, long after he'd loved her and then fallen asleep. She picked up the sewing box and looked inside, wondering how difficult sewing could be.

She did not know, for she never had a needle before. She never had thread or something as wonderful as these scissors.

She set the box aside, stood and crossed over near the bed to get a candle. She lit it and looked around the room until she found Roger's saffron cotte, the shirt he had worn under his mail and tunic. It was smocked, with large sleeves, and it had rips and tears in it from when she tried to remove his heavy mail shirt.

She took the cotte and candle, and trying to be quiet as a mouse, crossed over to the window and sat down. She leaned over the candle and threaded the needle, which took a while, until she figured out that if she snipped the thread sharply with her scissors, the ends were less frayed and easier to stick through the needle eye.

Then she began to sew.

Every so often, she would stop and look at Roger, sleeping there in her bed, his arm slung back over his head and his face showing no expression because he was asleep. And she would smile.

It took her most of the night to finish mending the shirt. And when she was done, when she had folded the shirt in her lap, she stayed there, her chin resting in her hand while she was thinking about him, and every so often watching him, just doing that and nothing else, because doing so made her feel better than a whole night's worth of sleep.

Roger awoke to find Teleri was already up and his cotte was folded and sitting next to him on the bed. He looked at the shirt in the daylight. She had patched the holes with the black thread. He had awakened the night before and had watched her when she thought he was asleep.

By the weak light of a candle, she had mended his smocked shirt, her face close to the needle, her tongue poking out of the corner of her mouth in deep concentration. She had flinched each time she jabbed the needle through the fabric, and he'd had a hard time not laughing once he'd realized what she was doing.

But here in the morning light, he saw that the stitches were all different sizes and meandered across the fabric like a trail of ants. They were nothing like those of his mother or sisters, who prided themselves on the fine and delicate quality of their stitchery. They sewed tiny, invisible stitches in perfectly straight lines.

Their buttons never fell off, their ties were strong enough for a man to yank and they would never break, the seams would not fray or come unstitched. They were fine seamstresses and had always fished for compliments whenever they made him a new tunic or shirt.

But the quality of those stitches mattered little to him. It touched him much more that Teleri, someone who obviously did not sew well or often or perhaps never had sewn before, had done this especially for him.

* * *

By late morning Merrick and Roger were outside, Merrick atop his horse with his pack loaded. He was returning home.

"You are certain you wish to stay here?" Merrick asked him again.

Roger nodded. "For a while longer. I want time alone with my wife before we leave."

"I will talk with Edward and send word to your family. Neither Edward nor I will let anyone else know you are here and are well."

Roger thanked him just as Teleri came outside, drying her hands on a cloth. She stood next to Roger. "I will show you the closest path out. It will take you to the eastern edge of the woods so you will not have to ride around them."

She took Roger's hand and they walked into the woods with Merrick and his horse following behind. The trail was not far, close enough to see the meadow, but was hidden behind a copse of brambles and birch and holly and where the undergrowth was solid.

Roger would have never believed that there was a way through that tangle, until he saw Teleri brush some branches aside and a path appeared almost as if it was made from the magic of her touch.

She turned and smiled. "This is the way."

Merrick gave her a kiss that was not overlong, then he clasped Roger's arms and shook them. "Farewell. Both of you." He stopped. "I almost forgot this." He reached inside his tunic and handed Roger a bag of coins. "You might need these," he told him. Then Merrick gave him a small and ragged piece of parchment.

Roger unfolded the paper and read it. "What is this?"

"Another gift." Merrick looked at him. "'Tis the names of the village lads who stoned her."

Chapter
36

Teleri sat behind Roger as they rode Horse toward Bleddig. Her hands locked together around his waist, and she rested her cheek against his back, but she could feel none of his warmth, only the hard links of his chain mail through the fabric of his tunic.

In the distance, she could see the village cottages huddled together like gossiping women. Her hands then locked a little tighter around Roger.

He glanced over his shoulder at her. "I will not let anyone harm you, love. I swear."

"I know." She said quietly, but still it was difficult for her. Silently they rode past the empty farm field, where the grain had already been harvested. The wheat sheaves stood in tall yellow bundles where the black-birds perched and cawed over and over, as if to say, "Go away. Go away!"

There was an apple orchard to the left filled with mossy old apple trees, heavy with ripe fruit on sprawl-ing branches above the thick and gray-weathered trunks. Those tall old trees were lined up in rows that faced the road and looked like the village elders already scowling at them as they rode by.

"Look! Look!" shouted someone from behind the orchard. "'Tis the witch of the woods!"

An old woman stepped outside her small home with a rake clutched in her hands. A hound barked and ran in circles with its tongue lolling out of its mouth.

"The witch! The Woodwitch!" someone shouted and soon people were coming out from barns and stables and cottages, whispering and hiding their mouths behind their hands.

A stone flew past them and Teleri jumped.

Roger cursed under his breath and reined in. He drew the sword Merrick had left him and held it before him so all could see the huge and gleaming blade.

Some of the villagers gasped and stepped back.

Roger pinned them with a look so black even Teleri drew in a breath. "Who dared to throw that stone?"

No one spoke a word.

"I said! Who was the fool that threw the stone?" he bellowed in a voice so loud and harsh it sounded like God. He stared down at the villagers, huddled together in a crowd, all looking afraid to speak. "Another stone comes near and I will use this sword swiftly."

He waited, then prodded Horse forward toward a huge chestnut tree that spread shade over a good third of the village green.

The people moved along the road, more slowly and apprehensively than before he had drawn the sword, but still they followed, quietly chattering among themselves.

Teleri could hear some of the things they were saying:

"Who is he?"

"Why is he with the witch?"

"She has cast a spell over him," someone whispered loud enough for them to hear.

Roger began to laugh. He turned to the crowd. "Do you believe Sir Roger FitzAlan of Wells is so feeble-minded that one small woman can control him?" He laughed again, as if that were the most stupid thing he'd ever heard.

A short distance more and he reined in, then brought his leg over the pommel and slid to the ground. He reached up and grasped Teleri by the waist. She planted her hands on his shoulders as he lifted her down.

He turned, then slipped his arm around her and faced the crowd, which had been following them. His free hand was on the hilt of his sword; his feet were apart and his stance challenging.

Teleri looked at the faces of the people in the village. Some of them she had known when she was small and when there had been no talk of her, no saying she was a witch.

"Hear me, all of you! This woman was walking in the woods." Roger paused. His hand tightened on Teleri's shoulder as he scanned the crowd without saying a word.

He pulled back her long hair and exposed the left side of her face and brow. "Do you see the bruises on her face?"

There was a low murmur and some people nodded, others just stared, looking almost afraid to speak.

"She was stoned." Roger's voice was cold and icy. He pulled a piece of parchment from his belt and opened it. "Young Morgan Cull! Owain Lewis! Will Tydder! Morris Powell! Rhys Madox!"

There were gasps and cries as each name was called.

"These names are those of the lads who did this. Step forward each of you whose name I called."

The hum of the crowd talking was in the air like bees in May, buzzing and hissing, some of them closing into smaller groups and rapidly whispering.

Then one woman with bright red hair dragged a reluctant and frightened boy forward by his ear. "Here is Owain Lewis!" She shoved him in front of her and held him by the shoulders. "I am the Widow Lewis. He is not a bad lad, sir. He is my only son. His father died two winters ago. I beg mercy for him, I do."

"And you others?" Roger spoke to the crowd, looking from young boy to young boy. "Come forward."

A tall boy of five and ten came from the crowd. "I am Will Tydder." Two more boys came forward, each giving his name.

An old man with a huge floppy woolen farmer's hat joined the boys. "I am Daffyd Madox. Rhys is my grandson and he is with his father to the north. They went for salmon in the river. I swear to you, my lord, he is not here this day."

Roger nodded, then he released Teleri and walked in front of the boys, stopping and looking at each one. Not once did his expression look as if he liked what he was seeing.

The boys fidgeted with their hands or rocked on their feet; not one of them could look him in the eye.

He stepped back and stood there, waiting for something, but none of them knew what. Then he drew his sword and the whole crowd gasped.

Even Teleri was afraid he might harm the boys.

"Roger. No. Please," she said quietly.

The boys paled and some began to cry silent tears.

Roger stuck the sword in the grass, and leaned on it, then he looked at the first boy. "Did you throw stones at this woman?"

The boy was crying, tears streaming down his cheeks. He nodded, then looked down, wringing his hands.

"Why?"

The boy looked up. He sniffed, then mumbled something.

"I cannot hear you," Roger said in almost a growl.

"Because she is a witch and if she looks at you, you will turn to stone," the boy said, his face pale.

"She is looking at all of you and I see no stone

276

statues." He turned to Teleri and placed his hands on her shoulders and said, "Look at me. Look me in the eyes."

Teleri looked into those blue eyes of his and saw what she always saw, the eyes of the man she loved, the man who vowed he would protect her.

Roger turned back and looked at all the people standing there, then at the boy. "Look at me, Owain Lewis."

The boy slowly raised his head.

"Am I stone?"

"No, sir."

"Do you still believe she is a witch?"

The boy shook his head.

"You!" Roger bellowed again at the next boy. "Will Tydder?"

The tall one who looked to be the eldest of the boys nodded. He tried to stand taller, but sweat was beading on his brow and his color was weak.

"Why did you stone her?"

"She is the Devil's child."

Roger laughed loud and hard. "This one small woman? Do you think the Devil would father something so small and puny?"

The boy frowned as if he could not answer that.

"Does she have cloven feet?" Roger lifted her gown up and showed Teleri's bare feet. "Does she, Tydder?"

The boy shook his head.

"You!" Roger said to the next boy, who almost jumped from his skin. "Who are you?"

"I am Morris Powell."

"Did you throw stones?"

"Aye."

"Why?"

"For the same reasons as the others. We were afraid of her. They say if her shadow crosses your path you will turn into a bird. And the wheat will not grow."

"I think you were not afraid, but only wanted to hurt

her to make yourselves feel more powerful. Like you were men. But men and warriors do not hurt women. They are not cowards who run away and hide."

The boy swallowed hard, but did not deny it.

"I saw the wheat in the fields along the road. It looked tall and fat to me."

The crowd mumbled about it being the finest harvest in years.

"Do you truly believe this woman is a witch?"

"No. I never did," he admitted. "I will not throw stones again, I swear, sir."

Roger did not say anything, but went to the last boy. He was the youngest. "Your name?"

"Young Morgan Cull. And I did throw stones, too," he admitted before Roger could even ask. Then he looked at Teleri and then up at Roger with wide eyes and added, "But I missed her. By a whole lot, too."

"Do you know why you threw the stones?" When the boy did not readily answer Roger asked, "Because of the stories about her?"

The boy nodded. "All those things the others said and more," he admitted. "Be leery of Teleri was what they always told me. Will Tydder swore that if the witch kissed you then you would turn into a toad."

Roger turned and pinned the tall boy with a pointed and angry look.

The boy swallowed hard.

Then Roger turned and lifted Teleri up into his arms and the crowd murmured behind them. He had moved so swiftly and caught her so off guard that she clasped her hands to his head as he looked at her. He slid one hand behind her head and kissed her in front of all of Bleddig.

It went on and on, that kiss, and Teleri was vaguely aware of the villagers, talking and watching. It was over almost as quickly as it had begun. He set her down on the grass. He faced the village and his gaze wandered over the crowd. He looked at the youngest boy. "What do you see, lad?"

"I see a knight."

"No toad?"

The boy shook his head.

"Hear this, all of you! I have come to Brecon by order of King Edward. To oversee the building of one of the King's castles here, up in the hills. Once the site is complete, I will be your overlord."

Teleri looked at Roger and frowned. He had said nothing of this castle or King Edward. She did not know if he was saying such to intimidate the village or if it was the truth.

"I will have no one stoned. Ever again. This woman is not a witch and as God is my witness I swear I shall severely punish anyone who says she is." He turned and held out his hand to her, then pulled her to his side, his hand clasped tightly around hers. "Understand all of you people of Bleddig. This woman is no witch. She is Lady Teleri FitzAlan, my wife."

Roger walked along the path, past the dirt rows where the cabbages and turnips once were. Now pumpkins and acorn squash grew there instead. He moved on toward the bridge and the brook, where Teleri stood waiting for him. It was almost twilight and a few moments before she had gone outside the cottage to let Pig and some of the other animals roam before putting them back inside for the night.

As he approached, he saw that Teleri stood with her hands resting on the stone bridge and she was looking down at the water below.

He came up behind her and put his hands around her waist, then leaned down with her, staring at the bubbling water. He gave her a small kiss on the neck. "You are very quiet, my love."

She did not answer him immediately, but stayed as she was, looking down into the brook as if the answers or words she needed to find were down there somewhere.

He waited and occupied himself by breathing in her

scent. She smelled of the richness of the woods and spring, like freshly mown grass. A clean and clear and natural scent that reminded him of life itself.

"Today was difficult for me."

Roger turned her around to face him, bracing his hands on either side of her. "I had no choice but to make certain they understood that I will protect you, and that I will never let anyone harm you again."

"You made that point clear enough, with the sword, I think."

"Did you truly think I was going to slice up those children?"

"Aye. You looked so angry and so fierce."

"I was angry. I still am angry, very much so, at what they did to you. And I do not forgive easily. The villagers need to remember my words. Fear of me will make them remember what I said. And I'll wager that no one in Bleddig will again be telling their children tales of witches."

She had turned back to look at the water and he realized that this was where she came to think. It helped to stand there and listen to the water and the quiet sounds of the insects and the last calls of the birds. It was peaceful here.

Pig trotted over the bridge and sniffed at their feet. But Teleri did not greet him as she always did, as if that silly pig was so special and she had not seen him in the longest of times.

"You still seem preoccupied."

"I was just thinking about that threat you made about building the castle in the hills."

"That was no threat, love. 'Tis the reason I came here, to scout the site for Edward. The castle will be built there, and I will be lord of Brecon."

The look she gave him was puzzled and a little hurt, as if she thought he was hiding it from her. "But you never spoke of this before."

He shrugged. "I was not hiding it. The reasons for

my being here in Brecon never came up between us. Did they?"

"No, I suppose not."

"You do not want to live in the hills? In a castle?" he paused. "With me?"

"I will live with you anywhere. You know that."

"Aye, but I was just making certain. Your voice is uneasy, love."

"I do not know how to be a lady."

He laughed. "You will learn. Look how quickly you learned chess, and everything else I have taught you." He gave her a devilish grin.

She gave him the oddest look, as if he had just grown a second head. "Roger, I can barely sew, much less run a castle."

"You sew fine. See?" He pointed to the lopsided stitches on his shirt. "Besides which, my mother and sisters can teach you what you need to know about sewing and castles, as well as can Merrick's wife, Lady Clio."

She looked as if that was doubtful, but Roger knew she could do whatever she set her mind to do. She was a strong woman. An independent woman. And he loved those things most about her. "The plans will be finished in the spring. Building will start soon after that. Then whenever you go into Bleddig you will do so as the Lady Teleri FitzAlan of Brecon."

She turned and faced him, leaning back against the stones. "I do not think I will ever be comfortable in Bleddig."

"Then you should keep going there until you no longer fear it."

"I do not know if I can do that. Think. Is there no place that has ever frightened you? A place where something bad happened and where you are not certain you could ever go again?"

Now he was the one staring at the water. He had his own fears to overcome. His hands had stopped shaking, but he still trembled inside when he thought about the hanging. And every morn, when he shaved, he saw the scars on his neck, a constant reminder of what he had gone through.

"Aye," he said quietly. "There is such a place. But if I must go there again, you will have to take me."

She frowned. "Where?"

"The place where I was hanged."

Teleri suggested they should wait until morning, since it was night, and there was a new moon.

But Roger refused. He told her he needed to go now. She looked long and hard at him and saw clearly that nothing she could say would change his mind.

So they left the cottage, each carrying a torch. Teleri held his hand tightly as she led him through the forest, down the paths that could be dark enough during daylight, but were even darker and more eerie at night.

Some of the tree branches were spindly and low and looked like claws because they had lost so many leaves. The air was getting colder and it felt good to have the torch in her hand, because it kept her fingers warm.

They went deeper into the woods, where the brush had grown brittle. Twigs from bushes and brambles scratched at her skin as if they were trying to hold her back.

They came to the old oak tree, the place where they wed, and she stopped. "You are certain you wish to do this."

"Aye. I am certain."

She squeezed his hand tightly and took the path that led to the dark side of the woods. It did not take long. She moved swiftly, and once past a turn in the path she saw the tree branch, lying on the ground. It was covered in fallen leaves and twigs, but above it, on the huge tree trunk, she could still see the place where the branch broke, where the wood was pale and new.

She turned to Roger. "We are here."

He lifted the torch higher and stood there, staring at

the place. He looked at the tree for the longest time, almost as if he were reliving the whole thing in his head all over again.

She searched his face for some sign of what he was feeling. There was no emotion on his face that she could see, which surprised her. But the light was odd, coming from their torches. It would flicker and turned their faces and skin colors that were impossible, red and gold and sometimes even blue, and it could easily hide what someone was feeling.

He dropped her hand so he could step closer to the tree. Her fingers grew cold and icy almost before he had let them go. He walked over to the tree trunk and touched the place where the branch broke, then he knelt on the ground and brushed aside the leaves.

"It looks like nothing but a broken branch," he said.

"Did you think there would be something else here?"

"The rope. Where is it?"

"At the cottage. I used it to make a sling and tie you to Horse, so he could drag you back to the cottage."

He was quiet again, thinking, then he looked up. "You used it to save me."

She nodded.

He straightened and turned in a circle. He began to laugh, but it had a strange and hollow sound to it. "I thought it would frighten me to be here." He looked back at her. "But it is only a tree." He put his foot on the branch. "'Tis only a broken branch." He walked over to her and held out his hand. "Look. It does not shake. My hand does not shake."

"No," she agreed. "It does not shake." She did not understand why he told her that. But she did understand that he was experiencing something very different from what she experienced in Bleddig.

He almost looked happy to be there, relieved. He laughed again, harder this time and it was real laughter, as if there had been a jest played on him.

He turned to her and held out his hand again.

"Come, love. Take my hand. I am not mad, I swear, but I thought coming here would make me so." He pulled her close and slid his arm around her, then dropped a kiss on her forehead. "Thank you, my love. Thank you for bringing me here. Thank you for saving me when you had no reason to. Thank you for loving me."

He bent down and kissed her and she kissed him back, each of them holding a flaming torch that surrounded them in a golden glow, and at least for that moment, all darkness seemed to disappear.

They spent the night loving beneath the old oak tree. Roger built a small fire and they lay there naked, ignoring the cold air, for when they were loving, neither of them was ever cold.

But that was not the case the next morning. Teleri awoke in Roger's arms, and even though they had slept in their clothes her feet were like ice. She wiggled a little and pulled her knees to her chest, then slowly tried to sneak her feet under Roger's shirt and against his warm belly.

"Jesu!" He shot upright. "Your feet are freezing!" He drove a hand through his hair and shook his head a few times as though he needed to do so to wake up.

She grinned at him. "Aye, and your belly is warm." She moved her bare feet closer.

His hand flew out and grabbed them, keeping her and her freezing feet at bay.

She grinned, because as long as he was holding her feet, they were warm.

"Is it morning?" he asked, looking overhead.

"Aye," she nodded.

"I am not certain I should ask you, woman," he grumbled and stretched his back and rolled his shoulder. "You rise the instant the sun does."

"And you sleep until half the day is gone."

"This ground is hard."

"We shall go home, now." She pulled her feet from

his hands and stood, then dusted as much of the dirt and leaves as she could off her gown.

He scattered the coals and covered the few that were left glowing with damp leaves and stones and then he straightened. "Are you ready?"

She nodded and started to lead the way.

"I can find the right path," he insisted.

"You can?"

"Aye," he said in a firm voice. "Follow me."

And she did; she followed him right down the wrong path, grinning.

Much later, after they had come to seven dead ends and false paths, Roger had stopped and was scanning the sky and trees as if he thought that would guide him in the right direction.

"Are you certain you want to take that path?" Teleri asked him.

"I know where I am going."

"Uh-huh."

He stopped and turned, his stance challenging. "You think I don't know where I am."

"No. I did not say that."

"Good." He went farther down a path that she knew led in a circle.

"I'm certain you know where you are," she said as she followed him.

She was quiet and it must have annoyed him because he turned back and scowled at her. "I know where I am."

"Aye." She grinned. "You know you are lost."

He did not laugh, but she did. Then she finally began to suggest the directions. He trudged ahead of her, slapping branches out of his way and muttering that this did not look like any path he had ever traveled.

She was still laughing when they finally came to the outskirts of the meadow, and he stood there for a long time, then turned back to her and said, "I was lost."

She laced her arm through his and laughed. "I know."

They walked over the bridge laughing and talking.

Roger stopped so suddenly Teleri almost ran into his back. She stood back and peeked around his shoulder.

There in front of the cottage stood a mounted troop of knights all in mail. Their leader was a regal looking man who sat tall in his saddle, and who was looking straight at Roger.

The man rode slowly forward, then stopped and pinned Roger with an icy cold look. "Well, look here, men. If it isn't my son, the villein."

Chapter

37

~

Roger could not move. All he could do was stare at his father. "How did you find me?"

"Your friend, Merrick, came riding up to Camrose as we arrived. Otherwise, I suspect I and my men would be still combing the Welsh hills for you." His father cast a quick glance at Teleri, who was standing behind Roger, and must have found her lacking his interest, because he then looked around the grounds as if he were studying a pig pen.

But Roger had talked to Teleri about his father and she knew that they were estranged, even though she never could completely understand how Roger felt. She had no father and would probably never know his identity. But Roger knew in spite of that she would support him.

True to his belief, she stepped bravely forward and stood by his side, then easily slipped her hand into his.

His father looked back at him and waved a hand. "Enough of this . . . this playing farmer. You will come home. Now."

287

"Playing farmer?" Roger wanted to hit him.

"What else should I call it. Philandering? What? As usual, you have found yourself a willing wench, then spent all this time with her, ignoring your duty to your king. You have not changed, Roger. You have no honor. You are still as irresponsible and foolhardy as you have always been. You play at life while your king, your friends and your family believe you are dead."

"You know nothing of my life!"

"I gave you your life!"

"Then 'tis you who have made me what I am."

"You will come home, Roger." His father's voice was flat and cold.

"No."

The battle line was drawn with that one word. And Roger did not care, for over the years, there had been too many battle lines to count.

"You have no choice. If I must, I will have you tied and dragged back home."

"I will only speak to you inside," Roger said and walked past him and around the corner, pulling Teleri with him.

"Leave the whore!" His father shouted.

Roger spun around and would have pulled his father from his horse if Teleri hadn't grabbed his arm.

"No! Do not!" she said in a hiss of a whisper. " 'Tis only a word."

Roger barely made it inside the cottage door. He stood there, with one hand flat against the wall. His head was down and his breathing was fast and furious.

The anger ran through him so fast, as if it were part of his blood. And for just a moment, he could not even see. He let go of Teleri's hand, and an instant later he drove his fist into the wall. Plaster crumbled to the floor, but he did not see it; he only heard it fall.

She jumped back. "Roger. Please. Do not do this. Please." She reached out and put her hands on his shoulders, then slid them under his arms and clasped him to her, resting her head against his back. "Do not let him do this to you. He is trying to make you angry."

"Go into the other room."

"I shall stay here with you."

"Go. If you love me. Go."

"I love you and I shall stay. He cannot say anything that will hurt me. Do not let him see that his words hurt you."

"They do not hurt me. They make me want to kill him."

"He is your father."

"He is a bastard."

Roger's father stepped inside. He looked around the cottage, then looked at the dirt floor and the animals in their cages. Pig was in the corner and snorted at the baron.

His father's arrogant look changed to one of disgust. He shook his head, a gesture that said this was all very avoidable, then strode past them.

He took his place, standing in the center of the room as if he owned this place and they were only his villeins, there to hear his most important proclamations. He looked from Roger to Teleri, then coldly back at him again. "So son, speak."

"You will not call her a whore again. She is no whore. She is my wife."

The silence in the room was brutal. Taut threads of emotion stretched out from father to son like the strings of a Punch puppet, and all one of them had to do was yank on it to cause hurt and anger and disbelief between them.

Then his father burst out laughing. It was a cruel and belittling kind of sound, meant to cut.

He looked at Teleri. "Your wife? She is not even fully clothed. God in heaven, Roger, the girl has no shoes." He laughed some more.

From the corner of Roger's eye, he saw Teleri raise her chin. He pulled her close to him, wanting to protect her and shield her from his father's cruelty. "She is my wife. I will have you treat her as such. She is the Lady Teleri and she will be the mother of your grandchildren." Roger paused. "Remember that, old man."

His jibe cut straight to the bone. His father's bitter smile faded and his eyes narrowed. Roger knew he did not like to be reminded that he was past his prime and, too, that he truly had no control over his son, for Roger was a knight in his own right and a favored vassal to the King.

"Then bring your . . . wife home with you." His father stood. "But come home you will. I swore to your mother I would bring you home. I will do so." He crossed the room, heading for the door.

Roger stood taller as his father came closer and closer, looking as though he would just stride right through the door without another word. But something stopped him. He stood barely a foot away. "What is that on your neck?"

Roger reached up and jerked the neck of his cotte down, tearing it past his collarbone. "This? Can you not tell what this is?"

His father did not move. He did not speak either. He just looked at his neck.

"They are rope burns from being hanged from a tree in these woods. Here, where you think I am playing farmer."

"Roger," Teleri's voice was soft, but it held a warning.

"Someone ambushed me and tried to kill me. They would have succeeded if my wife, the woman you have insulted repeatedly, had not found me and saved my miserable and unhonorable life."

For just one moment his father's hard look faltered. It was in the eyes; they were not as Roger remembered. They aged in almost an instant, suddenly old and fragile. The color was the same; they were still cold blue, but they looked like thin ice.

Roger refused to believe the emotion he saw there.

He knew his father and how he thought. That could not be the Baron Sander FitzAlan Roger saw. Never. Never.

And while Roger was denying what was there before his eyes, his father opened the door and walked outside without another word.

Teleri had learned something important about families that morning. When someone was in love, there were times when even that powerful love cannot heal a family that has been broken.

She walked over to the brook, where she was hidden from the FitzAlan men by the weepy old tree. She sat against the trunk and hugged her knees to her chest.

Shouting her love to the countryside, swearing it before all of Wales, or wearing her heart on her sleeve, none of those things would help Roger and his father stop the pain their stubborn pride was causing one another.

But just the same, the man she loved was hurting and she could not take that hurt away. She felt it deeply, perhaps too deeply, for now she could smell the odor of it on her skin, as if her husband's pain was making her rotten inside.

She leaned down and washed her arms and hands in the brook, trying to wash it all away. But she could not, for she loved him, even though she had a choice to make. His mother needed him and Roger loved his mother.

He needed to leave. She wanted to stay.

This was her home. The place where she felt safe. She did not know what the world outside was like, all she knew was that it could hurt, hurt so much that people could rot inside. People could change in an instant.

She had changed the moment she found Roger, perhaps the moment she found Horse, all those years ago. Her life was no longer what it had been. She had let down her guard and let him into her private, secluded world—a place she so cherished it was like letting him see inside her heart to her deepest and darkest secrets.

And now she had to choose: to follow him into the world outside or to stay where she would try to live as she had before. Safe. Alone. Living in dreams.

She could still talk to the animals, but they could not hold her the way Roger did. She could do everything just as before but it wouldn't be the same. She wouldn't really be there, because her heart would be wherever he was.

She knelt down and took a drink from the brook. She cupped the water in her hands, but by the time her hands reached her mouth they were empty, just like the rest of her life would be if Roger was not part of it.

Chapter

38

⚓

It took them four days to get to Wells Castle. Teleri sat next to Roger in the plank seat of a lumbering wagon filled with everything she owned and loved.

In the wagon bed behind her were all the cages of animals, the three-legged hare and the blind badger, the fox and the other animals that would never survive in the wild woods. Horse was tied to the wagon gate and he trotted along behind, with Hawk riding on his back, and Pig was sleeping on a small bed of straw. Every so often he would raise his head and look at the country-side and grunt.

They agreed to leave the cottage as it was, for Roger promised they would come back in the spring, so Teleri took only her personal things, the trunk with her few clothes and her wedding gifts. She packed her rocks and shells and kept her red leather pouch tied to her waist so she would not lose it.

There was little talk between Roger and his father. Her husband spoke more to some of his father's men-at-arms, whom he had known for years. His father stayed away from both Roger and Teleri, choosing to eat and sleep isolated in a small striped silk tent, while his men erected a larger one for Teleri and Roger.

It was late in the day when they came over a plump hillside. Teleri looked up. A vast gray thing loomed before them, looking like a mountain.

"That is Wells Castle," Roger said, slowing the wagon team.

Teleri turned and stared at him. "That is where you grew up? That is your home?"

"Aye."

The castle was so huge that it looked like a walled town, rather in the way she imagined London would look—vast and busy.

From the watchtower at the center of a seemingly endless curtain wall came the sound of heralds, and as they approached the gatehouse a huge drawbridge with planks as thick as forest trees lowered over the moat, which was the size of a lake and wrapped around the curtain wall for as far to the east and west as she could see.

The portcullis creaked open, looking like the giant jaws of some monster and Baron FitzAlan rode through ahead of them, with the wagon and his men behind.

Teleri sat there silently watching Roger who had been quiet for most of the day. He was coming home, but there was no anticipation in his expression. He sat straight and stiff, isolated, as if he did not want to be there.

Once inside it seemed that everyone was talking at once. People in the bailey stopped and waved to the men and to Roger. They all approached the keep, which was tall and wide and had true glass in some of the windows that sparkled like stars embedded in the dull gray stone.

The huge oak doors of the keep flew open and a group of women came running down the steps, most of them young, but the eldest was a breathtakingly lovely woman with deep red hair. She ran up to the wagon calling, "Roger! Roger!"

He jumped down from the wagon and opened his arms to the small woman that Teleri knew could only be his mother. She was crying as she held her son, her hands holding his cheeks as if she had to look into his face to believe he was truly there and well. "You are alive, my son. Thank God."

"I am well, Mother." He held her tightly, then his gaze flicked up to Teleri, still sitting in the wagon. She gave him a small smile that she knew quivered a little because she was so very, very scared.

His mother looked at him, then she touched Roger's neck. Tears rolled down her cheeks and she began to cry, saying, "My son . . . My son . . ."

"I am well, Mother. Cease this. Please." He paused and Teleri could hear his voice crack some. She could feel the tears gathering in her own eyes.

"Cease all this crying. I am well and home!" Roger said, holding his arms out from his sides as he looked at his mother and sisters.

He turned his head for just a moment, his eyes locking with Teleri's. She could see him start to move toward her. But before he could reach out to her his sisters crowded around him, crying and chattering. All of them speaking at once.

Teleri watched them and wondered how any of them heard what the others were saying, since they all spoke at the very same time.

Finally Roger pulled himself away from them and took his mother's hand and turned her toward the wagon. "Mother, I have someone I want to introduce to you. Someone special."

Roger's mother stared up at Teleri from curious but kind brown eyes.

"Mother, this is Teleri, my wife."

His mother tore her gaze from Teleri's face and stared at Roger with a stunned expression.

Teleri's stomach dropped. Now both his parents would not like her. She tightened her fingers in her lap and forced the smile to remain on her face.

"You are wed?"

"Aye."

"Oh finally! I am so pleased." She turned to Teleri and held out her hands. "My new daughter! This is wonderful! Oh! Help her down, Roger." She slapped Roger lightly on the arm. "You should not leave her sitting there while all of us rudely gape at her."

The moment Teleri's feet touched the ground, Roger's mother was hugging her. She smelled of cloves and roses and kindness. "Welcome, Teleri. Welcome." She threaded her arm into hers. "What a lovely name you have. Is it Welsh? You must tell me of it, and of your family, and how you and Roger met. My name is Lillianne, but you may call me Mother if you wish. I would so like it if you did. You know, my dear, I had fretted so for years now that I would never see my son wed. I am so pleased."

She almost dragged Teleri up the stairs and away from Roger. "Come inside. You must be exhausted from the long ride. Where did Sander find you both? He sent word but did not tell me of you, my dear. He must have wanted it to be a surprise for me."

Somehow, Teleri doubted that was why Baron Fitz-Alan had not told his wife of Teleri's existence.

Roger's mother led her through the doors saying, "You must tell me everything. My dear. Just everything."

The next morning, Roger came down the stone steps from his bedchamber in the west tower. He had not slept well and was stifling a yawn as he passed by the entrance to the solar.

"Roger!" his mother called out to him.

He came around the curtain that closed off the entrance to the solar, frowning. "All my life you have always known when I was coming down those steps. How do you do that?"

"A mother knows her child's motions, his voice and his way of walking."

He stifled another yawn.

"Did you not sleep well?"

"Not very well."

" 'Tis a strange bed. You have not been home for over two years."

He could hear the hurt in her voice.

"I had duties, Mother."

She looked at him long and kindly. "And there is your father, I suppose."

"Aye, there is that," Roger did not deny it. "But this morn, I am only tired from sleeping with that pig."

"Roger! That is horrid! You should never speak of your wife in those terms. What is wrong with you? Teleri is the sweetest thing. That is no way to talk about a woman, Roger. I am your mother and I will not allow it. I do not care if you are a man grown."

He burst out laughing, then explained about Pig.

She made him sit down next to her and tell her all about Teleri. He spent a long time telling her everything. About the animals, the woods, then told her of his hanging. His mother cried when he told her. He cried when he told her about Teleri's stoning.

Roger could always talk to his mother. She would listen, unlike his father. She would let him finish and not interrupt him. She was not quick to judge and she never made him feel as if he was a failure.

"You love her very deeply."

"I do," Roger admitted.

"I am happy for you, my son. That is all I have ever wanted for you. That business with Elizabeth de Clare was not good. She was not the right woman for you. Both your father and I knew that." She looked at Roger. "You seem to know that now, too."

"You can tell that from only looking at me?"

"There is a peace about you that has not been there before. A mother understands this, son." Lillianne sat a little straighter in her chair and looked around the solar. "Now tell me, where is Teleri? She did not come down with you?"

"Margaret and Marian are up there with her, trying on gowns and such. They chased me out."

"Then come." His mother stood. "You can take me belowstairs to break our fast. The girls will bring her down as soon as she is dressed."

The girls did not let Teleri out of her room until she had tried on every dress they owned. And no one could have possibly owned so many gowns. Both of Roger's youngest sisters were about Teleri's size and height. So when she came down the stone stairs to meet with her husband and his family, she was dressed in a flowing green silk gown with a thin overtunic of gold and green and deep, crimson red thin silk brocade.

On her head she wore a golden circlet with a huge ruby in the center, and her hair was braided with red and gold silken ribbons into thick plaits that fell down past her waist. And she felt like a stranger.

She let his sisters drag her into the main hall, where there was a crowd of people who were mostly strangers, sitting at groupings of long tables. The girls brought her before their father like a piece of prized fruit and Margaret said, "Look. Is she not the loveliest thing? See, Father? I told you she would clean up well."

"Margaret!" Lillianne said. "Sit down and fill your silly mouth with something other than your foot."

Roger had risen and led Teleri by the hand over to an empty wooden bench made for two. He seated her and leaned over and whispered, "You are the loveliest woman I have ever seen."

She smiled at him, suddenly feeling much better about the strange clothes she was wearing.

Then he added, "But you are limping. What is the matter?"

She leaned back a bit and lifted up her gown so he could see her feet. She wore tight red slippers with ties that wrapped around the ankles.

He frowned. "They look to be the softest leather. Do they hurt?"

"They are soft. But the stitches in them rub my feet and heels when I walk."

He patted her hand. "You will get used to them."

"Apparently your father gave your sisters orders that I was to be 'shod.'"

Roger slid his arm around her and said, "Do not wear them for me. I do not care if you go bare-footed. I am not my father, love."

She nodded.

A servant came by carrying a platter filled with bacon and ham and kidneys. She stared at it with her mouth open. She had never seen so much meat on one plate in her life. And she thought she might be ill. Luckily the servant placed the platter at the opposite end of the table.

But just as she was settling back another servant brought in a roasted pheasant, its green and blue tail feathers placed back in the cooked bird so it looked as if it were only sleeping.

The man set the meat between Teleri and Roger and she gasped. She sat there looking at that poor bird in front of her. She could feel the tears coming.

"Take it away," Roger ordered sharply.

There was a sudden silence. Everyone was staring at them. Roger handed her a goblet of wine and said, "Here, drink this. Take small sips. 'Twill help you calm your belly and dry your tears."

"What is wrong with the bird?" his father bellowed.

"Nothing," Roger said.

"There must be something wrong with it. You sent it away."

"I only wanted it away from my wife, Father."

"Why?"

"She does not eat meat."

His father scowled at Teleri. "Does not eat meat? I have never heard such foolishness. No wonder she is so pale and small. Tell me, girl, why will you not eat meat?"

"Tell him," Roger said. "Tell him what you told me the first time."

"No, Roger. Please."

"Tell him."

"Aye, girl. Tell us all." His father bellowed.

"I cannot eat meat, my lord," she said quietly.

"I asked you why."

"Sander," Lillianne placed her arm on her husband's. "Do not badger the girl. She can eat what she likes."

"I want to know."

"Tell him," Roger said again. "Go on. He wants to know."

Teleri raised her chin and looked squarely at her father-in-law. "Because, Baron, I could never eat anything that has a face."

The silence in the great room was so heavy she could have cut clear through it. Then, at that exact moment, two more servants came into the hall carrying a huge, whole roasted boar with a bright red apple stuck in its mouth.

No one ate it.

Chapter

39

❧

Things had gone rather smoothly for about five days. Teleri adored Roger's mother and sisters. She tried to avoid his father, but so did Roger. Late one morning Teleri and Lillianne were talking in the solar, something they did almost every day.

Roger came striding in through the west entrance. "Teleri, I need you to come to the stables and take a look at the coops I had made for your animals."

His father came in through the east door. "Lillianne! I cannot find my ledger books. Have you seen them?"

"Do sit. Both of you." Lillianne directed her maid to bring up some wine and fruit.

Both men looked as if the last thing they wanted to do was sit in that room together but they did.

Teleri found it rather amazing the way Lillianne controlled the men in her life. She did so with calm and no nonsense. She did not let them badger her. She spoke her mind, but did so calmly. And she did not accept the word no from any of them.

"Teleri and I were just talking." She waved her slim hand. "Continue my dear."

"I do not know who my father was. My mother died when I was born."

"What a tragedy, my dear. No mother or father. Well, you must now consider us your family. Right, Sander?"

The baron coughed and grumbled something.

"I want to know who my father was," Teleri told Lillianne. "You see, my mother loved him and swore to keep his name only in her heart."

"How very tragic." She leaned over and patted Teleri's hand.

"It was. But before she died, she told my grandmother that the answer to who he was is in a huge blue stone ring near where I was born."

Roger choked on his wine and spilt the goblet right in his lap. A servant rushed over to clean it up. But by then he was scowling and brushing it off himself.

"You know the ring, don't you, Roger."

"I know the stone ring." He looked as if he wanted to be ill. "I need to change," he said swiftly, then stood and left the room without looking at Teleri or his parents.

Lillianne just ignored her son and turned to the baron. "Did you know that Roger and Teleri handfasted?"

"They did what?"

"They wed under an oak tree in a handfast ceremony. It sounds lovely, Sander."

He stood up. "You mean to tell me you two were not married in a church or a chapel?"

"No." Teleri said.

"You had no Mass? There was no priest?" With each question his voice grew louder and louder.

Teleri shook her head.

"Roger! Roger FitzAlan, I want to talk to you!" A second later Baron FitzAlan strode out of the solar.

* * *

Teleri came downstairs the next morning. With each step the blisters on her feet rubbed against the leather on the sides of those horrid shoes.

By the time she was halfway down the first set of stairs she sat down on the cold landing and sighed, staring at the red tips of the shoes poking out from beneath her crimson and blue gown embroidered with stars and moons.

But all the stars and moons on all the gowns in all of England could not make her toes or her heels slip comfortably into shoes.

Her feet were killing her. With her chin propped in her hand, she stared around her at the tall stone walls with their huge tapestries, at all the wealth in the FitzAlan castle.

There were even likenesses of saints carved into niches in the walls. In fact, right there in front of her was the Virgin Mary holding the Christ child.

Teleri leaned her head back and stared up at the Virgin; she was bare-footed.

Teleri wondered what Baron FitzAlan would say if the Virgin Mary came into his castle without shoes.

She sat there a little longer, but her heels were red and sore and she did not even want to stand up, much less go in to break her fast.

All she knew was that she could not take another moment with her toes crammed into those instruments of English torture. So she bent down and began to untie the laces.

Roger could hear his father shouting Teleri's name right through the thickest walls of Wells Castle.

"Teleri!" Baron FitzAlan bellowed.

The hunting dogs ran from the great hall, yelping and scampering to get out. Servants stopped in place as if they were frozen by the north wind, then they moved swiftly, like chickens when a fox is after them, and they disappeared into small doorways.

303

Roger's eldest sisters Maude and Nell winced and the younger ones eyes grew wide; they all ducked behind some drapes in a nearby archway. Lillianne stiffened in her chair.

The baron came storming into the great hall. "What is this, Roger!"

"What is what?"

"How did your woman's shoes end up on the carving of the Virgin Mary?"

"What are you talking about?"

"These!" His father shook Teleri's red shoes by the laces. They were on the feet of the statue of the Virgin Mary!"

His sisters giggled and Roger was suddenly aware that Teleri was hiding behind him. "Lower your voice, Father."

"I will shout if I want to shout. This is my bloody home!" He scowled at Teleri. "I do not like to be made the brunt of a jest."

Roger turned to Teleri. "Were you making fun of my father."

"No," she shook her head.

"My wife says she wasn't making a jest."

"I have told you she is no wife. Until you are married in the chapel, I recognize no marriage."

" 'Tis a legal marriage. And I will not marry again just to satisfy your pig-headedness, Father. Merrick witnessed the marriage. Your own priest said the marriage is valid."

"I will not be defied on my own home. Your woman is to wear shoes. Peasants run around bare-footed, not ladies, and not the *wife* of my only son!"

"I thought you did not recognize our handfast marriage?"

"Do not twist my words. I forbid your wife, your woman, to come into the hall without shoes. Do you understand?"

"Sander," Lillianne said. "They are only shoes."

"Do not interrupt me."

She stiffened and her eyes narrowed. "You need not bellow so. None of us is deaf, dear."

"I am not so certain. As I remember it, I ordered you to see that the girl was properly attired."

"Ordered? You ordered?" Lillianne's eyes narrowed.

His father lowered his voice somewhat, then waved a hand. "You know what I mean."

"I believe I know exactly what you mean, Sander FitzAlan." Lillianne rose with all the grace and poise of the noblewoman she was. "Come girls. All of you. You, too, Teleri. We will go to the solar and leave your father to bellow the walls down if he so wishes."

Then Lillianne left with her women and daughters following her like ducklings up the stone stairs.

And that eve, when the most important meal of the day was served, there were only men in the great hall. The hounds were asleep by the fire, even the female servants were not to be seen.

The men sat there, looking a little lost, sipping their wine and tapping their fingers.

There came the soft swish of silk and soon every woman began to walk into the great hall in a long line, headed by Lillianne, who calmly walked up to her husband.

"Good eve to you, Sander," she said brightly. Then she made her curtsey and lifted her skirt clear to her ankles. She was bare-footed.

And every one of them stopped before the baron and made her curtsey, holding up her skirt to her ankles so he could see their bare feet.

The cook came out, barefooted, along with all the kitchen help. Every maid, every single female in Wells Castle made her curtsey to the Baron FitzAlan that night. And not a single one of them wore shoes.

Chapter
40

Roger and Teleri had been at Wells for nearly a fortnight when Sir Tobin de Clare and Payn Godart led Roger's men-at-arms through the castle gates. They greeted him with cheers and claps on the back.

Baron FitzAlan and Merrick had waited to let Roger's men know he was alive and at Wells and now the men celebrated in the great hall with food and drink and stories. Teleri wore shoes for the occasion, at Lillianne's request, who said she liked to keep the baron confused. Lillianne had taken one look at Teleri's blistered feet and ordered special shoes made for her from silk, lined with lambs wool and with soft leather soles and shorter laces.

So Teleri moved through the crowd, smiling, as she was introduced to each one of Roger's men. It was a little overwhelming, to have so many men kneeling at her feet, vowing to protect their lord's lady with their very lives.

But afterward she was able to talk to each man and she found they were not frightening, even though their size and manner were that of warriors.

Teleri was just sipping some wine and listening to Payn Godart and John Carteret tell tales of Roger, when a guard came running into the hall. "My lord!"

Baron FitzAlan turned around.

"Bigod and his men are at the gates. He states he has business with Sir Roger."

There was a odd kind of hush and the baron looked at Roger, who said, "Let him in. I would speak with him, too."

"You will not speak with him alone," his father said.

"Don your weapons, men," the baron ordered and the men began to strap on their swords and hilts. They moved almost in unison toward the doors, then lined up on the steps to the keep.

Teleri and the women were sent abovestairs, where Margaret and Marian showed them a nave above where they could watch.

The FitzAlan men were waiting when Hugh Bigod, a tall man with dark hair and a beard rode into the inner bailey.

Roger stepped forward. "Bigod." He gave him a nod.

"FitzAlan." Bigod nodded back. "I have business with you."

"What kind of business?" the baron said, stepping in front of Roger.

"I would like to talk privately," he said.

Roger nodded before his father started a battle there on the steps. He thought his hands might be shaking and he wondered if this was the man who had hanged him. He wondered if he should watch his back, but his own men were so close that Bigod would be a fool to act.

"We can speak in here," Roger said, and opened the door to the castle chapel. "We leave our weapons at the door."

Bigod nodded and they both unstrapped their swords and went into the chapel.

Bigod turned and faced him. "I heard you have married."

Roger nodded, his eyes sharp, keeping on the man's

hands in case he had a weapon hidden, though it would be foolish of him to try to kill Roger in his father's house.

"I have also heard something else."

"What?"

"That someone tried to kill you in Brecon."

Roger's palms began to dampen. "Aye." He reached up and pulled down the neck on his tunic.

Bigod stared at the marks on Roger's neck.

"Edward has told me of this. He also has told me that he thinks I could have done this. I have told him and I am here to tell you, I did not try to kill you."

"I believe some might think you have reason."

"I love my wife. What has happened was truly none of her doing. She was told I was dead. I do not blame her and I do not blame you." He looked away for moment.

Roger saw how difficult this was for this man. He thought about Teleri and how he would feel if the same thing happened with them. He did not know what he would have done.

Bigod turned back, his head high. "But I want to know it is over between you and Elizabeth. For good."

"I also love my wife. I do not want yours."

Bigod gave a sharp nod.

"Come," Roger opened the door. "You and your men are welcome. We have enough food and drink for a hundred more men."

And they left the chapel.

Teleri leaned closer to Roger. "Is everything well?"

"Aye," he took a long drink of wine. "All is well. He loves his wife and I love mine." Roger put his arm around her and laughed. "Besides, I doubt Hugh would harm me even if he wanted to, with my father and mother keeping him thoroughly entertained and underfoot.

Teleri saw that what he said was true. Lillianne and the baron were across the hall. So Roger and Teleri moved through the crowd. A short time later, Sir Tobin came over and spoke with Teleri. They talked of Brecon and of the hills and the woods and the plans for the castle.

De Clare lifted his wine goblet and took a long drink. " 'Twill be a fine site for a castle. After those blue stones are taken down."

"What?" Teleri looked at him. "What did you say?"

"I said the site for the castle will be perfect once those huge stones are removed."

Teleri turned to Roger. "You are going to tear down the stones? The ones in the stone ring?"

He looked from her to Sir Tobin and his face grew taut. His eyes narrowed and he looked ready to punch the younger knight.

" 'Tis true isn't it, Roger? I can see it in your face. How can you do that to me?"

"I did not know about the stones and your mother and father until you told my mother that morning in the solar."

"You cannot tear them down, Roger. Not the stones! You cannot!" Then she turned and ran from the room.

She ran away, unable to believe that love could hurt. It was worse than having stones thrown at her. It was more painful. The stones bruised her and cut into her skin. But this went deeper. It went into that part of her where she kept her secrets, her desires, and her dreams.

She kept running, out through a door in the rear section of the keep and across the middle bailey, then on to the orchard. She ran through the rows of trees, where the branches were long and shaded the ground and made her feel as if she were back in Brecon Wood.

She stopped and leaned her back against a huge apple tree, her breath fast, her chest heaving from running without stopping. High above her, light shone down from a mullioned window in the east tower—their bedchamber.

"Roger," she said his name on ragged breath. It sounded like velvet being torn in two.

As if her bones were melting, she slid down the trunk

to crouch at the base of the tree. There was ripened fruit all over the trees and the air smelled like cider, but all she could taste was the bitterness of betrayal.

There, at the base of the apple tree, with her knees pressed to her chest and her arms wrapped tightly around them, she cried the deep sobs of someone lost. And she kept crying until there were no more tears and the branches of the tree began to droop.

Roger looked everywhere for Teleri, but he could not find her. He called himself a fool a hundred times over for not talking with her about the stones and the new castle, for ignoring the problem as if it might just go away. He knew better. He walked up the east tower, to their bedchamber, which was empty, so he went up the iron stairs in the tower to the battlements above.

He heard her voice before he reached to top of the stairs and stopped. She was talking to his father and it sounded as if they were walking up the outside stairs toward the same battlements. Roger ran the rest of the way up the stairs, but paused before going through the archway.

"You must talk to my son."

"Why?"

"Because he loves you and will do anything for you. I know my son. He is not an easy man, but if he loves you, he loves with all his heart. He does not do things halfway."

"If you know your son so well, why do you goad him and belittle him, Baron?"

"I want him to be the best man he can be. I do not want him to make the foolish mistakes I did." He gave a soft bark of laughter that was humorless. "The mistakes I still make."

"Roger is the bravest and most wonderful man in the world." There was fierceness to Teleri's voice as she spoke to his father. "My husband is no little boy for you to try to mold. He is a man grown. Free to love and to wed who his wishes. He is a knight. He is not perfect. Far from it."

"Will you find him? Talk to him? Work out this problem with the stones? You should not have run off from him."

"Aye, I will talk to him. Later. Not now. He has hurt me. He kept something important from me."

His father did not respond, but then what could he say? Even Roger knew he was wrong.

"You call me baron," his father said to her.

"Aye."

"Why?"

"That is simple," she said in that way she had that made you feel foolish for asking. "I call my horse, Horse, and my hawk, Hawk. You are a baron. I call you Baron."

"I am also a lord."

"You want me to call you, my lord," she said in a flat tone.

"No." His father sounded annoyed. "I do not want you to call me, 'my lord'."

There was a long stretch of silence.

"I am also a father," he said to her.

Roger could not believe this was his father speaking. Was he asking her to call him father? It sounded like it.

"I shall tell you something before I leave you. When you start acting like a father, Baron, then perhaps someone will call you *Father*."

A moment later the sound of her footsteps echoed back to him. He came out of the dark and shadowed archway in time to see her disappear down the stone steps of the west tower.

His father was still standing there, leaning his arms on the stone crenels and staring out at the land beyond.

Roger stepped closer to him and he turned.

"How long have you been standing there?"

"Long enough."

His father turned back and looked out at the land again. "Your wife is a spirited thing, isn't she?"

"My wife? Are you conceding that we are truly married?"

His father was quiet. He just rested his hand on a crenel. "I do not like it, but I will acknowledge it," he said in a gruff voice. "Your mother would have liked to have seen her only son married."

"Mother was fascinated with hearing about the ceremony we had. She said it was romantic and she was glad we married in such a different way."

"You mother can be a trial to me." His father sighed, then added, "I expect that wife of yours will do the same to you." He looked at Roger.

"Aye. She does have spirit."

"I would have liked to see my only son wed."

Roger looked at him. "You were not there. I did not want to lose her, Father. I was afraid if we waited she might change her mind."

His father nodded. "Then I suppose I will have to understand your haste." He looked at Roger. "You settled things with Bigod, I take it?"

"Aye. He wanted me to know he was not the one who tried to kill me."

His father nodded.

A voice came from behind Roger. "That is because I am the one who wants you dead."

An arm almost crushed Roger's throat. An instant later a knife tip was pressed just below his chin.

Roger tried to fight, to struggle, but the man dug the knife blade into his skin.

"You!" His father looked from Roger to the man holding him by the throat. " 'Tis you?"

John Carteret laughed. It was evil and an ugly sound, like hatred calling out.

It was the same laugh that haunted Roger in his nightmares and his memory.

"Why would you do this?"

"Why?" Carteret repeated in a sick and madly quiet voice. "Why? You do not know why, Baron FitzAlan? Look close. Look at my face."

His father shook his head. "What am I supposed to see?"

"My mother. I look like my mother."

Baron FitzAlan shook his head.

"She was called Jane Tilly. Now do you remember?"

"You are Jane's son?"

"I am your son."

"Roger is my only son."

Carteret shook his head. "No. My mother died, but I found out that it was you who left her with child."

"That is impossible. There were many knights staying in that village. It was not I."

"No. 'Twas you, Baron FitzAlan. And all of Wells should be mine. I am the eldest."

Roger's eyes flicked to his father, watching for some sign. His father was watching him, then his gaze darted back to Carteret.

Roger waited.

His father raised his hand as if to beg with Carteret for Roger's life.

Roger jabbed his elbow into the man's ribs. The knife blade slipped down from his chin and cut the scars on his neck. He spun around, pushed hard, and jumped away.

He faced John Carteret. But Roger had no sword to draw.

Carteret came at him, his jaw clenched and the knife raised high.

"Roger! Move!" His father pulled his knife from his belt and came at Carteret.

But Carteret drew his hand back and threw the blade.

"No!" his father yelled. "No!" Then he stepped in front of Roger.

The knife went into the baron's chest.

Teleri heard the baron shout. She ran back up the outside stone steps onto the battlement. There in the shadows, she spotted Roger fighting hand to hand with a dark-haired man, John Carteret, one of his own men.

She looked down.

The baron was lying on the stones, curled in a pool of blood. She knelt down and cradled his head in her hands. She could hear the sound and shouts of men running up the stairs and over the battlements.

Suddenly there were FitzAlan men-at-arms everywhere. She turned just as they dragged John Carteret away. He was laughing. It was an awful sound.

Roger knelt by her side. "He stepped in front of me. The knife was meant for me and my father stepped in front of me. He saw it coming."

Roger looked down at his father as if he did not know him, as if he had lost part of himself. "Father?"

The baron did not move.

"Father! Jesu! Do not die on me now!"

The baron opened his eyes and looked at Roger. "I swear you are my only son. I knew Jane Tilly years ago, but I never touched her, I swear it."

"I do not care, Father. You saved my life, you foolish, brave old man."

The baron took in a deep breath and winced. He looked at Roger. "You caught my signal."

Roger nodded. "I saw you lift your hand, as if to plead with him." Roger gave a small laugh. "My father does not beg for anything."

"Aye, son. But I would have. I would have begged for your life."

"I think I know that now. Come, let us lift you and take you downstairs.

"Wait! I am sorry. I do not know how to be a father to you." Sander FitzAlan looked at Teleri. He gave her a small smile that was a half-grimace. "I love my son."

She put her hand to his damp brow. "Tonight you were more than a father."

The baron sighed and then closed his eyes.

Epilogue

❧

Brecon Beacon, Wales, 1289

It took eight years to build Annest Castle, a year longer than originally planned. By order of Sir Roger and with the approval of King Edward, new plans were drawn for a different concentric castle, built around a ring of huge blue stones that now stood in the lower bailey. The castle was strong and safe, and on a sunny day you could see clear to the sea. Baron FitzAllen recovered from his wound, and John Carteret was imprisoned in London, where after two months he hanged himself.

Roger and Teleri and their three children had lived in Annest for a year now, and many of the people from the village of Bleddig worked at the castle.

There were no tales in Brecon of witches, only the same old tales of the Devil Himself, of King Arthur and his famous knights, and of fairies who hide under the trees, just the same old tales that had been told for hundreds of years.

This day, Teleri was sitting on a bench in the middle of the lower bailey watching her children, Audry and Bryce, chase eight piglets around the ring, bare-footed. She leaned back against the bench, because she was tired, more tired than usual. She was with child again, which always made her sleepy and listless and teary in the first months.

Roger had told everyone who would listen that he always knew when she was increasing because he awoke before she did.

But now, he was inside with their eldest child, David, who was eight years old and bright as the summer sun. He learned to read at three and could write at age four. He spoke Latin, French and Welsh, and he could beat anyone and everyone at chess or draughts or any such game, including his grandfather, the Baron FitzAlan, who brought his grandchildren new shoes every time he and Lillianne came to visit.

Roger and his father were close, closer than anyone expected. They were so much alike in many ways and once Roger had realized that his father loved him, there were no more battle lines to draw. They were both strongly opinioned men, but their women kept them in line.

A shadow blocked the sunshine and Teleri opened her eyes to see her husband's face smiling above her. "Tired, love?"

She nodded, but she was not only tired. She was frustrated. For all these years she and Roger had come to the stones, looking for clues. There never were any.

She had stood in the middle of the stone ring when it was summer solstice and fall equinox. They had tried everything, had searched every square inch of the stones' surfaces. Roger had even climbed on top of the stones and looked there. But there was nothing.

No signs. No words carved into the stones. No name of her father. Nothing.

David came running outside and skidded to a stop in front of his mother, out of breath from running across two baileys. "I beat Papa!" he told her.

"Of course you did." She reached out and ruffled his red hair. "I could tell because your father isn't crowing over winning as he usually does."

"I do not crow."

"Yes, you do, Papa," David told him very seriously. "But you don't win often either so I wouldn't worry over it."

Roger gave an smile. "Humble lad, isn't he?"

"Just like his father," she said with a smile.

"Here are your healing stones, Mama. The ones you let me play with." He handed her the red leather bag.

"Thank you, my love." She took the bag and started to tie it to her belt.

"Did you know, Mama, that those marks on the stones spell something out when you turn them backward and upside-down?"

Roger and Teleri looked at each other.

"What?" They both spoke at the same time.

David took the bag and opened it up. "I shall show you. Watch."

He took the stones and examined each one, then turned each one over in his hands until he found what he was looking for. He lay the stones out before them on the ground.

"There!" he said, dusting the dirt off his hands. "See?"

Teleri looked at the stones and put her hand to her belly. "Roger. . . ." she whispered.

But her husband could not speak.

David looked up at his father who was standing so still that it was almost as if he had turned to stone. "Papa?" David tugged on his father's hand. "Papa? What does Pendragon mean?"

Roger looked down at his son. " 'Tis the family name of King Arthur, my son." Then he raised his gaze to his wife, who was looking at him from misty and wondrous eyes. He turned and looked out at the distance past the walls to the hills and valleys of this wild land and he knew then that what they said was true. Legends were born here.

Dear Reader,

I sincerely hope you have enjoyed Roger and Teleri's love story. I have to say there were days when those two would not cooperate with me at all. But characters do that sometimes, just take off and try to write their own tales with me limping along behind them.

But characters aside, now I need to thank some real people. My daughter, who, when I read a scene to her, blithely points out redundancies, wrinkles her nose, or contorts her face into some other vile look that sends me running back to the computer muttering. A very special thanks to my sister, Jan, who was chased by a headless chicken a long, long time ago and lived to tell the tale.

Historical notes:

> The Arthurian Legend was very much a part of medieval Wales. The Welsh believed in the Second Coming of King Arthur and his knights, all of whom, according to legend, lived in a huge cave set amid the Welsh hills, until that day when they would ride back to save Wales. There were rumors of sightings and those who claimed they saw mysterious silhouettes of men riding over the hillsides. Wales is filled with places that are named for Arthur—hills, rivers, wells, and caves. Some are based on sightings and others on local legend, but like the stone rings, they all remain a mystery even to this day. I wanted to use this legend in my writing, because when I see a wildly imaginative tale such as this, I want to walk right into it and live the legend myself.

By the time you read this, I will be happily writing—or quite possibly limping along behind—Sir Tobin and Lady Sofia, in their story, titled *Wicked,* which Pocket Books will publish sometime in 1999. I have a hunch Sofia will make things as difficult for me as she will for Tobin de Clare, but I know I'll have fun. And I think Sir Tobin's life needs a little shaking up, don't you?

Enjoy living the legends, my friends,

Jill Barnett

Proof-of-Purchase

1581

**POCKET BOOKS PROUDLY
PRESENTS**

WICKED

JILL BARNETT

**Coming in 1999
from Pocket Books**

**Turn the page for a preview of
Wicked. . . .**

Since the age of three, Lady Sofia Beatrice Rosalynde Anne Therese Howard had been ward to Edward Plantagenet, her autocratic and much older second cousin, who also now happened to be the King of England. And therein lay the problem, for you see, Lady Sofia acted as if *she* were king.

At three, she had been a lovely child, cherubic and striking with her pale skin and dark hair, but willful and full of mischief. As each year passed, she grew lovelier. And more stubborn.

By the age of thirteen, one glimpse of her fair face would cause grown men to stick in their tracks like deer frozen in a blizzard. She had long and shiny hair that was as black as onyx. Her eyes were the true blue of a hedgesparrow's egg.

While some English beauties were known to have skin that was ruddy and sallow, Lady Sofia's was fair like snow and summer cream, set off by cheeks the color of one of the Queen's prized roses.

And her lips were full and lush. They forever looked as if they had been stained with the richest of French wines. She was small in stature, no taller than a short man's chin, yet when she came into the room, all were aware that she was there as surely as if she were as tall as Longshanks himself.

Troubadours sang of her beauty. Brave lords and knights who caught only mere glimpses of the fair Sofia's profile in the Queen's carriage or at a tourney claimed they must have her to wive. As Edward's ward, she came heavily dowered, which combined with her exquisite beauty made her the prize of the land.

Until the fools met her.

Many times over recent years, the sound of King Edward's bellow had echoed off castle walls. "She is responsible for every single one of these gray hairs," he would say, shaking his fists in the air as he paced and muttered the Lord's name in vain. The castle priest would then cross himself and speak in prayer while Edward ranted on, "She has burned my brain with her foolery and now no hair will grow from my head that is not white!"

One time, after a spurned betrothal between Lord Geoffrey Woodville and the fair Sofia, the King called in Italian physicians to examine him. He swore to the archbishop of Canterbury that his brain was boiling and the next hairs on his head would grow in the color of the flames of hell. For a week, no one dared mention the Lady Sofia's name in Edward's presence.

And to think that this speech had been only after Lady Sofia's *first* offer of betrothal.

She was fifteen at the time of the match, which was considered by all to be a splendid one. Lord Geoffrey was the son of a royal duke.

Lady Sofia, however, was not pleased and considered nothing about the match splendid. She told Queen Eleanor that Lord Geoffrey Woodville had a face like a hatchet, a mind the size of a flea, and was as cocky as the bandy red rooster that crowed every day upon the bailey wall.

When the orange-haired young lord came to seriously court Sofia, she rubbed pork fat in her shiny hair so it was stringy and hung in dirty hanks. She scoured her face with willow leaves so her skin turned sallow and was tinged a greenish color, then she wore a gown so pale a green it seemed to blend with the tint on her skin. She made her footsteps slow and shuffling, like the mad old hag that begged for buckets of gold at the castle gates because she thought she had died and gone to heaven.

Upon first meeting Lady Sofia, Lord Geoffrey raised the question to his man if the girl was not in truth very close to death. To King Edward's frustration and Queen Eleanor's constant amusement, Lady Sofia spent most of the supper meal cackling like a witch at Lord Geoffrey's vapid jests. Whenever the King wasn't looking, she would cross her eyes and stick food in her ears and nose.

Lord Geoffrey and his entourage left in a rush before Matins and under cover of night, for he did not want to displease the King. But even for royal favor and blood bond, he vowed he would not marry and breed sons with the castle idiot.

The next offer came from Spain. A prince, no less, who sang love poems beneath Sofia's window and sent her precious oranges and jewels. The love poems bored her. The oranges gave her spots and made her nose run.

But she liked the jewels. She was, after all, no fool. She just didn't like the man who sent them.

Prince Ferdinand followed her everywhere, singing to her and praising her beauty. If she rounded a corner, he was there, winking his beady black eyes. He would purse his thin lips and work his jaw in a strange fashion—one that made his stringy mustache and pointed beard twitch and stick out like the hairy chin on one of the masticating castle goats.

Worse yet, he would strike a pose, his feet crossed so his pointed-toed shoes curled up slightly. Sofia looked at him and decided that if he'd had a spiked hat with bells, he could have juggled for her.

He would cock his head, flutter his eyelashes, and slyly walk toward her with mincing steps, then hold out his soft, woman-like rouged hand and tell her, "Comes with me, my lovely little plum. I shall take zee to hay place where za moon and za stars wane before zuch heavenzent an angelic hay faze!"

Lord, but the man liked to hear himself zzpeak!

Once he got going, Sofia decided that he could postulate on his great romantic prowess and praise her nose and ears and lips for hours. Finally, came the rueful day when Prince Ferdinand tried to kiss her. He grabbed her, bent her over one arm, and began his assault by nibbling on her neck and ears. She pushed Prince Ferdinand into the Queen's cabbage roses, and when he tried to take her with him, she dumped a bucket of horse manure on him, since it was conveniently sitting close by.

She almost caused a war.

For the next two years Lady Sofia frightened off her suitors in the most inventive and calculated of ways. Edward threatened banishment, but secretly continued to raise her dower prize by vast amounts of land, gold, and jewels.

Nothing would persuade the poorly abused suitors to have her once she got done with them. Word of Sofia's true nature spread throughout the continent, until there was no one brave enough to dare an offer. She offered to wed God, but Edward said he'd tried and the Church refused to allow her into any of their orders.

So of late, Lady Sofia had no lovelorn men to plague her. The only thing that plagued her was dire boredom, something she could never tolerate for more than a few drips of a water clock. She almost wished for another suitor to keep her mind sharp, and to keep time from moving more slowly than honey in winter.

Sofia had spent the entire morning in the Queen's solar with the other ladies, stitching hangings of infamous battles and poking her fingertips with the needle, until they were bloodier than the battlefield bodies depicted on the tapestry. Finally managing to escape, she went in search of something that would truly amuse her.

Her friend, Lady Edith, who was fifteen and betrothed to a lord who was on a diplomatic journey to the north, was in one of the tower rooms in the Gloriette at Leeds, sitting by an arched window that opened to rays of warm and precious sunlight. She was bent so her head was lit by the sunshine and she was working intently on a lovely and intricately embroidered wedding shirt for her betrothed, should he ever come back to wed her.

The doors flew open and slammed into the plastered wall with a loud bang. Lady Sofia shot inside quicker than an arrow from a crossbow. She turned to close the doors, her gown whipping around her ankles in a flurry of rich scarlet silk trimmed in threads of finely spun gold. She turned back around, hid her hands behind her, and pressed her back to the doors.

She gave Edith a devious and wicked little smile that, had the King spied it, might have caused him to lock her in the tower room before something dire befell them all.

Edith put down her sewing and stood. "What do you have?"

Lady Sofia grinned. "A surprise that will clear all the dullness in this day, Edith."

"What? What is it?" Edith came closer, stretching her neck and trying to see what Sofia was hiding behind her.

"Fetch that water ewer from the table and I shall show you."

Edith brought over the water so quickly she was sloshing it onto the tile floor. Sofia pulled her hands out from behind her and gaily tossed two handfuls of pink, flaccid objects on the Queen's daybed.

Edith squinted her eyes and bent over the mattress. "What are *those* things?"

"Pig bladders," Sofia said with a laugh of impish glee. "I stole them from the kitchen."

"Why?"

"I spotted them tucked inside a tin the other day when I was looking for that apple to shoot off Lady Juliette's head."

"Has Lady Juliette recovered yet?"

"No. She is still having a witch's fit." Sofia's voice was filled with disgust. " 'Twas only one small scratch. One would think I'd skewered her, when in truth, the arrow only sliced through the sleeve of her gown just a tad. Besides, she was stupid enough to let me try the shot. I was nearly successful, too." Sofia chewed on a nail thoughtfully.

"What are you going to do with pig bladders? And be aware," Edith added in a rush, "that I will not let you aim your bow at me nor will I be the stand for any kind of target."

"Of course not, Edith." Sofia clasped her friends hand and patted it reassuringly. "I would never expect that kind of silliness from you." Sofia turned and picked up a bladder and dangled it in front of Edith's face. "What say you?"

Edith crossed her arms and eyed Sofia suspiciously. "Explain your plan."

Sofia stretched the bladder wide, staring down into it as if it held something curious. After a moment she turned to Edith, holding open the bladder. "Here. Now you fill it with water."

Edith tilted the water pitcher slowly and began to fill the thing as Sofia stretched it open even more.

"Look! It's swelling. And swelling!" Edith paused and tilted the ewer upright.

"Do not stop yet. The thing needs more water."

"I must stop." Edith's eyes grew almost as round as the bladders. "It will surely burst!"

"That is the point. It must be stretched taut. We should fill it to bursting." Sofia held it up and eyed it, then instructed Edith to pour a little more water inside until the bladder had swelled so she could see the water inside.

"Stop." Lady Sofia lifted the bladder, which was almost stretched clear, for she could see Edith's worried face right through it.

Perfect! She tied off the bladder and carefully set it

on the mattress, then grabbed another one and stretched it open. "Now fill this one, Edith."

Soon they had filled and tied ten bladders into plump and sloshy balls which were stacked in a pile of buoyant lumps on the bed.

Sofia picked up one of the balls and rolled it from one palm to the other, grinning. She looked up and handed it to Edith. "Here."

Carefully Edith took the ball and cupped it in her two small hands. She eyed it as if she expected it to pop open any moment.

Sofia picked up another one. "Follow me." She walked over to the arched window. "Look outside, Edith. Do you see that chalk mark I drew on the stone steps?"

"The circle with the mark in the center?"

"Aye. 'Tis a target, like in archery. The object of this game is for both of us to drop the bladders at the same time, and whoever comes closest to the mark wins." She paused and moved over. "Come now, let us hold out the water balls and start the game."

Edith moved carefully, balancing the bladder and soon both girls were bent over the window casement, the balls extended in their outstretched hands.

"When I say drop we let go at exactly the same moment. Understand?"

"Aye."

"Edith?"

"Hmmm?"

"I believe you stand a better chance to hit the target if you open your eyes and take aim at the mark."

"I don't like heights."

Sofia shrugged and said, "Drop!"

They both let go. The balls fell like missiles from

heaven and burst open on the stone step with a loud *splat!*

"Look! Look! Mine was closer!" Edith was jumping up and down, laughing and pointing and apparently forgetting about her fear of heights.

Sofia frowned, noticing that her bladder had bounced just a little before it burst and missed the mark by a good arm's length. "Aye. You did particularly well, for unlike you, I had my eyes open. It did not seem to help." She spun around and grabbed another, this time making certain this bladder was filled to capacity.

'Twould never bounce, she thought as she walked back to the window. "Come, let us do this game again. Whoever has the most target hits by the time we have dropped them all, will win."

"What is the prize?"

Prize? She had not thought about a prize. She'd had another purpose. Without missing a moment she said, "My pearls."

Edith's eyes grew wider, for the pearls were tear-shaped and a rich blue color, a gift from the King himself. They were the loveliest of anyone's except the Queen's. "So if I win, you will give me the pearls?"

Sofia nodded. "And if I win, you must be the one to accompany the Queen to confession every eve for a fortnight." Sofia looked at Edith. "Agreed?"

"Agreed."

Soon plump pig bladders were falling from the tower window. The young ladies had an equal number of hits when they finally were ready to drop the last two bladders.

"Whoever is closest wins." Sofia said as she leaned way out of the arch and eyed the target, stalling for a moment, before adjusting her feet a little to the right. "Now do not drop it until I say to do so."

"I did better with my eyes closed," Edith admitted and squeezed her eyes tightly shut.

"I have an idea, just to make this more interesting, let us both close our eyes."

"Fine," Edith agreed with her eyes still shut.

They both leaned out the window.

"Close your eyes tightly, Edith." Sofia said, leaving her one eye open just a smidgen and looking intently downward. "On your mark . . ."

Sofia waited a little longer.

"Make ready . . ." Sofia finally closed both eyes when she felt she had the bladder right over the spot she wanted.

The door below creaked open.

"Drop!" Sofia whispered.

They both let go at the exact same moment.

'Twas also the exact same moment that two of Edward's knights walked out the scarcely used western doors and stood directly atop Sofia's chalk target.

In unison the girls leaned out the window to watch, each gripping the stone casement in their hands and looking downward.

There came a grunt of male surprise.

Splat! Splat!

The pig bladders hit the two knights square on their heads.

"God's blood!" came the cursing from below.

Edith's mouth fell open and she stood frozen.

But not Sofia. She grabbed Edith's hand and jerked her away from the window, then she ran to the doors, dragging her friend with her as she ran down some back stairs and hid in a small dark-shadowed niche two floors below.

They could still hear the men swearing.

Edith looked at Sofia. They both began to giggle.

"My Lord in heaven," Edith gasped. "Who was it, do you suppose?"

Sofia began to laugh hard. "I know the one in the blue cloak."

"You do?"

"Aye." She giggled again. "'Twas Gloucester's eldest son."

"Sir Tobin de Clare?"

Sofia nodded, now laughing so hard she was making snorting noises into her hand.

"Wasn't he the arrogant young knight who insulted you at the Miracle Plays?"

Sofia grinned wickedly. "Aye."

Edith studied her for a long time. "Did you know he was in the castle, Sofia?"

"Know he was here? Me? Why Edith! Are you suggesting that I planned this whole game just so I could hit him over the head with a pig bladder full of water?"

"Aye, I am. I have known you for many years, which is why I did not volunteer to put that apple on my head, dare or no. I would not put it past you to do something like this."

Sofia drew herself up into a stance she thought showed her indignance. "Truly, Edith, what is the likelihood that he would come out those west doors of the tower? You know yourself that no one ever uses those doors."

Edith was silent for a pensive moment, then she searched Sofia's face. She sighed and said, "I suppose even you could not invent so intricate and devious a plan."

"Aye." Sofia said clapping her hands. "But what good fortune it was that he merely happened to choose those doors at that particular time."

The bell rang announcing None, and the girls left the tower to meet the Queen in the solar. 'Twas later that day, though, well after Vespers, that Sofia accompanied the Queen on her evening visit to the castle priest.

After Queen Eleanor was through, Sofia went inside the small, dark confessional. Once there, she blithely admitted with no remorse that it was she who had given the arrogant and cold Sir Tobin de Clare the wrong direction.

So as the Lady Sofia knelt in the chapel, her head bent in one of the hundred and thirty-three prayers she must say for penance, she smiled, for that one single look on Sir Tobin's arrogant face—his wet and red face—was well worth a night of sore knees.